# CONVERGENCES

## JOHN VANCE

**Black Rose writing**

This is a work of fiction. Names, characters, businesses, places, events and incidents are either the products of the author's imagination or used in a fictitious manner. Any resemblance to actual persons, living or dead, or actual events is purely coincidental.

ISBN: 978-1-61296-681-6
PUBLISHED BY BLACK ROSE WRITING
www.blackrosewriting.com

Printed in the United States of America
Suggested retail price $16.95

*Convergences* is printed in Book Antiqua

Special thanks go to Reagan Rothe and Dave King of Black Rose Writing; to my children Hope and Jimmy for their support; to my wife Susan for her enthusiasm and keen editorial eye; and to Hugh and Allie for their friendship and our Canadian adventures.

# CONVERGENCES

# CHAPTER 1

Less than two miles away was the repository of his complete history—with all its successes, failures, surprises, hopes, and memories. Less than two miles away was his country. The country he once loved. The country he had left.

Ethan Brooks stood on the shoreline just off the Thousand Island Parkway looking south across the St. Lawrence toward Waterston Point State Park on Wellesley Island U.S.A. It was a pleasant late September day—in the low 60s he guessed. Or rather around 16 or 17 Celsius. He would have to get used to Celsius and kilometers now. In any event, it was likely fifteen degrees warmer in Washington D.C., and there the fall was not as advanced as it was here in Southern Ontario, where the yellows, reds, and oranges had begun to blend into delightful bouquets of autumn colors. How he had looked forward to the fall season on that humid summer morning almost three months earlier when he had his last civil conversation with his boss--the President of the United States.

Brooks rubbed the sleeve of his flannel shirt, and out of habit his hand started up to check the knot in his tie. But the flannel shirt was open at the collar, and he hadn't worn a tie since that stifling July 7th, when he stood in the Oval Office moments after he had stunned the president by refusing to do as he was asked. As Brooks later bitterly joked, the day began with the compliment that among the president's staff he was the most able and it ended with his being banished like some modern day Cain.

The two month's growth of his beard and hair had done a good job of changing his appearance, as did the exclusive use of contact lenses, rather than the glasses he was required to wear in his old job. Working out and running had toned his body and put some definition to his muscles. His weight was down twelve pounds since the mid-summer, and he remembered how he had felt the shelf of the podium pressing into his loose flesh as he looked through his black framed glasses at a room of anxious, insistent, and confrontational men and women—whose respect he had rightly earned for his honesty.

This marked the seventh time he had come to this spot off the 1000 Island Parkway to gaze toward New York State. He wondered what he expected to feel each time he stood on the northern shore of the St. Lawrence and contemplated his separation from his "homeland," as he characterized it in the more poetic style. He waited for the longing to overcome his indignation, but as of yet it had not.

Betrayal. Was it not a two-way street? He knew he was still being castigated for abandoning a president, his party, and by extension his country. And he was sure no one saw it as the other way around.

Brooks crossed the parkway and began running on the bicycle and pedestrian path that paralleled the road. He ran approximately half a mile to the east before turning and heading back west toward his car. Further to the west was his current place of residence—Kingston, Ontario. He liked Kingston. "A really neat town," he had told his younger sister Holly when they talked on the phone a week earlier. He was comforted by his sister's soft lilting voice, even while she was arguing with him.

"Ethan, you know you have to come back eventually."

"No, Holly, I don't know that."

"You're still upset. It may take some time for everything inside you to die down. You'll move on from it."

"No, Holly, *you* don't know that."

"I still say you should come back. You can keep growing your hair and beard. No one's going to recognize you."

"Holly, I've got to--"

"I want you to spend your birthday in Vermont--with us." Ethan smiled at her lifelong habit of interrupting him when he was about to make a contradictory point. "Jeff's all for it, and the kids want you to come. Ethan, we're all the family you've got."

Yes, his birthday on October 13th—when he would turn 34. He hadn't given the approaching date a single thought. It was as though he had his birthday on August 1st—the day he left the States and came to Kingston. Three weeks earlier than that, as he left the Oval Office and headed out of the White House, he had tried not to look at the stunned and angry faces of friends and co-workers, who couldn't believe what he had just done—men and women who might even then have begun to realize how their lives would be affected by the changes that were sure to come. But he couldn't avoid the voices of those who waited until he passed before remarking with confusion, "Ethan, how could you?" or with bitter sarcasm, "Thanks for fucking up everything, Brooks" and "Do hope you can live with yourself, you son-of-a-bitch."

Since that day, memories of his recent past encroached regularly on thoughts of his present reality. He didn't wish for these memories to cloud his mind; they simply came of their own volition. The events of the previous July followed him like a shadow, and there wasn't enough shade or darkness to make that shadow disappear. The constant shifting back to his Washington experiences so often fatigued him and lessened his spirits that it was impossible for him to look forward to a brighter professional and personal future.

Sprinting the last hundred yards of his run, Ethan felt one of the few unqualified moments of pride he experienced since early July by recalling how far he had come with his cardiovascular stamina the several weeks after starting a stricter running regimen. He did quite a bit of running around when he was presidential press secretary, but the exercise was of a more debilitating kind. Now the feeling of his chest rising and falling at least suggested that there was something vital left in him—a feeling of health and of purpose. He had just reached for the bottle of water he had left near his car when he heard the beep of a horn.

The window of the white Toyota Corolla slid down. "Perfect timing, *eh?*" Brooks smiled at the woman's playful reminder of his ignorance of and his trite assumptions about Canada, its customs, and what Americans thought were its linguistic idiosyncrasies. Thirty minutes after their initial meeting five weeks earlier, he had teased her by saying, "I love how you mispronounce 'controversy.'" Had he been a little more sober and less drained of emotion on that afternoon, he would never have risked insulting the friendly and quite attractive Blair Babineaux.

"How was your run, Ethan?" Ethan could barely hear the question, given the volume of the Norah Jones song coming from the car's CD player. Norah Jones—yet one more reminder of his former occupation. She was going to perform at the White House at the end of January, and he had spoken with the acclaimed artist briefly on the phone.

"The run was good. What brings you way out here, Blair?"

"You, of course."

Ethan could only muster a brief smile at Blair's brash attempt to make clear how she felt about him, because he was far too cautious, if not distrustful, when it came to their relationship. He couldn't get it out of his mind that she had reached this point in her affections after a mere thirty-four days of knowing him. After all, he reasoned, she might simply be somewhat over the top in general, and such gestures as driving out to find him, while flattering and most appreciated, didn't necessarily mean she was fully committed to him. He wondered if she guessed he was in no condition--after all that had happened, about which she knew nothing--to give his heart to anyone, let alone trust a woman other than his sister with his deepest feelings and vulnerabilities.

"I thought we could stop at Gananoque before going back to Kingston. I was so sure you would say yes that I drove out here to meet you. Besides, I knew I might get lucky and see you actually breathing hard—if not gasping."

Brooks winced at her *double entendre*, prompted by his cautious approach to their romantic activity. At first, he pleased her by exhibiting "1950's gentlemanly behavior" when she seemed willing to accelerate the pace of physical affection. Surely she guessed that he recently suffered a romantic disappointment and might still be playing torch bearer for a lost love. He was grateful that she only tried to tease him out of his caution.

"How about it, Ethan? Can we head to Gananoque for pizza and beer before we head back to Kingston?"

"Isn't it a little early, isn't it? At least for the pizza?" It was just 11:00 a.m. She offered a Cheshire-Cat grin.

"All right. I assume you want to go to Moroni." He had pronounced it with a terminal long "e."

How many times do I have to tell you, Ethan? It's Moroni—with a long "i."

"Sorry, where I come from we say things like "macaroni and cheese"—with a long "e.""

"And where I come from, it's pronounced "*Macaroni et fromage.*""

Within fifteen minutes of their first meeting, Ethan learned that Blair Babineaux was born in Évry, France—in the southern suburbs of Paris--and that when she was six she moved with her family to Montreal. Brooks had informed her truthfully that he was born in Vermont almost thirty-four years ago. But he hadn't told her much more than that about his background, although he did mention his married sister and his two nieces. Blair volunteered nothing about her age—which he guessed was late twenties to very early thirties.

"Well, Ethan? Do we rendezvous at Maroni?"

"Sounds like a plan."

"I'll obviously get there before you, and I'll go in and get us a seat, my darling Mr. Matthews."

Ethan wiped his face with a towel and took a long swallow of water. "Mr. Matthews." He wondered when it would be that he could admit to his real last name. But hadn't someone he deeply cared for told him before he left Washington that his last name would be forever vilified because of his unconscionable act of selfishness? An act that wouldn't be relegated to whisper and innuendo, but would instead be broadcast and noted by those writing about this period of American political history.

# CHAPTER 2

Ethan glanced out toward the St. Lawrence as he began his trip to Gananoque, about a half hour's drive from Kingston. He had gleaned from one of the locals that the Thousand Islands actually consisted of 1,864 islands and that to be deemed one of the official "Thousand," one square foot of the land mass must remain above water every single day of the year and must include at least two living trees. Brooks also learned that every one of the islands is entirely in the U.S. or in Canada. Most captivating was the dynamic of powerful flowing water splitting apart as it confronted the impediment of rock and earth before it, only to reconnect once that object was passed. Ethan wondered if his separation from his country was simply a temporary disconnection from the course his life would take. Or had he in fact torn his present and future from all he had done and been--forcing him to begin anew?

As he further contemplated the St. Lawrence and its islands, he recalled a quotation he came across in his reading. It was a line from an obscure seventeenth-century French writer: "Honor is like an island, rugged and without shores; once we have left it, we can never return." Previously, Brooks had the consolation of believing that what he had done in early July was honorable—and that his subsequent actions had been influenced by principle. But the Frenchman's words suggested otherwise. Ethan had not taken himself *to* an island, far removed from all that he now despised and despised him; rather, he had been banished *from* the island, the symbol of honor in this case, and could never return—the exact point made by those he once served. Brooks completed the rest of the drive to Gananoque looking only at the road ahead of him.

. . .

"How about another pint, Ethan?"

"Now, now, Blair. We have to drive back to Kingston, remember."

"Two beers do not a D.U.I. make, my dearest. By the way, which do you in the States prefer? D.U.I. or D.W.I.?"

Ethan grinned at her expression of rapt attention, as if he were about to offer his view on the Black-Hole theory. Ethan loved the many faces and vocal inflections of Blair Babineaux—most of them hardy matching the question asked or the assertion made. He didn't yet wish to tag her with the label "incredibly fascinating," but he was losing the battle to resist doing so.

"We've been going more with D.W.I. since the new millennium."

Blair took another bite of mushroom and pepperoni pizza and spoke before the piece was adequately chewed. Even as half a slice of mushroom bounced harmlessly off her chin onto the table, she lost none of her femininity or articulation. "I never say D.W.I. It doesn't roll off the tongue as well as D.U.I., especially for a French girl. Ethan, what's wrong?"

He was frowning at having said, "We've been going..." He hardly felt qualified saying "we" now. It might have been more accurate to say, "In the States, they've been going..."

"Go ahead. Finish your thought."

"Sorry. I was just debating whether I'd like another pint."

She rubbed the back of his hand, and he relaxed at her touch. He noticed that her nail polish matched the color of her sweater. "No, don't stop. Keep rubbing. It feels nice."

"What do you know? There's life in the old boy yet, even though he's lost his short-term memory."

If only he could have eradicated his *long*-term memory, but the ring of a patron's cell phone pushed into Ethan's mind the call he received two days after the election the previousn November.

"Mr. Brooks?" The woman on the phone sounded pleasant enough.

"Yes?"

"Will you hold for a moment? I have the President-Elect on the line."

Assuming he was on the threshold of a practical joke, Ethan spun his desk chair right and left, more amused than annoyed.

"Hello? Ethan Brooks?"

He stopped spinning and dropped his smile. The voice sounded very familiar. "Yes, this is he."

"This is Jack Peterborough. I want--"

"Yes, sir. Congratulations on the big win yesterday." Ethan couldn't believe he interrupted the president-elect and congratulated him as though Peterborough had just won a bowling tournament. "Excuse me, sir. You were about to say?"

"I appreciate the congratulations, Ethan. If you voted for me, I want to say thanks. If you didn't, well--I won anyway." Ethan in fact did vote for Jack Peterborough and was especially pleased that the man revealed a comfortable presence on the phone, in addition to a good sense of humor. Still, Brooks couldn't imagine what the president-elect wanted from him. "What can I do for you, sir?"

"Ethan, I want you to become my press secretary."

Blair's poking the back of his hand jolted him out of his memory. "Are you communing with dead people, Ethan? I'll ask one final time. Would you like another pint?"

"I'm sorry. Yes, yes. Another beer."

"You still don't get it, do you?" She rolled her eyes in mock frustration.

"What?"

"'Would you like another pint?' was the very first thing I ever said to you. Remember? I had just come on my shift, replacing dear old Angela, who couldn't possibly appreciate you the way I could."

As he had with Jack Peterborough on the phone, he and Blair had indeed "hit it off" as soon as she approached his table at one of Kingston's favorite brew pubs.

"Blair, that was almost five weeks ago."

"Such cruelty. You don't have sentimental bone in your body, do you, Ethan?"

"I never drank enough milk as a child."

Blair's belly laugh drew the attention of every patron at Moroni. "Ethan I'd love to hear more about your boyhood. I know so little about you. It's not fair, really. You know so much about me."

"I only know a few things, Blair."

"Such as?" He hesitated just a moment. "See, Ethan, you've forgotten every single thing I've told you."

He felt her freshly manicured nails turn inward and playfully dig into the back of his hand.

"I have not. I know that you were born near Paris and came to this country when you were six. You lived in Montreal until you moved to Kingston seven months ago."

"So far, so good."

"You're bi-lingual. You're five feet six and half inches tall—but you refuse to disclose your weight." This time he felt those newly manicured nails not-so-playfully dig into his flesh. "You enjoy sunrises, cold weather, jazz and pop classics, and Christmas nutcrackers. You hate mayonnaise, butterscotch, pettiness, and politics—especially American politics. You've traveled to seven other countries besides Canada, but you've never been to the States. Your favorite color is green, and the greatest day of your life was when you were seventeen and first saw Nora Jones perform at the International Jazz Festival in Montreal."

Blair leaned over and kissed him. "How sweet. You remembered. Too bad I don't know that much about you."

"You know that much about me, come on."

"I only know that you've never been to a hockey game, that you love red licorice, and that you're far too contemplative for your own—and my—good. Everything else about you is one big dark secret. I don't even know what your college major was. But I've figured it out. You're C.I.A., aren't you? Spying on us peace-loving Canadians, right?"

Ethan looked at her seriously, the smile gone from his face. Blair laughed at what she assumed was his playful response to her C.I.A. joke. He could take no pleasure in holding back two significant facts about his life, each with the potential to destroy his and Blair's relationship. Even her reference to his love of red licorice dragged forward the past. When he had begun his job as presidential press secretary, still utterly amazed that he had been chosen to serve, the chief of staff told him to remove the clear glass jar of licorice from his desk and never to be seen chewing the candy because of the impression it would leave. "We can't let anyone think we're a bunch of young neophytes who don't know what the hell we're doing." Ronald Reagan's jellybeans wouldn't serve as an acceptable precedent, Ethan realized. That's also when he was told never to be seen without his glasses.

Blair once more pulled him from his reminiscence. "Ethan, I love being with you."

Her expressive green eyes as well as her sweet compliment finally shook him from sobering memory. "Same here, Blair. I really mean that." He wasn't yet able to say he loved her, regardless of his growing feelings, but he felt free enough to speak honestly about being with her.

As the second pints arrived, Blair excused herself, leaving him to ponder the reason why he hadn't told her what he majored in at Champlain College and what he studied for his Masters at the University of New Hampshire. Journalism had been a long-time interest ever since he produced a four-page news sheet while in middle school. A four-year stint with his high school paper, a summer internship with a city publication, and editing and writing tasks in and outside of his classes prepared him well for his graduate work at New Hampshire, following which he did some reporting and for the next several years writing for papers in Burlington, Vermont; Concord, New Hampshire; and finally Albany, New York.

Ethan caught sight of a young girl, about the age of six or seven, sitting at a table with her parents. She was staring at him. Even here, in Gananoque, Ontario, with a new beard, longer hair, and without glasses, he expected to be recognized and then approached by a member of his former journalistic brethren. The day after he walked out of the White House on July 7, he began suspecting he would be discovered, pursued, caught, and then made to defend himself--verbally or physically. Shaking his head at the absurdity that he might have been identified by one so young, he smiled at the young girl, who waved and then returned to her pepperoni pizza.

It seemed that everything he saw opened the portal to his past — even pizza. It was some twenty months ago, when he plied his journalistic trade in Albany. Brooks was about to shove into his mouth the crust end of his fresh basil and prosciutto combo when he received a call that would launch an investigation ultimately leading to the resignation of two New York State Assemblymen and a governor's aide. The call came from the Legislative Office Building and identified one of the two assemblymen suspected of fathering a "petition mill" — a type of bankruptcy fraud that purported to keep financially-vulnerable tenants from eviction. Interviewing several victims of the scheme, Brooks learned that each believed he or she was being protected from eviction by a "consulting service." Instead, the so-called "service," without the tenants' knowledge, filed for bankruptcy anyway, charged outrageous fees, drained the tenants' savings accounts, and greatly damaged if not completely ruined their credit ratings.

He also learned that one assemblyman once owned the apartment complex in question and moreover discovered that the legislator still had a financial connection to the structure, even though he claimed to have sold his interest at the time of his first election to the Assembly eight years earlier. But Brooks kept digging and uncovered two accomplices in the petition mill scheme — one being a fellow assemblyman and the other an aide in the governor's office. When Ethan approached the first assemblyman about his findings, the man reacted as expected. He denied having anything to do with the scheme. "I left the landlord business eight years ago," he protested, and when confronted with some of the evidence, he leveled a personal attack at Brooks, noting the reporter's youth and inexperience and threatening to have him fired from the paper. "You little prick, you run with this and your ass will sit in biggest sling you ever heard of" was the assemblyman's parting shot, and Ethan did all he could not to laugh at the metaphor and the perverse combination of epithets.

The paper ran with the story, the resignations shortly followed, the governor thanked the paper and Brooks in particular, and the story received full national attention. Ethan proudly wore the "Woodward and Bernstein" tag bestowed on him, and the *New York*

*Times, Chicago Tribune, Atlanta Journal, Boston Globe, L.A. Times, Time* magazine, and a dozen other lesser publications spoke with him about a position. Ethan Brooks was a hot commodity at age thirty-one, and he realized that he had better make a move now, because he was unlikely ever again to be involved with a story as big as the one he had covered in Albany. Little did he know.

# CHAPTER 3

"Miss me?"

"More than you know."

Blair kissed him. "You've made my day. So when am I going to see your place?"

"Soon. But remember, it's not my place."

When he realized in July that he had to leave Washington D.C., Brooks toyed with the idea of going abroad, at least for a few months, but the idea was impractical and financially prohibitive. He thought it fate, then, when one of his good friends called from Kingston, Ontario and offered the use of his house for nine months, rent free. Richard Montrose, a professor in Queen's University's School of Business, met Ethan when the Canadian came to Skidmore College to give a lecture and spend several days on the Saratoga Springs campus. Brooks was sent from Albany to interview Montrose because of the latter's controversial article damning one of the companies on which he served in an advisory capacity. The company had several ties to New York State, particularly the Albany area. The two men liked each other immediately and continued to correspond after Montrose returned to Kingston. They met again when Montrose came down to Washington a few weeks before Brooks left the city in July.

Montrose knew he would be leaving Kingston at the beginning of August for a nine-month visiting position in Great Britain. A week after the press secretary's dismissal, he invited Ethan to come to Canada spend a few days with him before he left and offered the free use of his house until his return in May. "Think of it this way. Tina and I would feel much better if we had someone staying here, looking after things." After receiving an assurance that the Montroses would reveal to no one the identity of their house sitter, Ethan agreed to spend the next nine months in Kingston.

Although he initially felt a little out of place at the house, which was meticulously and artistically decorated by Tina Montrose, he found the basement apartment to his liking, since it had more of a Spartan feel to it. It also provided a sense of isolation and security, which he needed. But he couldn't resist spending plenty of time in the modern kitchen, which Tina had designed and had added to the existing structure. And then there was Richard's pride and joy, the recently completed two-level deck on which Ethan sought to relax while watching the cavorting black squirrels that used the tree-lined rectangular backyard as their playground. Ethan often sat there enjoying a bottle or two of Schooner's Lager or Moosehead, which Richard had stocked as a parting gift. Ethan hadn't yet popped open the award-winning *La fin du Monde* Blair presented him after their first formal date. It was her favorite beer to order whenever she would travel to Quebec City, and she noted that a common description of the beer also depicted her perfectly: a "cloudy blonde with a golden hue." That one translation of the name meant "the ends of the earth" made the beer seem like a beverage of last resort to him. Something to drink if he needed to go elsewhere after the Montroses returned in the spring. He fancifully imagined the Yukon Territory serving well his desire for escape.

When he felt too restless to enjoy the kitchen, the black squirrels, and beer on the deck, Brooks found peace and physical exercise in his runs and long walks through the Queen's University campus and the lively downtown area of Kingston on the edge of Lake Ontario. He assumed that when he first came to Washington D.C., he would often make the trek on the Mall from the Lincoln Memorial to the Capitol, but there never was enough free time or the required energy to do so.

Blair poked him on the arm. "You're not answering me, Ethan. Did your friend specifically forbid you to bring female company into the house, even if the purpose was nothing more than tea and chat in two separate and widely-spaced chairs?" He couldn't help laughing at both her image and the facial expression that accompanied it.

"Blair, I promised the Montroses I wouldn't entertain any wild women or have any wild parties at their place."

"Well, that leaves me and all my friends out. But what if I come accompanied by a stuffy clergyman and his holier-than-thou wife?"

"As I said, I'm not supposed to have any wild parties."

Ethan was grateful for Blair's reaction to his wit. She was the outlandish one; he much more subdued in his humor. Yet their differing elements combined to make a perfect chemistry between them. And how badly he was in need of a witty and humorous exchange that August afternoon when he first walked down Clarence Street and entered Kingston's most popular brew pub. If any establishment required one to leave his or her troubles at the door, this was the place. It seemed that every square inch of wall space contained photos, logos, and bottles. The small bar with its brick façade was jammed with exuberant imbibers, rubbing shoulders and clanking bottles and glasses—deliberately and otherwise. The tables were of differing sizes and in unique placements. There was nothing "cookie-cutter" about this place. Ethan's growing beard and longer hair length matched the appearance of half the men in the pub, and no one gave him a second glance as he sat in the area near the bar. Regardless of the others standing just a few feet away, Ethan felt the table provided him a snug little retreat. He enjoyed watching the convergence of disparate looking and animated men and women, bouncing into each other while they waved their arms and hands, causing full pints of beer to spit out some of their contents through the air and unto the floor.

On that initial visit, he ordered food and was brought a pint by another server, but then Blair Babineaux took over service at his table and the two of them started bantering. Ethan assumed she was the same with all of her customers, but he hadn't been this entertained by such an amusing and attractive woman for quite some time. Blair's playfulness relaxed him and made his food and the next three pints as enjoyable a meal as he could remember. And all along he had thought that the dinner ten months earlier in the Willard Room on Pennsylvania Avenue would never be topped.

There were five of them at that dinner that night in Washington-- two other men, both in their mid-thirties, and a woman, who was twenty-seven, six years younger than the thirty-three-year-old Ethan Brooks. The host of the dinner, the incoming president's brother and chief of staff Owen Peterborough, was a formidable presence--a bulky man impeccably dressed with a rather large emerald tie-tack centered on his pale blue tie. Somewhere in his mid-fifties, Peterborough's short hair was equally salt and pepper--his eyes iron gray. Having met him briefly the previous day, Ethan observed that only slightly beneath his hail-fellow-well-met personality was a driven and impatient man—and certainly not one to cross. Brooks had arrived at the table first, joining Peterborough, who looked at his watch when he caught sight of the younger man.

"I'm a little early, I know."

"No problem, Ethan. Rather a mark in your favor. I just ordered a drink. What will you have?"

Disappointed that he hesitated, Brooks felt pressure regarding his choice of cocktail. Ordinarily, he would have selected a draft beer or bourbon, but he had never before dined at such a marvelous venue or with someone with such a high national profile.

"You should have an Old Fashioned. None made better than they are here."

"Sounds good." He appreciated Peterborough's suggestion but feared he lost points by failing to choose on his own.

"Ever dined at the Willard?" Peterborough asked as though he well knew the answer.

"No. Never have. I am really looking forward to dinner." With this staggered start to the evening, Ethan felt fully out of place.

"No other hotel in this country has such a history." Peterborough gazed around the room. "Lincoln holed up at the Willard right before his inauguration in 1861. They feared he'd be assassinated before he could take the oath—so he did all of his pre-inauguration business in the hotel."

Ethan also learned that MLK wrote his "I Have a Dream" speech and Julia Ward Howe the words to the "Battle Hymn of the Republic" at the Willard. He was impressed by Peterborough's command of the hotel's history and the famous literary names who once stayed there, such as Dickens, Twain, Emily Dickinson, and Walt Whitman.

Peterborough checked the time and added to the august list of Willard guests P. T. Barnum, Buffalo Bill, Samuel Morse, and ten U.S. Presidents—from Zachery Taylor to Warren Harding. Brooks wondered if Peterborough had arrived at the Willard planning to display his knowledge of the hotel or had simply launched into these details inspired by the structure's impressive history. Still, it seemed to Ethan that the older man would never do or say anything without a purpose of some kind.

Peterborough stared at his younger guest, obviously expecting a response or reaction. Ethan obliged. "Makes me feel a bit intimidated just sitting here."

"Glad you see it that way, my boy. The past has the ability not only to teach but to awe—or to intimidate, as you say. It's a smart man who understands that. An Old Fashioned for the gentleman, please." The server was still five steps away from the table.

Once more, Brooks debated whether Peterborough was playing his part as host or demonstrating that the young man would have to get used to having others speak for him, even though as press secretary he was supposed to speak for others. He was bothered by his apparent suspicions. Could they be attributed to the suddenness of this incredible opportunity or could it be nagging second thoughts about having accepted the position?

The two other men arrived before the cocktail was delivered. Ethan stood, while Peterborough remained seated. Brooks shook hands with Mark Lattimore, who was coming in as deputy assistant and associate counsel assistant to the president; and Jim Conley, the new director of speechwriting and assistant counsel to the president.

As soon as Lattimore and Conley ordered their drinks, Ethan noticed Peterborough staring at his watch, apparently waiting for it to reach a designated point before he would continue speaking.

"She's now officially late," Peterborough offered coldly. "Never wise, gentlemen. Never wise at all."

Ethan tapped the ice in his Old Fashioned and anticipated a fuller lecture on the importance of punctuality. But suddenly Peterborough rose from his chair and blandly pronounced, "Well, she's made it after all."

The men also stood and, with his back to the approaching dinner guest, Ethan could tell from the brightening expressions on the faces of Lattimore and Conley that he was about to meet a lovely woman. He turned and found his assumption verified.

"Gentleman, I'd like you to meet Aashna Malini, who will assume the duties of press secretary for the First Lady."

She had luxurious dark hair cut just below her shoulders, with light brown eyes that seemed speckled with gold. But what struck Brooks most about Aashna Malini was the light caramel texture of her utterly flawless skin. He was of course surprised at her appearance because he hadn't expected the fourth dinner guest to be such a beautiful woman, but surprise topped surprise when she spoke.

"I'm so sorry I was late. The parking was impossible. . . It's very nice to be here with all of you."

In the brief moment he had seen her before she spoke, Ethan expected her to possess a deliberate and somewhat dark voice, tinged with an Indian accent. But the voice was quick and bright and reminded one more of Manassas than of Mumbai.

As Peterborough made the introductions, Aashna walked around the table and shook each man's hand. Still, she carried herself regally, befitting her stunning appearance. She came to Ethan last and extended her hand. "So happy to meet my alter ego." Her face registered a look of befuddlement at the incorrect metaphor.

Brooks did what he could to rescue her. "I was about to say the same thing. Two press secretaries for price of one." She smiled, appreciating that his metaphor was worse than hers.

"Not unless only one of you is eating." Peterborough's eyes widened at his own attempt at wit. But he returned to his terse and business-like demeanor when the server arrived with Lattimore's and Conley's drinks. "Aashna, what would you like to drink? It seems we're ordering in shifts." With that observation, Peterborough let her know that he didn't appreciate her being a minute late. Ethan wished to say something in her defense, but nothing came to mind.

After Aashna ordered a glass of sparkling wine, Peterborough gestured for everyone to sit. Ethan and Aashna were seated next to each other at the circular table at the rear of the impressive Willard Room.

"I wanted to meet with the four of you together because you all have an interesting bond. Each of you is coming into this administration without any political experience whatsoever. The president-elect—and the First Lady in your case, Aashna—wanted each of you for that very reason."

Peterborough reiterated for the sake of everyone at the table what had impressed the president-elect about each of them—that they had achieved at least regional recognition for their efforts on behalf of justice or a noteworthy cause. Ethan glanced at Aashna, who subtly revealed her impatience. "I'll start with a short bio on Ethan and discuss the rest of you in the order you arrived." Ethan felt sympathy for Aashna when her eyes dropped in embarrassment. After praising Ethan's exposure of and dogged reporting on the corrupt activities in Albany by two New York State Assemblymen and an aide in the Governor's office, Peterborough summarized the legal career of Mark Lattimore and the literary one of Jim Conley.

Peterborough paused for several telling seconds before revealing that Aashna Malini was born in Virginia to parents who had come to the States from India three years before her birth. "And I've pronounced your last name correctly, accent on the right syllable, haven't I?" After she nodded, he went on to joke about how she might expect the media to make an Italian out of her by emphasizing the second syllable of her last name. Ethan tried to catch her eye to offer support, but she kept her attention focused on Peterborough, who continued with her bio and education. Brooks found most interesting that after she completed her Master's Degree in Broadcast Journalism from the University of Maryland, she proved a popular on-air presence—first as a field reporter and then in the studio--in Lynchburg and Charlottesville before moving to an anchor spot in Richmond. Ethan noticed that she braced herself for something she expected would make her most uncomfortable. "It was there that she did a two-part interview with the next First Lady right after the convention this past summer," Peterborough continued. "Apparently it was Kismet, and at twenty-seven Aashna was soon offered the position of press secretary." Now Ethan understood Aashna's reaction. There was nothing in Peterborough's account that spoke to her efforts on behalf of justice or any noteworthy cause with which she was involved. Her being hired was just plain luck, according to the incoming chief-of-staff.

Peterborough paused to order a second round of drinks for everyone. When the drinks arrived, Brooks assumed that the nature of the conversation would be less embarrassing to Aashna. He was wrong. Peterborough trained his eyes on her. "Aashna, I hope you know that the new First Lady chose you before she even picked her chief of staff." Ethan easily detected the lack of pleasure in Peterborough's tone as he offered this bit of information, but she held her head slightly elevated with her eyes directed at Peterborough's. After another moment's silence, Peterborough smiled and with a weak attempt at charm offered, "I am fully confident you'll serve the new First Lady well. As I'm sure you gentleman will serve the new president with equal skill and loyalty."

Throughout the soup and salad courses and the entrees of Maine Scallops, Shenandoah Lamb, Stuffed Veal Breast, and Fillet Mignon, the four guests spoke barely a word. School was in session, with Peterborough, who said he had eaten earlier, holding forth, taking only brief pauses to sip his Old Fashioned.

Ethan and the others were reminded that the president-elect had a rough time during the primaries and the presidential campaign with the mistakes and overall image left by several of his staff members, the biggest offender being his long-time spokesman and press secretary. "Fourteen electoral votes were likely lost because of this man's incompetence, making the election results much closer than they should have been." Brooks was struck by the anger reflected on Peterborough's face. There could be no doubt that the new chief of staff wouldn't permit those who deceived or disappointed the incoming president to do so with impunity. "And Aashna, you have a first-hand knowledge of how difficult and down-right arrogant the outgoing First Lady's press secretary and communications director have been. If you gentlemen don't know, Aashna was twice denied an interview with the current First Lady for no stated reason, although we guess it was because Aashna here was too young and attractive— or even ethnic, perhaps."

Once more, Ethan marveled at how Aashna suppressed her anger and embarrassment. He felt that Peterborough's addition of "or even ethnic, perhaps" was particularly gratuitous and inappropriate. Brooks briefly touched Aashna's forearm below the table line as a supportive gesture, and she smiled back at him. After further explanation of the president-elect's "impressive and inspiring" life story, Peterborough leaned forward and glared at each of them in turn. "Nothing is more important than loyalty to the president, but what comes close is that we stay true to the message. Even the slightest deviation causes more headaches than you could possibly know at this point. Think of your job as protecting the president, Ethan—or First Lady in your case, Aashna. Remember that every one of you is expendable if you become a liability to the president--a consequence that's already been demonstrated by the staff changes made this fall, which of course has resulted in all four of you being my guests tonight."

By the time the pastry trolley made its way to the table, Peterborough had emphasized that each of them had also been selected because the president-elect wished to inject more youth and charisma into his new administration. "All of you have been chosen to blunt criticisms expressed during the primaries and campaign regarding the incoming president's legal advisers, speeches, and media relations—not to mention the perceived lack of youth on the team. Already we've been getting some good reviews about the changes we've made and about the commitment of the president-elect to correcting previous errors. We want all of you to do your part in keeping these solid reviews coming."

By the time the dessert and coffee were served, Brooks was impatient with Peterborough's refusal to change the subject. None of them could have doubted or misunderstood anything the president's brother had said. Ethan feared he had sighed audibly when Peterborough added, "One last thing. The president's integrity and image, lady and gentlemen--let those two words guide all that you do. Don't ever do anything—in your duties to the president or in your personal lives--that puts his integrity or image in jeopardy. As chief of staff, I will of course talk individually to you in the weeks and months ahead, and I hope to offer each of you words of praise and encouragement along the way. But if you foul up, I'll be the last person you'll want to see, I can promise you that. I've protected my younger brother all his life, and I'm not going to stop now simply because he's going to be the next president of the United States."

Aashna departed the Willard Room before the four men, who stood as she shook each of their hands. Without a genuine smile, she also thanked Owen Peterborough for the meal and his advice. Ethan wanted to escort her outside, but Peterborough had requested that he remain for a minute or two after the others left. Before he could explain why, Peterborough received a call, which led to postponing their talk until the next day. As the chief-of-staff and older brother of the incoming president walked out of the Willard Room still conversing on his cell phone, Brooks took one more look around the grandly opulent surroundings, still incredulous that only two weeks earlier he had been more than content to dine at any of the leading chains, "The Ruby Apple Olive Bee's" as he generically collapsed them.

The night was compelling enough to justify another drink. Rather than remain at the table, Brooks chose the Round Robin Bar, another noteworthy spot in the Willard. Entering, Ethan found the circular bar with its stacked display of prime offerings both inviting and slightly intimidating, especially when observing on the walls the framed portraits of the famous patrons of the hotel.

Seeing an open spot at the bar, Ethan stepped forward to take the seat, but was prevented by a young Washingtonian dressed in a dark gray suit of impeccable construction and cloth. "Sorry, but I'm holding this seat, unless my friend gets lucky. If he does, I'll give it to you--promise." The man pointed to one of the tables at the exact moment his apparently unlucky friend turned and headed back to the bar. "Sorry, he's going to need his seat."

Ethan caught sight of the woman the other man had unsuccessfully attempted to join. It was Aashna Malini. Ethan couldn't resist indulging in a playful assertion of masculinity. As he headed toward Aashna, he whispered to the dejected suitor, "Let me try my luck."

"Ethan? I thought you left the hotel. Please sit and keep me company." She looked even more beautiful to him sitting in the throne-like chair. On the table before her was a Mint Julep, the specialty of the house. Ethan couldn't believe his good fortune. When she left the table in the Willard Room, she gave no indication that she was in the mood for another drink.

Brooks cast a glance back to two friends sitting at the bar. The foiled suitor was shaking his head; the other man lifted his glass in a form of salute for a job well done.

"I'm lucky you turned away your previous caller."

"I told him I didn't wish for him to sit with me," she sighed. "I utterly hate lying, even in social situations. One of my weaknesses, I'm afraid, is that I don't always consider other's feelings when I speak my mind. I just think blunt honesty is preferable to charitable deception."

He couldn't tell if she was being completely serious. At this moment, it didn't matter. Her appearance and the sound of her voice captivated him. "I'll just stay a minute, Aashna—I promise. I don't want to blow your cover."

He was quite surprised when she tapped her index finger on the top of his hand. "Again I'll be blunt. Keep me company for a half hour or so, all right?"

Her accompanying smile was superfluous. He couldn't have been more charmed. "How do you like your Mint Julep?"

I've only taken one sip. It's made with Maker's Mark, or so I was told by my first gentleman caller. He asked if he could buy the drink for me, claiming that it cost fifteen dollars."

"I'm sure it does. Without the tip."

"Really?" Her reply was so understated that Ethan found it richly comic.

Ethan ordered another Old Fashioned. Without expecting to, he had come to like the drink recommended by the irrepressible though not especially lovable Owen Peterborough.

"Aashna, I'm sorry Peterborough embarrassed you at the table. I thought he was out of line." Ethan averted her eyes. If he knew Peterborough's remarks to be offensive, why didn't he stand up for her? He knew why he didn't—and so did she.

"It's all right, really. You can't afford to get off on the wrong foot with the incoming chief of staff." She again placed her index finger on the back of his hand. "But I really appreciate your saying that." Shifting her legs under the table, she briefly touched the bottom of his leg. He knew that what he felt and entertained at the moment was as improper as anything Peterborough had said to her. For the moment Ethan indulged the thought of kissing her neck and touching her lush black hair.

"So, Aashna, do you want to compare notes as incoming press secretaries, or. . .?"

She answered without hesitation. "I'll take rain check on that. For the time being how about sharing how each of us ended up drinking a fifteen-dollar Mint Julep and whatever it costs for your Old Fashioned in such a splendid place as this?"

Ninety minutes later, they left the Round Robin Bar and went outside to get a cab to their respective hotels. Ethan was grateful not only for the exquisite time he spent with Aashna Malini but also for the fact that they were staying at different places. This way he wouldn't have to beat himself up about *not* trying to kiss her good night at the door of her hotel room.

# CHAPTER 4

"Ethan, please stop by tonight so I can at least spend some time with you. I'll save you a table and promise you utterly superb service—provided you tip the full twenty-five percent. And I won't take no for an answer." Blair kissed him and headed into her townhouse apartment. Ethan had followed her back to Kingston to make sure the two beers she had at Moroni hadn't affected her ability to drive. He laughed at his concern over her safety. It would take more than two pints to impair the driving abilities of one who served beer for a living--surely.

Yes, that living of hers. He hadn't yet asked why was she working at a brew pub—even a first-rate one—seeing that she seemed to him so intelligent, witty, talented, and incredibly personable. He had always assumed that women like Blair Babineaux delivered beer and chicken wings while they were studying for a graduate degree or seeking a big break in the New York theatre world. He also wondered but hadn't yet gotten around to inquiring where she had worked before she came to Kingston. Such reticence was part of his personality—a strong dislike of prying into the personal business of those he liked and cared for. His talent for ferreting out information leading to a journalistic revelation stemmed from an idealist's antipathy for corruption--a crusader's and avenger's prompting that sustained him during the tedious hours spent tracking down even the most innocuous of facts. This trait led him to respect genuinely those he addressed in morning press gaggles and at the more formal White House afternoon briefings. He had been especially gratified in the first four months of his tenure as press secretary when he received glowing reviews and off-the-record compliments from his journalistic "adversaries." When he belonged to their fraternity, there were lines he wouldn't cross when it came to the subject of his investigations. It was only later that he found himself trapped inside the kind of story he previously would never have even approached.

Driving down to King's Street at the southern edge of the city, Ethan decided he'd wait until Blair probed him more fully about his own work history before asking about her career choice. All she knew was that he'd been a reporter for a paper in the States and that he was spending at least nine months in Kingston house sitting for a friend and doing research for a book on journalism in the northern border states and the neighboring Canadian provinces. Though uncomfortable playing loosely with the truth, he just wasn't ready to reveal his true identity. Fortunately, she hadn't asked him for which paper he wrote, therefore postponing any desire she might have to look up what "Ethan Matthews" had penned, and since she cared nothing for American politics, his notoriety might well be unknown to her, although Brooks couldn't shake the feeling that almost everyone — even in Canada — knew what had occurred in Washington almost three months earlier. As for the fiction that he was researching a book on U.S. and Canadian journalism, Richard Montrose had brought up the subject before leaving Kingston as a topic for which he personally had some interest. Ethan knew his meager half-step toward honesty was pathetic at best, but it had the added benefit of giving him a plausible excuse for leaving Kingston if he needed some time away. Libraries in Toronto, Ottawa, and Montreal might need consulting, after all. He of course found it painfully coincidental that these three cities were on the itinerary for the president's Canada trip later this fall.

"Ethan, have you been to Canada often?"

"Mr. President, believe it or not, but I've never once left this country."

"And you're from Vermont and worked in upstate New York?"

"And in New Hampshire, sir."

Jack Peterborough laughed as he opened the Oval Office door and headed toward the Red Room, where on that early spring day the president was going to pose for pictures with the Canadian Prime Minister and where the two men would make a rough outline of Peterborough's visit to Canada in December. As they traversed their way from the West Wing down the West Colonnade to the Red Room, the president praised his press secretary's work in the new administration and reiterated the hope that Ethan would remain with him as long as he was president—whether for four years or eight. "Little I wouldn't do for you, Ethan. I'm afraid I already regret half a dozen of my appointments, but not my tapping you for this job. My brother likes you a lot, and the First Lady adores you. In fact, we may have to adopt you." The president tagged his remark with a loud guffaw that put smiles on everyone in the White House who heard it. Ethan felt flattered, humbled, but also somewhat invulnerable. How much more secure could one be than to be in so tight with the president of the United States?

But now months later, he felt threatened by exposure and some amorphous act of retribution. Perhaps that was why he wished to spend time today at historic Fort Henry, just a short drive across the water from Kingston. Since he had come to the city, he determined to learn as much as he could about the country that was generously harboring him, as he thought of it. But driving up to the elevated Fort also reminded him of every summer between the ages of ten and fifteen, when he accompanied his energetic paternal grandfather to famous Revolutionary and Civil War historical and battle sites. Dan Brooks dearly loved his only grandson and spent his final years making up for the absence of his own son, Ethan's father, who remarried after divorcing Ethan's mother when Ethan was nine. Trent Brooks chose to make up for his failure as a husband and father by devoting all his time to his new wife and her three children from a previous marriage. He was responsible when it came to supporting financially his first family but simply damnable when it came to spending any time with Ethan and Holly. On their birthdays he would send fifty dollars folded inside a card with printed wording saying how proud he was of the recipient. Ethan would wonder why his father never wrote out those words in his own hand. From what he was told, Trent Brooks kept photos of his biological son and daughter on the mantle of his new home—a gesture Ethan found far more wounding than gratifying.

Ethan's grandfather had turned seventy when they began taking historical tours, which included the battle sites at Yorktown, Lexington, Concord, Ticonderoga, Saratoga, Gettysburg, Manassas,

Antietam, and Charleston, among the most famous locales. Ethan also knew that the senior Brooks had known battle intimately, having survived the hell that was the Battle of the Bulge. The boy would never forget his reaction to his grandfather's tale about Christmas Eve 1944. Dan Brooks and several other members of his unit were briefly captured by the Germans on that night, but owing to their ingenuity and daring they escaped in the wee hours of Christmas morning. Each Christmas Eve from that time forward, Dan Brooks left the warmth of his Vermont home and strode out into the frigid weather to be alone with his thoughts of that night in 1944. Ethan learned from his grandfather that it was important to spend time reflecting on one's past, enjoying the wonderful memories and learning from the mistakes and misfortunes. Ethan had been doing much reflection lately, but it was almost exclusively about the mistakes and the misfortunes.

He made his turn on Fort Henry Drive and approached the historic landmark, recalling what Richard Montrose had told him—that the Fort was originally constructed during the War of 1812 as protection from a possible attack from the United States. Ethan laughed when heard that because it seemed so preposterous. Why would Canada have anything to fear from the United States? But when Montrose reminded him that the relationship between the two countries, especially in the early nineteenth century, hadn't always been one of mutual respect, Brooks found the motive to build the fort far less absurd. Walking further toward the west, he gazed at the scene below the Fort. Kingston—fully visible from his elevated vista. He saw Kingston Harbor, the north channel of the St. Lawrence, and the entrance to the Rideau Canal. The Fort's strategic importance was easily evident, but Ethan's thoughts had already shifted to the purely symbolic. Having no desire for a guided tour of the fort on his first visit, Brooks wanted to stand alone and indulge in a promontory view of the area. Had he gone to the other side of the Fort and looked southward toward the United States, he might have further pondered his past and the decisions he had made. Instead he viewed his present in the peninsula city and the water that snuggled up against it. Yet he was teased by the thought—did Kingston also represent his future? With only a few cars in the parking area and several children pointing to the sign advertising Fort Henry's Halloween season activities—"Fort Fright"—Brooks felt enough alone to allow for other contemplations, such as the associations between his frequent thoughts of Ethan Allen and his present situation.

Before the events of the previous July, Brooks believed he had come to share the famous Vermonter's desire for praise and reward—and wasn't at all ashamed by the connection. Nothing pleased him more than the affection with which he was held by the president and the frequent pats on the back by Jack Peterborough's brother, the chief of staff. But even more gratifying was the general approval of the press corps with whom Brooks conversed and whom he faced daily in formal briefings. Throughout the spring, Ethan pondered the next step in his career, filling his mind with hypotheticals and possibilities about whether he'd stay on for a second term and if so, if he would prefer to oversee all facets of media relations as White House communications director. He had even researched the web for any evidence of former press secretaries who ran and won races for national office. And more intimately was the attention he had received from Aashna Malini, from morning greetings as they passed each other in the corridors of the White House to the serious and agreeable conversations over meals about present and future political events—and finally to the feel of her body in moments of passion and slumber during the nights they spent together.

Ethan Allen's characteristic impatience was also reflected in Ethan's relationship with Aashna. He fell in love the night they had drinks at the Round Robin Bar, and the intensity of his feelings remained unchecked, regardless of how many times Aashna cautioned him about moving too fast romantically. She held off sleeping with him until the end of March, yet comforted him by admitting that she wasn't seeing anyone else. Not for one minute translating this nod to fidelity as reflective of her general hatred of complication in her life, Ethan joyfully informed her that he had always been a one-woman man and insisted that her decision about monogamy was enough to make their marriage "inevitable"—although he wanted their nuptials to take place before the end of the year, whereas she countered that they had to get through Jack Peterborough's first term before they could even consider anything permanent. Ethan found the difference of their time tables something he could negotiate, and with charm, romantic pleading, and a few nicely timed gifts, he managed by June to secure Aashna's promise to address the question of marriage "after the mid-terms" some seventeen months away. At the time he read little into her lack of enthusiasm for the agreed upon date.

Looking back toward the fort, Ethan observed one of the cannon projecting over the wall and imagined it being fired at a vessel sailing toward the city or to the entrance of the St Lawrence. But the only movement he detected in the distance was of two kayaks gliding over the tranquil water. It was easy for him to reset the scene below to the 1830s, when the present fort was constructed. His mind rife with fancy, he thought of his own crisis and whether, if he had been in the administration of Andrew Jackson and had made the same decision he made this past July, he would have been summarily dismissed for his disloyalty to the president. He was sure he would have been, but he couldn't imagine the repercussions being as devastating to him then. Who at the time would have trumpeted his deplorable act to an entire nation? Who would have harassed him through the media and encroached on his privacy? Turning back to the fort, Ethan stared at the walls as if they encircled not a military structure but a prison. Similar to Ethan Allen's capture during the Montreal fiasco in 1775, Ethan Brooks felt incarcerated—captured and intimidated by an aggressive political machine and by his own conscience. As a final and most bitter historical correlation, Ethan Allen had his unfortunate connection to Benedict Arnold—then and forever since the quintessential emblem of betrayal. Was it self-pity or a simple but sad and justifiable fact that prompted Brooks to think of himself in the same terms? Would the day come when he could be ransomed and permitted to return forgiven to his country? Or was there some way he could transfer allegiance, even if reluctantly, and find his peace here in Canada?

All these historical reflections and connections were interrupted by the sound of tourists making their way toward where he presently stood and the sound of motor boats cruising on the water below. A moment later Brooks was startled by the unexpected ring of his cell phone.

It had to be Blair or his sister Holly in Vermont. Richard Montrose wouldn't be calling Ethan's cell from across the Atlantic, because he intended to leave all messages via email. No one else had Ethan's cell number. He checked the incoming call. It began with the 202 area code—the District of Columbia. He hadn't a clue about the identity of the caller—since no name appeared with the number. It wasn't from the White House or from any other number he recognized. He waited for a message, but after four rings the line went dead. His conclusion was inescapable--someone knew where he was.

Before leaving the States, Ethan had taken precautions to make sure he couldn't be reached by anyone other than his sister. He cancelled his previous phone service and had Holly add a new phone to her bill—under her name. All forwarded mail from Washington was sent to her address in Burlington, and she either sent it to "Ethan Matthews" at a postal box in Gananoque or read the contents over the phone. They had talked about his driving down to Burlington—a trip of some 250 miles—or her visiting him in Kingston. Ethan knew his sister had endured the frequent and annoying demands from the media for her brother's whereabouts, which initially she had politely declined to reveal. When her patience ran thin in later August, she began saying she assumed he was in San Francisco but that she hadn't heard from him. Much to her and Ethan's relief, requests for his whereabouts tapered off dramatically in early September, but periodically she would receive a call or a knock on the door to let her know that the media was still interested in her brother.

Brooks realized there was a record of his being in Canada, although he was surprised when he was asked for his passport when he crossed into Ontario. He had assumed from past experience that he had only to show his driver's license. But the rules had changed in 2009, and a passport was now required for entrance. Fortunately, he had renewed his passport in the spring after Jack Peterborough promised the Canadian Prime Minister that he would be coming north to pay a visit.

Coincidentally, in early July Ethan had just made the announcement to the press that the president would be going to Ottawa in the second week of December when he accepted an invitation that ultimately led to the events that wrecked his life. The president had just taken him along to Los Angeles, San Antonio, and Denver as part of an effort to highlight the administration's new initiatives on immigration and to improve Peterborough's standing among Hispanics, who gave him just forty-six percent of their vote in the past election. Drained of his usual stamina from a summer virus, Ethan managed the press gaggles on Air Force One well enough, but the president's whirlwind pace while they were in the three western cities was more than he could handle. The president even insisted that his young press secretary take a nap when they were in Denver, much to Ethan's embarrassment. By the time they returned to Washington at 9:00 p.m. on the 6th, Ethan knew he needed a long hot bath and some loving attention from Aashna Malini, followed by eight solid hours of sleep. But Aashna had left the day before with the First Lady for a two-day visit to Boston. As a result, Ethan was forced to settle for the bath, a brief phone conversation with Aashna, and the needed sleep. Even so, the next morning he arrived at the West Wing, as the president's personal secretary described it, "dull-eyed and droopy-tailed."

"Jesus Christ, Ethan, you look like hell." Owen Peterborough examined the younger man's face. "You missed a spot under here. Come on, I've got a razor in my office." True to character, the chief-of-staff took perverse pleasure in these not-so-subtle inspections of White House staffers' physical appearance and usually expressed his displeasure at any cosmetic or sartorial malfeasance no matter who might be standing nearby. Yet he had never dressed down Ethan for one of these violations. As Brooks never forgot, even as early as their dinner meeting at the Willard, the chief of staff had taken a strong liking to the press secretary, which caused Ethan to defend himself from the playful charge that he was spared Owen Peterborough's wrath and censure because he was the chief of staff's snitch when it came to identifying those with shirts inadequately pressed or shoes improperly buffed. Although said in jest, the charge still bothered him because of his aversion to gossip, spying, and revealing when it came to a person's private life or habits. He tried always to hold to the adage of speaking well or not at all.

In his office, the chief of staff once more pointed to the small patch of stubble a few inches under Ethan's right ear and jaw line and handed the press secretary a disposable razor. "Tough going on this trip, Ethan?"

Brooks took off the stubble without wetting the blade. "It was, Owen. I got some kind of summer bug I'm having a hard time shaking. Just hope I make it through today."

"Just splash some cold water on your face and stride bravely forth, my lad."

"I'll do my best. Thanks for the razor, Owen."

Peterborough grabbed Ethan by the arm as he attempted to leave. "I want to say again that you've done a stand-up job as press secretary. As I've told the president, you've been a good deal responsible for the extended honeymoon period we've had with the media. They like you and believe you're not going to jerk them around. I know you've had to dodge a bit here and there, but they understand that."

"I'm not so sure they all do, but thanks for the kind words, Owen." Brooks found most gratifying the chief of staff's latest demonstration of his approval.

"Ethan, you do know that it's normal for a president to have more than one press secretary during his time in the White House?"

Brooks couldn't resist indulging his impish side. "Same is true for the chief of staff, or so I've heard."

Peterborough laughed. "That's right, you little bastard, but you and I are going to keep our jobs for every god-damned minute of my brother's two terms."

"That's easy for you to say, Owen—you're family." He couldn't believe he was bantering with the normally tactless and hard-nosed Owen Peterborough.

"And you're lucky enough to be on my good side, Mr. Press Secretary."

"I am indeed, sir. I am indeed." Perversely, Ethan imagined the pain of being punched in the face by the overweight, yet still powerfully built chief of staff.

Peterborough wrapped his arm around Ethan's shoulder. "Look, let's have dinner and a few drinks tonight. We haven't had a one-on-one chat in a while. Besides, I'm in desperate need of a little R and R. This job has already taken its toll. I want to forget about work for one night and let the good times roll." Ethan had heard the rumors that the chief of staff was always one drink away from disaster. Peterborough laughed at the concerned look that came over the press secretary's face. "Don't fret, laddybuck. It's just going to be two soldiers scarfing down some grub and downing a few—taking a break from battle as it were."

As far as he knew, he was only one in the White House Owen Peterborough called "laddybuck"—a distinction Brooks would have gladly surrendered if asked. "Can we make it early, Owen? I'm not sure how much gas I'll have in the tank at the end of the day."

"How's 6:30 sound?"

"Okay, I should still have enough strength left to lift a fork to my mouth at that time."

"Good. I'll round you up a little after six."

As usual, there was no saying no to Owen Peterborough.

. . .

"Ethan, you've been here before, I assume?"

"No, I haven't. Heard great things about it, though."

"I'm surprised Ms. Malini hasn't insisted that you take her here."

Brooks diverted his eyes from Peterborough, who sat across the table from him at Filomena, Georgetown's highly acclaimed Italian restaurant. No one in the upper echelon of the administration had mentioned anything to him about his serious interest in Aashna, and Ethan had succumbed to a false sense that his private life was in this respect still private. But Owen Peterborough let him know otherwise.

"Don't worry. I'm not going to lecture you on the dangers of becoming involved with a fellow White House employee."

Peterborough let the remark simmer, and Brooks sensed that the older man wanted him to ask what those dangers were. But Ethan remained silent, and after a few moments the chief of staff smiled. "I've chosen to let it slide since she works for the First Lady and not the president. In any event, I hope for your sake that she likes Italian food. I happen to be married to a woman without appreciation for the world's greatest cuisine."

Ethan smiled but was troubled by Peterborough's remarks about his relationship with Aashna.

"Mr. Peterborough, how wonderful to see you again."

"Ah, here he is. Ethan, we got the luck of the draw. This gentleman is the best server in the city. Mariano, this is Ethan Brooks, the president's press secretary."

"A pleasure to know you, sir." Ethan nodded and extended his hand, which took the server by surprise. "So, gentlemen, can I start you off with a nice cocktail?"

Ethan recalled the only other time the men dined together some seven months earlier. He really wasn't in the mood for an Old Fashioned.

"Let's wait until we decide on our meal."

"Of course, Mr. Peterborough."

The server moved away from the table, as Ethan perused the menu.

"Ethan, you can't go wrong with anything here, but I'd recommend what I'm having--the *Gnocchi Della Mamma*. The Bolognese meat sauce is to murder for. Pork sausage, ground beef, veal, vegetables—you can't beat it."

"Sounds great, but the way I feel right now, I'd better stick with something a little less substantial."

Peterborough signaled the server to return to the table. "My usual, Mariano—*Gnocchi Della Mamma*. With that, I'll have the *Remo Farina Valpolicella*. The only red wine I drink, Ethan. It's a muscular wine, if you know what I mean. All right, let's give my young friend here the *Linguini Cardinale*. Good choice, right Mariano?"

The server looked at Ethan. "It's delicious, sir—one of our favorites," but his expression seemed to ask if that was indeed what the customer wanted. Ethan had his eye on the *Vitello Saltimbocca* as something his stomach could handle, but he chose not to reject Peterborough's choice for him. If this evening's conversation was about something important—something that might benefit his career--he didn't want the chief of staff annoyed with him for any reason.

"The *Linguini Cardinale* sounds perfect, Mariano."

"You won't regret your...the choice, Mr. Brooks."

Peterborough was most at home when he dominated those around him—which was always when his brother the president wasn't present. "Said to be Clinton's favorite dish, Ethan. The lobster sauce over the pasta will sit well on your stomach, don't worry. Now, you'll want that with a nice wine. Mariano, what's the best pairing with the lobster?"

Before the server could answer, Ethan interrupted. "You know, I think the only thing I should drink tonight is beer. It's what I best tolerate. Sorry, but I've been under the weather this week."

"Jesus, Ethan. Beer with this meal? In this place?"

"Sorry, Owen." Great. He had risked the chief of staff's displeasure after all.

"At least order an Italian beer, for Christ's sake." Peterborough smiled at his feigned outrage.

"Will do. Mariano, I'll have a *Peroni*."

Peterborough slammed his hand on the table. "Good boy. Let's have the calamari as an appetizer."

When the drinks arrived, Ethan was surprised to see a full bottle of the Valpolicella rather than a single glass. "Going to drink the whole bottle, Owen?"

"You never know. Besides, I can't drink wine without having a bottle on the table. It seems unmanly not to. My old man taught his boys that it was effeminate to order by the glass. See that couple over there?"

Ethan turned to his left and saw a young couple sitting side-by-side, both lifting a glass of red wine to their lips. The young man stared at the beautiful young blonde, his head tilted and his attitude one of complete adoration, while she gazed straight ahead, seemingly unimpressed by his attentions. He guessed what Peterborough was about to say—something along the lines of "Now that boy wouldn't look as subordinate or 'whipped' if he had a phallic wine bottle on the table asserting some form of male dominance." But he wasn't expecting what came from Peterborough's mouth.

"If that was me, I'd slap that princess-look right off her fucking face."

Other than the crude and graphic remark, Ethan found disturbing the way Peterborough had apparently taken personally the woman's attitude toward her companion. Ethan couldn't imagine the chief of staff merely taking the side of a fellow male. He didn't chuckle or exaggerate the remark to suggest facetiousness, and he hadn't drunk enough wine to forward inebriation as an excuse. Peterborough didn't look to Brooks for corroboration or comment, but stared at his wine glass, finished its contents, and poured himself another. He lifted his eyes and shifted to a discussion of the first five and a half months of his brother's term, and never cast his eyes at the couple again. Peterborough quickly regained his convivial tone, but Ethan wondered if the chief of staff would say anything else objectionable before the night was out—especially after having more to drink. Peterborough then informed Ethan that after their meal at Filomena, they would head to Martin's Tavern, a short walk away.

# CHAPTER 5

Taking a final glance at Kingston from Fort Henry, Brooks returned to his car and headed back to the city. The phone call he had just received from the D.C. area could have been a member of the media who somehow pried the number from Holly, although he was sure she wouldn't have betrayed his trust. Or might it have been a special plea from his good friend and Washington journalist Tim Gerard that convinced her? If so, why did the caller give up after four rings and fail to leave a message? Perhaps it was simply a misdial—the hitting of an 8 instead of the 7 intended by the caller. Yet Ethan couldn't believe the explanation was that innocent. He chided himself for once again entertaining the possibility that someone wished to exact revenge upon him in the form of physical violence. On the other hand, those who might wish to share their low opinion of the former press secretary would form a lengthy line indeed. Even though he refused to read or watch anything relating to the current political situation in Washington, he couldn't always avoid the headlines of a newspaper or a passing reference on television to the growing unpopularity of the administration. Brooks knew the day he became press secretary that the president's popularity would slip as the honeymoon period came to an end, but he couldn't shake the belief that the dip in the approval numbers were largely his own doing.

After parking downtown, Ethan spent the next hour and a half walking around Queen's University, absorbing the history of the older buildings and admiring the stone work, especially with the ivy attached like elaborate embroidery on a vintage garment, all of which mingled harmoniously with the stone and the multi-colored maples and the other deciduous trees on campus. It seemed different to him than the many autumns he had experienced in Vermont and New York State, if only because he was in another country—one that hadn't turned against him. In more poetic terms, he felt the city's arms opening to and then closing around him, providing a sense of comfort and security he had lost during the personally catastrophic July he had experienced in Washington and then, briefly, in Chicago and Atlanta, where he had gone to clear his mind and decide on his immediate future.

In both cities the media had found him, and although he refused all requests for a public statement while in Chicago, he agreed to speak briefly with a woman from the Atlanta Journal, who found him sitting alone in a hotel lounge in Decatur, on the eastern side of Atlanta. The woman seemed sympathetic to his situation and desire for privacy, and sympathy was what he sought most at the time. They sat at one of the raised circular tables in the center of the lounge area, with Ethan nursing bourbon on the rocks.

"What do you plan to do now, Mr. Brooks?" "Any chance you'll return to the political arena?" "How has all the criticism affected you personally?" "Do you think you've been treated unfairly?"

His answers were "I don't know," "No chance," "No comment," and silence.

"It's been reported that one of the news channels—and you can easily guess which one—might like to have you become a regular contributor. Would that interest you?"

"I doubt the report is accurate. But if it were, I wouldn't be interested."

Ethan flushed with anger when she mentioned such an offer being made. If true, the network would simply have wanted to trot him out as a prop—a visual reminder of all that was wrong with Jack Peterborough's administration. Even though he hadn't watched any political commentary since the moment he left the White House, he was sure the commentators on this network were "taking his side" only because it would serve their political interests. But Brooks also understood that another network would have made the same offer had he belonged to the other party.

"They just released a poll asking whether you betrayed the president and the administration. Have you seen it, and do you think the results were accurate?"

So much for her being sympathetic. "No to the first part of your question." In fact he hadn't seen it, but it was clear by the second part what the results were. "Look, I think that now I'd just like to sit here with my drink. Thanks for spending time with me."

He immediately perceived the absurdity of his final remark, but it was how he always dealt with the media—thanking them for their work, even if they demonstrated impatience with what he offered them.

The reporter attempted to elicit a more telling response with several more questions, but Brooks wouldn't bite. "Please don't ask me anything else. I'm really tired and a bit cranky, as you might have guessed. I don't wish to be impolite or disrespectful but..."

She thanked him for his time and left her card. She departed visibly delighted that she had secured a one-on-one interview with the man at the center of a major news story. Ethan's privacy was further disrupted by the click of two cell phones taking pictures. He saw a man and woman circling nearby like famished birds of prey, salivating at the fact that they had the former and now disgraced presidential press secretary directly in their sights.

The following morning, Ethan flew to New York and then to Burlington, where he spent two days with Holly and her family. He called Richard Montrose, accepted his invitation to come and housesit in Kingston, and drove to Ontario in his sister's car, which he promised to return at Thanksgiving, if not sooner.

It was hard for him to conceive that he arrived in Canada barely eight weeks ago. Standing now in front of Queen's Theological Hall, Ethan once more concentrated on the thick ivy that blanketed parts of the structure. Earlier he thought the ivy covered and protected, but now it seemed more to hide and suffocate. Kingston was presently doing the former, but might it come to represent more the latter? Was his sister right? Would he ultimately have to return to the States and confront the consequences of the decision he made in early July? Had he merely run away or had he gone to where he could find contentment—a place where now he belonged?

. . .

"Blair, are you okay?" Ethan had arrived at the brew pub as promised and found her emotionally upset.

"It's nothing. Just…just a little problem I've had to deal with. Glad that…do you want to eat…or should I just bring you a beer?"

Her eyes danced away from his. "Blair, did I do or say anything wrong?" Immediately he was disappointed in himself for such a clumsy and self-centered response.

"Of course not. It's just something I'm dealing with." She saw a hand beckoning her to another table. "I'll be right back." She daubed her eyes with her towel and made her way to the two men requiring refills.

The thoughts came quickly. Something to do with her health? A medical report she just received? Family issues? Ethan didn't know all that much about her background, after all. A work-related matter? Had she in fact been informed that they were letting her go? By the time she returned to his table, he had decided on what he would say next.

"Blair, I can see you're troubled by something. If you want to talk about it, I'm here to listen. Or would you prefer that I come back later?"

"No, no. Please stay as long as you can." She touched his arm. "I feel better having you here. We can talk after I get off work—okay?"

Ethan had his meal and nursed several beers until the pub was ready to close. He walked downtown until Blair called his cell to say she was ready to leave. He saw her heading toward him at a rapid pace. As soon as she reached him, they hugged, and Ethan felt her tighten her hold several times during their embrace. Those who walked past them smiled, assuming they were lovers who had just been reunited.

"Let's go to my place so we can talk. I need a drink—badly." She laughed in that soft and painful manner so typical of those who see humor and irony in their serious difficulties.

Ethan liked Blair's two-bedroom townhouse on Yonge Street, on the other side of Richardson Stadium, where Queens played their home football games. He thought her upscale living accommodations didn't match the kind of job she had, but he assumed that her family assisted her financially. He'd been inside her place on several occasions, but never when she was upset. Tonight he was determined to stay for an hour or so, until she felt better.

She looked up the staircase. "I just want to take a quick shower. Can I get you something?"

"No. Just get cleaned up and I'll make you a drink."

"My hero. Thank you." If she were in her normally playful mood, she would have invited him into the shower with her.

"Blair? What would you like?"

"Can you make me a vodka martini?"

His wrists and hands tensed. A martini. "What...how much vodka to vermouth?"

"Four to one. And please make enough so I can have a second one, okay?"

In the spring, Aashna Malini informed him that she'd prefer arsenic to a martini, but that memory wasn't the one affecting him at present.

"Blair, where do you keep...?" It was too late; she had already turned on the shower. Ethan made his way to the attractive stand-alone bar in her living room, which housed a premium selection of vodka, gin, scotch, bourbon, fine red and white wine, and several liqueurs. Once more he found odd a visible manifestation of one who was well-to-do--given her present occupation. Yet knowing Blair, she'd probably charmed enough men to encourage their buying prime brands for her or bringing them upon their visits and leaving them as proof that they once were in her life. On the other side of the cabinet were the vermouth and other mixers, along with a fancy cocktail shaker and other bar accessories. And in the corner of the cabinet were three bottles of champagne, two Piper-Heidsiecks and one Bollinger, again not what a woman on a limited budget usually calls affordable.

Brooks stepped into the kitchen for the ice, returned to the bar, and set about mixing the martini. He had never felt as uncomfortable mixing a drink as he did at present. Before July, Ethan had always enjoyed the atmosphere of bars and lounges. The colorful bottles attractively displayed. The sound of ice rattling in a near-empty glass. The generally cheerful countenance of the bartender. And later, the sight of attractive women in skirts and heels. He was sure his grandfather was also responsible for his affinity in this regard, because Dan Brooks liked to take his grandson into his favorite haunts and discuss with him the history of taverns and pubs as well as the genesis of various spirits. By the time Ethan was in his teens, he was ordering his cokes in short cocktail glasses, so he could simulate what he so looked forward to—his twenty-first birthday and a real night of sharing drinks with his grandfather. But Dan Brooks' death cheated Ethan of that long-sought pleasure.

Unable to get his mind off that July night with Owen Peterborough, Ethan had difficulty keeping his hand from shaking as he poured the vermouth into the shot glass and then into the shaker. If only he had parted from Peterborough at Filomena and not agreed to accompany him up the street to Martin's Tavern in Georgetown.

I'd like it shaken, not stirred, Mr. Bond."

Blair stood before him, the edges of her sandy-blonde hair wet from the shower and the rest of her clad only in an overly large red Montreal Canadiens hockey jersey, which came down to mid-thigh. He had never seen this much of her uncovered body, and the sight did much to clear his mind of painful recollections.

"I don't know, Blair. They say the shaken martini bruises the gin—or vodka in this case."

"You must shake it to release all tension and latent violent tendencies—and then the drink goes down smoother and doesn't get you as drunk. Besides, vodka tastes best when it's as cold as can possibly be."

"As you wish." Ethan shook the mixture and strained it into a martini glass. Its cloudy consistency testified to how well he had chilled the drink. "How about an olive?"

"No. The way my day has gone, it would probably get stuck in my throat. You made enough for seconds, I hope?"

"Indeed I have, your ladyship." He handed her the cocktail.

"Will you at least have a beer, Ethan?"

"All right." He stepped back into the kitchen and grabbed a bottle of Molson from the refrigerator. When he returned to the living room, Blair had almost finished her martini. Tears were visible on her cheeks.

"Please tell me what's wrong." After refilling her glass, he led her to the sofa.

"I'm scared, Ethan."

"Of what?"

"I need to tell you more about my past. The last several years of it anyway."

He was relieved that at least her problem didn't seem to have anything to do with her health or employment status. "I'm here to listen. Tell me whatever you want."

Ethan also encouraged her to start at the beginning, especially since he wanted to learn more about her history. She commenced by talking about her decision in college to forge out a career in either business or banking. After graduation she took an entry-level position in one of the larger banks in Montreal and after two years moved up to professional services manager.

"Were you happy in those jobs?" Ethan couldn't imagine someone with her outgoing and quirky personality being content in such an environment.

"At first, I liked it well enough, but after I was promoted I began to feel fidgety and, dare I say it, bored with the routine. I doubted whether I had made the right decision not to major in art, film, or another of the fine arts. I was making decent money and decided to stick it out at least another year or so. But soon I felt everything closing in around me to the point that I couldn't bear even to come to work."

"Then you made a wise decision to get out. Good for you." But why did she subsequently move almost two hundred miles to the south? The hockey jersey she wore was only one of several bits of evidence of her continued affinity for Montreal. Her place included several framed photos of her with friends at the *Château Dufresne*, the *Place-d'Arms*, and the *Jardin Botanique & Insectarium*. There had to be a significant crisis in her life before she decided to come to Kingston and serve food and beer.

She rose from the sofa and poured into her glass the last of the vodka and vermouth. She remained in front of the bar visibly struggling with her emotions.

"Blair?"

"I met someone while I was working at the bank."

Ethan was surprised he had such a palpable reaction to her announcement. It was evidently a flush of jealousy, although he had no justification to feel that way, since they had only been seeing each other for some five weeks and he had never admitted to himself that he loved her. He had recently loved deeply and wished never to feel that way again.

"Did the two of you get serious about each other?"

It wasn't the question his heart wished to ask, but it was all he could articulate.

"Yes." She remained at the bar, the martini glass rigid in her hand. "I can't believe it now, but I had wanted to marry him."

"But he broke it off?"

"No." She took a long sip of her second drink. "I did."

Ethan wasn't sure where this was going. Was she still upset at her decision—regretting it now to the point that she could weep for this lost love?

"When did you break up with him?"

"The end of June of this year."

So they had both made summer decisions that continued to haunt them, he thought. "I understand, Blair. Are you now regretting your decision to call it off? And have you found that he wants nothing to do with you anymore?"

She turned to him with an incredulous look. "No, Ethan, no. I don't regret my decision one bit. I'm just afraid he still wants *everything* to do with *me.*"

# CHAPTER 6

She partially reclined on the sofa before she continued. "His name was Jordan Essex." Her use of the past tense relieved Ethan. "He was an investment manager at the Montreal bank where I worked. He was thirty-nine when we met—about twelve years older than I was." Now Ethan knew her age--twenty-eight or twenty-nine, around five years younger than he. Ethan wasn't surprised that Essex invited Blair to lunch to discuss her "future with the bank." "I suppose my head was turned by his promise to 'see what he could do' to help me move up." Blair sighed wearily and finished the rest of her martini. "Ethan, can you get me a glass of water?"

He was glad she cut herself off, but she was already affected by the vodka and vermouth she had quickly consumed. After he returned from the kitchen with a tall glass of ice water, Blair informed him that Essex waited two weeks before he asked her to dinner "to discuss the status of my advancement. I agreed to dinner without hesitation, even though I knew he was married. But I was charmed and grateful for his obvious interest in me. I was just too stupidly vain and immature to say no."

"Blair, don't blame yourself. No one would have expected you to say no to his invitation—given the situation with your job and all that."

Blair eked out a brief chuckle as she took a long swallow of ice water. "My mother would have, Ethan. 'Never—not for any reason—get involved with a married man,' she preached monthly from the time I was fourteen."

"Involved with." Ethan knew what was coming next. She hesitated, but he encouraged her to go on.

"As soon as I received word I would be promoted to service manager, Jordan took me out to dinner at *Château Versailles*—my favorite hotel in Montreal—and after we drank two bottles of champagne, we went up to the room he had reserved for the occasion. And...oh God, Ethan. You don't need to hear all of this."

"Blair, I do. For your sake. You need to get this out. I want to listen and help if I can." He was surprised he could articulate what he truly felt but wished he didn't have to hear.

"But I don't want to make you feel bad."

Her consideration of his feelings meant a great deal to him, especially after his relationship with Aashna. "It's okay, Blair. So you spent the night in the hotel and after that you continued to be...intimate with each other?"

"Not intimacy as I always imagined and wanted it, Ethan. You have to believe that."

"I was just groping for a euphemism, Blair. I understand—I do. You said earlier that you had wanted to marry him."

She expelled a groan of deep frustration and sat up, but she dropped her head, keeping her eyes from Ethan's. "That's how naïve I was. Because we were having this affair, I believed that I ought to marry him, even when the excitement of being with him was being crowded out by my growing shame."

"And his wife?"

"I'm sure you can guess. I was taken in by the oldest line in the book."

Ethan couldn't help being amused by her comic tone and the exaggerated growl with which she tagged her comment. "So he said that he and his wife had been having trouble long before he met you and they had already talked of divorce. Am I close?"

"So you were hiding in the room at the time?" The lighthearted quality of the exchange freed her to raise her head and look at him again. "Don't think horribly of me, please."

"I won't. I couldn't." He insisted she take another sip of water.

"My mouth is so dry. A combination of vodka and nerves, I guess."

Taking her hand, Ethan knew that the next part of her story was going to be the most painful to relate. A year went by. She and Essex had lunch three times a week. He took her to dinner on the average once every two weeks. They spent the night together in Montreal only twice, and he took her with him on four weekend trips.

"And we often met for anywhere from a half an hour to an hour at my apartment just to…well, I wrote down every time we were together. And it shouldn't surprise you to know that he was continuing to make 'progress' in his separation and divorce, even though his wife remained at their home and accompanied him to every formal function he attended. And how I just *loved* all the obligatory phone calls he made to her when he and I were together."

Ethan kissed her on the cheek. It was the only gesture he could make that seemed appropriate at the moment. "So after a year…"

"A year was the deadline I set for myself, even though the love I had for him had dwindled considerably. All genuine affection had evaporated a month or two earlier. His demands on my loyalty and discretion were merely annoying until they began to frighten me. Naturally, I felt used, especially when he would lapse into one of his jealous moods and reasserted himself in bed." She winced and turned her head away.

"Blair, it's all right. Just keep talking to me."

"Ethan, I can't believe you still want to be here listening to this. I always thought I'd find a female friend to share all this with, but the simple fact is that I trust you — even if I hate myself for saying things that might hurt you or make you never want to see me again."

"Okay — I'll be honest. After tonight, I hope never again to hear about your love life with this jerk. I know you could define that as jealousy, but please don't equate mine with his."

Blair sighed — as much from playfulness as from fatigue. "From what wonderful planet did you drop down from?" She kissed him. "I'm almost done, and then we can snuggle." She told Brooks that on their one-year anniversary day, she asked Essex to meet her at the Montreal park where they often gone to be alone. "We took a walk down one of the lanes, and I told him I had to break off our relationship."

"Which he didn't take too well, I assume."

"He was quiet for what seemed like a full minute before he started laughing. For some reason I took that as a hopeful sign — as if he were about to say to me, 'This is funny, Blair, because I was just about to tell you the same thing.' But his first words were hardly in that vein. 'You ungrateful bitch' was his opening line—delivered in French, of course. '*Vous ingrats chienne.*' He went on to accuse me of impatience and selfishness and claimed I had used him and failed to appreciate his situation. That was just the prelude to demanding to know who I was seeing behind his back. Because we were passing others in the park, he put his hand under my hair and squeezed the back of my neck trying to force the name of the guy who was 'cuckolding him.' I hadn't heard the word 'cuckold' since my Shakespeare class at university. I finally broke free from his grip and threatened to make a scene. He apologized, said he was just shocked by my decision, and offered to drive me home and collect some of his things he kept there. As soon as we came inside he slapped me on the mouth as hard as he could, which drove one of my bottom teeth into the inside of my lip. I bled so much I was afraid I'd need stitches, but I didn't say anything. I was scared to death he would kill me." Ethan's stomach tightened. "He vowed he'd never let me leave him, and then he started stroking and kissing my hair. He paid no attention to the blood I was daubing with my sweater sleeve. He tried to kiss me, but when I pulled away he shook his head and said, 'You just need some time to think about what you've said to me.' He told me he'd be gone for three or four days to visit his wife's family in New Brunswick and that he'd come back to my place on Wednesday after work. I'll never forget the look on his face when he announced, 'I'll expect an apology. I really hope you understand how much you hurt me today.' He bent down in front of me so that our faces were on the same plane. He pressed fingers hard into my chin and warned me. 'Don't make me do something worse to you than slapping your pretty face, Blair. You and I are always going to be together.'"

Ethan was in his own way as drained as she was. He knew such men as this existed but it was hard to imagine that Blair Babineaux could have been subjected to such abuse. "So you left Montreal right away?"

"I know you think I should have called the police."

"I wish you had—yes."

"But I was afraid he'd tell them a story they'd believe instead of the truth." He was very well respected in the banking business and he was a pretty believable liar."

"Did you leave Montreal while he was in New Brunswick?" Ethan assumed she had, but he wished to guide the conversation now because she was still feeling the effects of her two martinis—her eyes closed for several seconds at a time and her head sagged.

"Yes. I left two days after he hit me. I didn't go back to the bank. I just called them and said I had to take a leave of absence right away owing to a family emergency. I told you before that I wasn't happy with my job, didn't I?"

"Yes, you did." His sympathy outweighing his desire to know the facts of her coming to Kingston, Ethan tried to place her head on his shoulder. "We can finish this tomorrow if you want."

"No, Ethan, I want to tell you everything now. If I lean against you, I'll fall asleep. Don't be mad with me, okay? I really, really don't want you to be mad or disappointed with me."

"Why on earth would I be mad or disappointed with you?" He guessed her final comment was the vodka and vermouth talking. "So you left Montreal and came here?"

"Yes."

"Did you tell your parents?"

"I didn't want to. They had just gone to France for the spring, the summer, and part of this fall. I didn't want them worried. But I knew I had to tell them."

"I assume you had enough money to make the move easier for you."

"Yes, my father occasionally sent me funds, and I had made good money when I was at the bank." She hesitated. "Jordan also made investments for me. It was all in my name—so I was able to transfer the funds in my accounts to a bank in Toronto. I drove there, retrieved the money, and deposited it here. I shouldn't have done that. Knowing him, he's probably discovered that I have an account in a bank here."

It dawned on Ethan that she was working at a pub because she feared the man would check with all banks at least in the larger

Canadian cities to see if a Blair Babineaux worked there. And Ethan believed he now knew why she was so upset tonight.

"Tell me. Did he contact you, Blair?"

"No. But I saw him today."

. . .

For the next hour, Ethan sat on the sofa with Blair's head on his lap. She was fast asleep, with her legs curled in the fetal position. Knowing that now wasn't the time to appreciate her lovely body, Ethan pulled the Canadiens hockey jersey down her legs as far as he could. Before she fell asleep she told him that after she had turned the corner of Ontario Street onto Clarence, she saw Essex coming in her direction on the other side of the street—and she knew she wasn't mistaken in her identification. She was certain he had been looking for her at the TD Bank or another of the financial institutions up the street from her work place. She rushed inside the pub and hid from the front window and door, terrified he would come inside. When she finally peered out to Clarence Street, there was no sight of him, although she remained shaken for the rest of evening until Ethan returned to take her home.

Ethan rubbed her brow each time she stirred in his lap, but she didn't awaken until her cell phone rang.

Ethan answered, ready to confront Essex. "Yes? Who? I'm sorry but there's no one by that name here. That's all right. Bye. She wanted someone named Morris." Blair finally breathed. "Blair I've been thinking. If what you say is true—that Essex was probably checking the banks—he'll finish doing that, if he hasn't done it already, and then move on to another city. He's surely looked in all the banks on Clarence Street. I'm confident you won't see him again. But if you want me to, I'll--"

"No, no. I don't want you to get involved with my problems. I shouldn't have told you." Feeing further effects of her drinking, she pressed her fingers against her temples.

"Yes, you *should* have told me, and I *want* to be involved with your problems." When he was in her position, he believed no one in Washington would be willing to assist or even hear him out.

Blair pulled at both his arms. "Will you spend the night here? Just tonight. I know I'll feel better tomorrow and won't be afraid of being alone."

"Of course." He shot a quick glance to the sofa. "Would you have an extra pillow and blanket?"

"Don't think so." She offered a playful smile, waiting for him to act on her unspoken invitation to share her bed. "Ethan, if you come up with me, I'll promise not to touch you."

Once more she punctuated her remark with one of her patented expressions—shoulders hunched up, teeth gritted, and eyes expanded—as if she had let slip a glaring profanity in mixed company.

"It's I who should do the promising, Blair."

The laugh they shared was liberating. Blair put her arms around Ethan and kissed him on the mouth. "We're still downstairs, Ethan, so I can touch you here without breaking my promise."

After escorting her upstairs, Ethan stood at the entrance of the bedroom until he saw her grab the hockey jersey to lift it above her head. As much as he wanted to lie next to her while she slept, he closed the door and found a pillow and blanket in the linen closet and made his way to the downstairs sofa. He reached the bottom of the steps when he heard her voice. He left the pillow and blanket at the foot of the stairs and made his way to her bed.

# CHAPTER 7

Blair kissed Ethan awake at 8:30 the following morning, apologizing if she spoke French in her sleep. Over breakfast, they talked further about Jordan Essex, and with Ethan's encouragement Blair arranged to have the next few days off to visit a recently-divorced university chum living in Toronto. Answering Blair's concern that Essex might go from Kingston to Toronto, Ethan countered that it was far more likely that Toronto was the first city in which he would have searched for her--after Montreal. Ethan couldn't know that for sure, but then he didn't know if Essex was in Kingston merely on banking business. And it was possible that the man was now involved with another bank employee and couldn't care less about his former lover.

After Blair began her three-hour trip to her friend's house on the western side of Toronto, Ethan headed out for a beer and something to eat. But most of all, he wanted time alone to digest all he had learned in the past twelve hours. He left Kingston and headed east on the Macdonald-Cartier freeway. Passing Gananoque, Ethan drove to a place in Prescott that Blair had recommended—The Red George Pub, a waterfront establishment complete with an 1812 ambience. He ordered food and a pint of draft and continued the task of sorting things out.

Ethan first considered the noteworthy similarities between Blair's situation and his own. They had both fled intolerable situations, and they both tried to erase the trail that led them to Kingston, Ontario—including listed phone numbers. They each felt embarrassment, shame, and helplessness over recent events. And they had no idea what their long-term plans would be. But there were stark differences as well. Blair had kept her full name; he hadn't. Unlike him, she remained in her own country. She had also told him the truth about her recent history, and he had avoided doing so about his. He still found it fortunate to incredible that she hadn't recognized him, given the maddening national publicity his leaving the administration drew. Although no fan of politics, Blair must have heard of the American president's press secretary committing an act of infamy—at least to the thinking of Jack Peterborough's party and its supporters. She might have even registered the press secretary's last name and saw his photo in a newspaper or on television. But with his new beard, longer hair, contacts, and false last name, Ethan apparently disguised himself well enough to prevent any connection she might have otherwise made. Yet now for the first time he wondered if she had heard him on television speak in his official capacity as press secretary and noted the vocal similarities between that man and her new love interest Ethan Matthews. Nursing his beer, Brooks decided to tell her the truth when she returned from Toronto—regardless of how it might affect their relationship. He owed her that much.

Scanning the sports section of the *Kingston Whig-Standard* left on a nearby table, Ethan was perversely tickled by the thought of how close in proximity the paper was to printing a major news story— "Former U.S. Presidential Press Secretary Found Hiding in Kingston." After receiving his food, Ethan realized there was another significant difference between his and Blair's situations. She had already ceased being in love with Jordan Essex when she left Montreal, but he was still much in love with Aashna Marini when he departed from Washington.

Ethan shifted his thoughts to the previous evening. Lying in bed with Blair, he had awakened to find that she had while asleep pulled the covers off him and half off herself. He gently tried to readjust the sheet and blanket, but the position of her body prevented him from doing so. There was just enough light coming through the window for him to see her short nightgown bunched above her waist, exposing her panties. This sight and the faint hint of her cologne made him desire her, which battled against his insistence that it would take more time for them to consummate their relationship— given the confused feelings he still harbored for Aashna. He pondered whether he had wanted Blair at that moment simply because he was a man and she was an attractive woman. Or could it be that he desired her as a substitute for Aashna. He found that possibility disgraceful.

Brooks was still old-fashioned enough to believe that sex should be the result of genuine love and affection, not merely physical attraction and a flush of lust. His grandfather had often teased him about being a "one-girl-guy," but Dan Brooks had it right, even when Ethan was a teenager. It was "all in" with every girl and woman he dated more than twice—and usually "all out" within a month or two after that. His string of ephemeral relationships after leaving college was long indeed.

Blair had resolved the matter the previous night by rolling on her back, freeing the covers, which Ethan pulled back over him. In these postures, they slept for the next several hours. Assuming Blair would be willing to make love, her playful teasing about the subject aside, Ethan easily concluded that she was anxious for them to commit to each other, in spite of the relatively short time they had been together. Sliding his pint glass back and forth between his hands, Ethan recalled his self-admonition when he started seeing Blair regularly—that he couldn't make a decision or take an action that was the result of his being on the "rebound" after losing Aashna. Unlike most lovers' quarrels, what occurred the morning after he left the White House for the last time could not be forgotten or forgiven. Aashna was at her apartment, packing for yet another overnight trip with the First Lady. She hadn't taken his calls the previous evening, and evidently hadn't expected him to show up at her door.

"Do you want to come in?" Her tone was distant and resigned.

"Why didn't you take my calls or call me?" He was genuinely stunned by her apparent and sudden change of heart and loss of affection.

"How can you even ask that?"

"Don't you understand why I had to do what I did?"

"No, Ethan, I don't. You could have easily said nothing and saved...never mind."

"They sat me down and told me the best way to handle it."

"Then why didn't you follow their advice?"

"They never gave a serious thought to what they were asking me to do."

"Ethan, you're not making sense." She stepped into her bedroom and resumed packing. Ethan's face flushed with disbelief. He moved toward the entrance of the room.

"Aashna, I thought you'd be on my side." She had made love to him fairly frequently; she hadn't rejected his talk of marrying her in the future. And now she was packing as if she was leaving their home for another man, and he still couldn't understand why.

"Ethan, you've ruined so much—don't you see that?" She forcefully shoved her dresser drawer closed. "You've caused so much harm to all of us. How could I ever forgive you for that? What really infuriates me is that you did what you did out of ego and selfishness—and please don't try to deny it. All of us have worked so hard for these past five and a half months. As you and I often discussed, so many have said we've gotten off to a better start than any other administration in recent memory. How can you *not* be ashamed of yourself? All you've done is damage our relationship with the media and with the voters. How could you be so stupidly naïve? And this is loving me? Because of you, I'm embarrassed and humiliated. Now I have to deal with questions about you and the nature of our relationship. I'm utterly sick over the whole thing. I'll be lucky to keep my job because of you."

She zipped her bag and walked to the front door. "Don't call or try to see me again. You can remain here until you finish collecting your things." She stopped and lowered her voice. "Ethan, please be sure the door is locked when you leave."

He looked around the apartment after she had closed the door, and saw that the large framed photo of the two of them had been removed. He opened the plastic garbage can in the kitchen and found his notes and some of his smaller gifts lying among the coffee grounds and other trash. He left her place without taking any of his belongings.

"Are you finished, sir?" Ethan nodded and the young woman picked up his plate. "Would you like another pint?" The server wore a concerned look on her face, probably seeing that her customer was contemplating something unpleasant.

He took a deep breath. "Sure, why not?" He saw from her tag that the server's name was Nadine—which he knew from Blair was the

French variation of the Russian word for "hope." He smiled at the uplifting "sign" — that is until he recalled what Aashna told him what her first name meant in India— "devoted to love."

Before the second pint arrived, his cell phone rang. 202 area code. It was the same number he saw at Ft. Henry. He didn't answer; it stopped again after the fourth ring. This time he realized that the caller wasn't necessarily in Washington D.C. He could be anywhere.

. . .

"I'm here, Ethan, and believe it or not, I still love you."

"Any traffic problems around Toronto?"

"Nothing more than expected. I just brought my bag into the guest room, and I didn't want to delay calling you. I had to find out if that wonderful man who stayed with me last night was real and not a figment of my martinis." At least Blair sounded like her usual playful self.

"I'm a figment all right, but of what consistency I don't know."

"Excuse me, Ethan. Lisa's trying to tell me something. Okay. Ethan, Lisa says hello and invites the *both* of us to come to Toronto the next time."

"So you told Lisa about me?"

"Two weeks ago actually. Hope you don't mind."

"Just as long as you didn't build me up to be someone I'm not." He couldn't believe he had phrased it like that. Ethan informed her of his lunch in Prescott.

"You went without me? I hate you. But if you want to make it up to me, and since you don't mind travelling outside of Kingston for lunch, how about coming to Toronto tomorrow? I understand the city has one or two places where one can get a decent sandwich and a bowl of soup. Wait. Lisa says you can stay here if you'd like."

"So Lisa is listening in?" he asked, more amused than concerned.

"I'm entertaining her with my inability to unzip my bag. But seriously, can you come over? Don't you remember that 70's classic that goes 'Please come to Toronto for the weekend'?"

"That's Boston and it's for the springtime."

"Heavens, I wouldn't want to go that far away, especially for that long. So how about Toronto—just for one day and night? You could follow me back on Sunday—or I'll follow you if you need to keep the engine of your masculinity stoked."

Ethan was relieved to hear Blair's personality running on all cylinders, as she might have phrased it. "We'll go to Toronto together soon, how's that? For now, I want you and Lisa to have a great time together. I don't want to be the third wheel."

"What would a tricycle do without a third wheel, Ethan?"

"I meant the fifth—never mind. I'll be here when you get back on Sunday, I promise."

"Ethan?" Her voice had dropped to a whisper. "You'll think I'm crazy, but will you stop by my place today and tomorrow—and early Sunday—just to check on things?"

"I understand completely. Of course I will. I'll take in your mail as well."

"Thank you. I love you. Bye."

She hadn't left him enough time to respond before hanging up. Brooks understood that she didn't want to hear him hesitate saying or fail to say "I love you too."

Pleased that Blair had regained her bearings, Ethan once more vowed to reveal his identity when Blair returned from Toronto. Yet she might determine that his having misled her were grounds for terminating their relationship. Although he wasn't sure how deeply he felt about her, he was certain he wanted her in his life. Still, how could he feel so strongly about Blair Babineaux so soon after loving Aashna Malini? What he felt for Blair wasn't the same; yet did that necessarily mean that he didn't love her?

. . .

Ethan retrieved Blair's mail and entered the apartment with the key she had given him. He checked the back door and then the stove to be sure none of the burners were on. Only Blair could have come up with the story of igniting the edge of her blouse when, during a dinner party, she leaned against the stove and without knowing it "turned on one of the burners with my fat *derrière*." Aashna had never indulged in any form of self-deprecation, even for a laugh. She was always immaculately dressed, coiffed, and made up—her posture perfect whether she stood or sat. Even when they made love, she was highly conscious of how her body was positioned. She wasn't formal or puritanical in her lovemaking, but she had to be in control, always ready for a quick transition to a post-coital activity, which she would of course perform perfectly.

Moving to the living room, Ethan noticed that the bar hadn't been straightened from the night before. The vodka and vermouth were sitting out next to his beer bottle and her martini glass. He took the glass and stared at it for several moments. It was impossible to divert the rapid and painful flow of memory—of the night he and Owen Peterborough were socializing in Georgetown.

# CHAPTER 8

"You can't end a meal at Filomena without a little Sambuca or Amoretto, laddybuck."

"Not sure we should, Owen. You said you wanted to go to Martin's Tavern, right?" Brooks was surprised that the chief of staff would risk mixing his spirits, but it was obvious that Peterborough was intent on unwinding.

"And we will. But as I say, you can't end a meal here without some Sambuca or Amoretto." Peterborough's bottle of Valpolicella was some four-fifths empty. Ethan didn't need anyone to tell him that a relaxed and inebriated public servant was a catalyst for a political disaster.

"Mariano, bring the lad here some Amoretto; I'll have the usual."

"Sambuca — yes, sir."

When the cordials arrived, Peterborough held up his glass. "Ethan, my uneducated wife calls this 'liquid licorice.'" He sipped. "Such a wonderful anise flavor. Like to try it?"

"No, no, I'm good." Ethan couldn't imagine how the Sambuca could complement the hearty Valpolicella.

When they finished, Peterborough paid the bill and the men headed a short distance up Wisconsin Avenue to Martin's Tavern, which Peterborough noted had opened in 1933, just as Prohibition was being repealed. "A number of presidents have come here — Truman, Kennedy, Nixon, LBJ, Bush. My brother is anxious to come, but we've decided to wait until next year's mid-terms are over."

Ethan was alarmed that Peterborough hadn't lowered his voice when he made the pronouncement, since they were stepping through the door as he made it. The chief of staff excused himself and went to one of the booths right next to the bar. He apparently knew the two men sitting there — and one of them did look familiar, although Ethan couldn't place him. Brooks had been in the White House for a little over five months and there were still so many faces he hadn't yet attached to names. Peterborough waved him over as one of the two men was signing a credit receipt. Introductions were made; both men were on the vice president's staff.

"Perfect timing. We'll sit here, Ethan. Close to the action." He and Peterborough took the booth the other men had just vacated. It was up against the left corner of the bar but the high wooden backing gave the booth a private feel.

"Really nice spot, Owen."

"Damn right it is. I hope that someday when you're showing another young laddybuck the best spots in Georgetown, you'll remember tonight." Enough with the "laddybuck," Ethan thought but refrained from articulating. Regardless, he caught the wistful tone in Peterborough's voice.

After the table was cleared and wiped, the server presented herself and asked if the men would be eating dinner.

"Not tonight," Peterborough replied, winking at Brooks. "But I'll bring this young gentleman in for lunch next week so he can have your burger. Best in Georgetown, Ethan. We'll just be having a couple of drinks tonight—although you can bring us something to munch on. Ethan what'll you have?"

Brooks had a hard time coming to terms with Peterborough's convivial and exuberant side—as well as his rapid-fire delivery. He wondered if he was the only one in the administration, other than the president, ever privy to it. According to his own and Aashna's observations, everyone lowered their eyes when the chief of staff passed through the White House halls. Owen Peterborough never so much as nodded hello to those who wished him a good morning.

As Ethan ordered a draft beer, Peterborough shook his head. "Jesus, Ethan. I really thought you were more adventurous than that."

"I'm still recovering from the western trip, remember?" In truth, he was getting very tired and wished to sleep, but there was no leaving the irrepressible Owen Peterborough—at least for the next hour or so.

The woman turned her attention to the chief of staff. "And for you, sir?"

"Martini—up with a single olive. Boodles or Tanqueray would be fine. But just rinse the glass with the vermouth and then toss it out—the vermouth, that is. Okay?" The server nodded and stepped toward the bar.

"What are you looking at, Mr. Press Secretary?"

"I'm just impressed by the way you ordered that drink."

"Many years of practice, son—many years of practice. It's been quite a while, however. I've had too goddamn much to do these past eleven months or so. Haven't been able to unwind since the fucking convention."

Ethan was amazed that Peterborough would add a martini to the Valpolicella and Sambuca. Was it proof of a Herculean tolerance for alcohol or some kind of death wish? For a brief moment, Brooks entertained the notion that he ought to be flattered by the chief of staff's possible desire to show off in front of him.

"Ethan, again I want to say that you've handled your job with skill, enthusiasm, and appropriate humor. The president recently told me that he has no apprehensions whenever you face the press."

"I really appreciate that. Well, so far so good at least. They haven't in any way let me off the hook, but they seem to understand the discomfort of my hanging there."

"All to your credit, my boy. There are a few ass-holes—mainly the young ones—who feel the goal of good journalism is embarrassing more than questioning their adversaries."

"I know, but they have a job to do, and I don't at all see our relationship as wholly adversarial."

"And that's why you're popular with them, Ethan."

"You know, Owen, I've received the advice of three former press secretaries who cautioned me not to assume my good luck is going to hold for much longer."

"Really? Well, they're just jealous of the fucking success you've had in the job, laddybuck."

Ethan paused, hoping that Peterborough would judge the hesitation as a reaction to the annoying pet name. "Owen, I can't tell you how much I owe the president for not putting me in any difficult situations. I understand the need politically to be less forthcoming than the media desires, but I haven't had to bend the truth to any degree—let alone to mislead."

"My little brother has never asked anyone to lie on his behalf—and he never will."

The server brought the beer and the martini. "The greatest first swallow in all of drinkdom, Ethan." Peterborough lifted the glass with his right hand and took the first sip in an almost ritualistic manner—with his other hand open and elevated as if he were hushing a crowd. "Rather delicious. I need to get you started on these."

"Well, I'm afraid it can't be tonight, Owen."

Peterborough laughed; his large head and muscular frame vibrated with glee. "How you holding out?"

"I'm fine." Ethan was hardly that. He still believed Peterborough wished to share something important with him, but he couldn't imagine what it could be.

"The president also appreciates your ideas on more effective public appearances and photo ops." Peterborough had almost finished his cocktail. It was odd. He seemed in one sense in a hurry yet in another quite settled in for a long evening.

"Not all my ideas, Owen. In April, I argued that he ought to appear, at least every so often, without the accompaniment of officials or citizens serving as a backdrop. It's become so much of a cliché for the past fifteen years or so. In my off-the-cuff talks with members of the media, I've been made aware that such displays have become laughable. But the president doesn't agree."

"And neither do I." Peterborough's face clouded up, and Brooks feared he had gone too far. But as soon as the chief of staff lifted his empty martini glass and signaled to the server, his demeanor once more reflected his convivial mood. "It's like the flag lapel pins, Ethan. You have to wear them—and you have to be seen on the platforms with the voters, the police, the firefighters, et al."

"I suppose so." Peterborough stared into his eyes, as if he wanted Ethan's understanding or approval. Aashna and anyone else working in the White House wouldn't believe this evening, Ethan thought. The intimidating chief of staff definitely in his cups—pleasant, conversational, jovial, profane, and perhaps vulnerable. Except, that is, for the strange and violent reaction to the young blonde woman in Filomena.

Peterborough continued to dominate the discussion with campaign war stories and the occasional anecdote from his and the president's boyhood. Brooks was pleased and honored to hear evidence of Peterborough's affections for his brother Jack, as well as his unqualified loyalty and belief in his brother's worth as president. Ethan also found it refreshing yet unusual that the older brother in this case had such admiration for his younger sibling. Of course, having an older brother as a president's chief of staff was rather peculiar in itself. But as Peterborough went on to yet another topic of the administration's concern, he also progressed to his third martini. Before it arrived he excused himself and headed to the rest room, moving a little more slowly, yet as steadily as he normally walked.

Ethan felt he should have one more beer—only his second since arriving—and try as tactfully as possible to keep Peterborough from his fourth cocktail. After the server set down the third martini and assured Ethan she'd be right back with his draft, she cleared out of the way and Ethan saw a man standing in the front of the booth.

"Just wanted to say hello." The man extended his hand, and the men shook.

"Hey. Good seeing you."

"Great place, isn't it, Ethan?"

"You bet. My first time."

The man looked at the martini. "Well, I don't want to intrude. See you around."

"Right." The man stepped away, and Ethan assumed he took an empty bar stool. He recognized the face, but he couldn't come up with a name or the context in which he had seen or previously met him.

When Peterborough returned, he took a hearty sip of the fresh martini, followed by a long breath. Ethan thought the chief of staff was trying to steady himself.

"Where were we, laddybuck? Oh, right. You know my brother and I usually didn't like the same things—which our mother found most helpful."

Ethan laughed, but Peterborough simply went ahead as if he hadn't offered anything amusing. "Jack was a high-school star in baseball; I in football. He liked the white meat at Thanksgiving; I had to have one of the drumsticks. He was the intellectual; I was more hands on. That sort of thing."

Ethan couldn't imagine where this was going. The server returned with his draft and saw that Peterborough had already consumed half the martini. She almost asked if he wanted another, but responsibly decided against it.

"Now, we both liked politics—obviously—but he always had to be out front, while I couldn't stand the thought of being a public figure. Damn it. I've spilled half the damn drink on my hand."

Brooks felt Peterborough's mild profanity was expressed a little too loudly. The amount of alcohol he had ingested was clearly having its effect. Could he somehow manage to get the chief of staff out before he fully embarrassed himself? "Owen, let's talk outside."

"Right, right. After I finish this."

Ethan felt more emboldened. "Okay, but this should be our last drink."

Peterborough leaned toward Ethan and attempted to lower his voice. "You're a good kid, Ethan. You know, don't you, that I took a liking to you at the very beginning. I feel I can talk to you and feel confident you'll keep what I say to yourself."

"You can trust me, Owen." Ethan prayed the man would go no further.

Peterborough's watery eyes danced as he took another sip of his drink. "Sometimes a man needs to vent a little, don't you think—even we few fortunate ones who run the damned country?"

It was time to get to the matter. "Owen, what are you trying to tell me?"

"God damn it, what the hell's the matter with me. I'm the chief of staff. I'm supposed to say what I mean. That's what everyone expects, right?"

"Try to lower your voice, Owen."

"Right." He once again spoke in a loud whisper. "My brother and I only had one thing we really competed for all our lives. Just one fucking thing." He paused, waiting for Ethan's response.

"Go ahead, Owen." It dawned on Brooks why the chief of staff wanted to share his feelings with the press secretary. Peterborough obviously knew of his family history and the early disappearance of Ethan's father from his life. Ethan braced for the painful revelation that the father preferred his younger and more outgoing son Jack to his older and more plodding sibling.

"Ethan, my brother and I both loved the same woman."

"I see." Ethan was wrong about his assumption but thought there was hardly anything surprising in the admission.

"No, I don't think you do see. The woman is his wife. The current First Lady of the United States."

# CHAPTER 9

Ethan finished setting Blair's bar back in order and for the first time took a careful survey of her furnishings. The colorful chairs and sofa were inviting, each covered in a durable and comfortable fabric. He saw no piece of furniture that would make him hesitate to sit on or place a glass upon it. The framed wall prints were all from the work of John William Waterhouse, all done around the turn of the twentieth century, yet all suggesting a time much earlier. The subjects were of women alone—romantic and wistful figures from literature and myth. Ethan easily recognized the artist—his sister Holly had a print of the popular *"La Belle Dame Sans Merci"* hanging in her home—but he had to examine each one to identify the titles. On the walls of the living room, hallway, and staircase were "The Shrine," "Narcissus," "Boreas," "Lamia by the Pond," "Pandora," "The Lady Clare," "Psyche Opening the Golden Box," and "St. Joan." Each female subject appeared lost in mediation and in her sorrow, suffering, and hopelessness, but each was also imbued with a haunting sensuality. These women seemed so far removed from the moods of the delectably effervescent Blair Babineaux. Yet, the previous evening, Ethan had seen her other side—one that made her part of the sorority of the Waterhouse women on her walls. How often had Blair viewed herself in the context of these subjects? There was so much more he wanted to know about her deeper emotions and fears. He chastised himself for having believed that he could maintain their relationship by not fully understanding who she was and what she wanted out of life.

Of all the Waterhouse prints, Brooks was most taken by "The Lady Clare," which he at least knew was the subject of a Tennyson poem. The subject had an eerie facial resemblance to Blair, although Lady Clare's hair was much darker. Surely Blair saw the resemblance—the location of the framed print above the fireplace in the living room directly across from the sofa suggested its privileged place as her favorite Waterhouse depiction. Lady Clare wasn't alone in the painting—a white doe shared the frame with her—but the expression on the young woman's face drew all of Ethan's attention. It seemed to him that the woman was awaiting an answer she expected would never come. Her face also appeared on the threshold of deeply expressed grief. Captivated by the work, Brooks felt helpless to assist this achingly lovely woman. His reaction was cathartic. Up until last night he had been chiefly concerned with his own situation and had judged his relationship with Blair Babineaux only through his own perspective. But now he felt humbled yet free from a debilitating self-absorption. Ethan realized that Waterhouse hadn't meant simply to convey the emotions of his subject to an aloof and objective viewer; he had also intended to elicit empathy from those who responded sympathetically to Lady Clare.

How different were Blair's furnishings than were the ones in Aashna's stylish apartment just outside of Washington D.C. White and gold made up the palette of each room. The art Aashna displayed was modern and abstract; there were no portraits on her walls. A dove-white short sofa and matching chair were the stars of her formal living room—designating an area she made off limits unless she was entertaining White House colleagues. Ethan never told her so, but as an apartment went, he only felt truly comfortable in her kitchen and in her bed. Regardless, he was impressed by her taste in decorating as well as in her personal appearance. Aashna had to endure the constant teasing of fellow White House staffers who warned her that the First Lady was sick of being outshone by her beautiful press secretary. Whenever they went out, Brooks took delight in the number of heads Aashna turned, and he felt badly that, of the two of them, his was the face known to the American public. Few outside of the White House and press corps knew her name, but whoever saw her walk by would never forget the impression she left.

To Ethan, Aashna was the epitome of beauty, grace, and control—that is, until that morning after his final visit to the Oval Office. He couldn't believe now that he had honestly expected her to suppress her anger and disappointment in him and agree to meet him and eventually re-open her arms. Instead, she wouldn't even take his calls. He would begin to leave a message and she would press the talk button and immediately hang up—just to let him know that she was at home. He couldn't bring himself, even after he left the city, to return and appear uninvited at her place and plead his case. Conceding that she wasn't going to forgive him—not now, not ever— he was also certain she wouldn't lose her job because of what he had done. Still he never, in the almost three months since he left Washington, attempted to find out whether she remained as press secretary to the First Lady. He refused to read any American newspaper in all that time, although in the past week or so his curiosity had been chipping away at his resolve. Ethan rationalized that if he read a recent copy of the *New York Times* or *Washington Post* and found no mention of him or the incident, he might feel better. But if it was still a national story, replete with columns and commentary, would he feel worse. On the other hand, he didn't think feeling worse was possible.

Brooks barely saw the shadow as he stepped into the kitchen to retrieve a bottle of beer from the refrigerator. Someone had walked past the window next to the kitchen door at the rear of Blair's townhouse. Ethan didn't think much of someone's being back there, since the units were all joined and the parking area extended around the side of the first apartment, two units to the left of Blair's. When he lived in upper New York, he had often seen cable technicians or electric company readers walking behind his place, as well as neighborhood kids taking a shortcut home or to the ball park. But the moment the name Jordan Essex popped into his head, he was no longer indifferent to the shadow behind Blair's townhouse. Ethan unlocked the backdoor and stepped onto the narrow rear patio area. He looked to his right and saw nothing. Jerking his head to his left, he saw a man heading toward a parked vehicle. The man didn't turn back but reached for the keys and opened the driver's side door and in a moment pulled out to the street. Brooks doubted if the man noticed him at all.

The car was a recent-model silver Lexus, but Ethan was too far away to get the tag number. The man seemed around forty, standing over six feet but not excessively tall—trim but well built. He wore charcoal slacks and black shoes. He had on a sweater with a pattern of alternating black and gray squares. His clothing certainly befitted a man with the Park Avenue name of Jordan Essex. The man moved at normal pace and the car left the parking area without undo haste. Just to be certain that no one had broken into Blair's apartment after he left in the morning, Ethan went upstairs looking for any evidence of a robbery, but everything appeared undisturbed. Was the man looking to break in—and was it indeed Essex? If so, he had at least narrowed Blair's location to this row of townhouses. Perhaps the man had seen Ethan inside the apartment and made the determination that Blair didn't live there after all—or that she was presently living with another man.

Yet there was one way to know if the man he spotted was Essex—that is, if Blair kept a photograph of him. The odds were long that she would have, but Brooks did a cursory exploration of her townhouse, this time looking into each room and on all surfaces for a photograph of the man. Ethan would have of course been troubled if Blair had a photo of her and her former lover on display. But she could have left lying about a stack of photos including one of Essex not yet discarded, possibly saved as a reminder of the mistake she had made. The last room Brooks looked into was the upstairs "office," in which Blair did her "scrapbooking"—a hobby she had started right after moving to Kingston. There were no framed photos in the room, but stacked on the desk were two closed scrapbooks, with another six placed on a bookcase next to her work desk. Ethan felt he might be justified looking through them because Blair had "threatened" to carve out an evening of "boring him to death" with some "necking and scrapbook looking." But his conscience got the better of him and he decided that he had no business peering into either dresser drawers or scrapbooks.

Ethan averted his eyes from the two scrapbooks only to catch a glimpse of several strips of newspaper that had fallen on the floor in the narrow area between the desk and the bookcase. He picked them up, and placed them on the desk—thinking he would tease the normally tidy Blair about being a poor housekeeper—and saw from the strips that one of the papers was local and the other was the *New York Times.* He couldn't fathom why she had the American newspaper, since he was sure she wasn't a subscriber. The Montreal

*Gazette* or *Toronto Star* he could understand, but not the *Times*. He opened one of the folded-over strips and found that she had cut out a large rectangle, removing what had been on the page. As far as he could tell, the remaining text dealt with rising fuel prices and the brutally hot weather. He guessed she might have found a caption or photo to go with whatever she had decided to include in the scrapbook. After all, Blair had informed him that whereas other people doodled, she wrote humorous and often naughty captions to go with magazine photographs. But then it hit him. Brutally hot weather? He looked again and saw the date on the top of the section he had just examined. It was from the *New York Times* dated July 9th of the current year—two mornings after the most consequential day of his life. He refolded the cut out and pushed it and the other scraps over the edge of the table to the spot where he had found them.

. . .

An hour later, Brooks stood on the back deck of the Montrose house enjoying both the quiet and the dropping temperature. Cradling an armful of split oak to feed the wood stove in the kitchen sitting room, Ethan had already started to boil some water in order to make himself a bowl of pasta, complete with the pedestrian accompaniment of a jarred marinara sauce. He would also cobble together a basic salad. He didn't wish to go out for his meal; tonight he desired complete privacy—that is, since Blair was in Toronto.

Ethan faced the rectangular back yard and watched two black squirrels come down from a tree and take a position facing him some twenty feet from the edge of the wooden stairs leading up to deck. They seemed to be waiting for him to make a pronouncement of some kind. This was the first time since the morning of his leaving the administration that he stood in such a configuration. On that day several months earlier he was about to announce the president's choice to replace the outgoing Chairman of the Council of Economic Advisors, who had recently lost his wife to cancer and was in no shape to continue his duties. But Ethan knew the press had no questions prepared about the incoming chairman. They were all anxious to get Ethan's response to what had only the previous evening been published by the on-line site "An Ear for Washington."

Brooks had chosen his friend, the journalist Tim Gerard for the first question. "Tim."

Gerard stood from his regular seat at the end of the first row. "Ethan, we're all shaking our heads at what Steve Jankowski put in his blog last night. We need to know more than what the administration released this morning." The question didn't surprise the press secretary. Gerard may have been a friend, but he was also damned good at his job. Ethan had nothing to do with the brief response released by the White House several hours earlier, part of which read, "The administration asks the media to remember that a web-site devoted to Washington gossip and innuendo can hardly be perceived as a trustworthy source for news. It is important to note that in a crowded social environment, the noise level often makes difficult accurate comprehension of conversation." Ethan understood the White House couldn't get by with that; therefore, as he expected, a differing response was crafted and given to the press secretary for the early afternoon press briefing.

"Ethan?" He hadn't realized how long he had remained silent after Gerard's request. "Ethan, regarding the release your office put out this morning, Jankowski responded by swearing that he heard everything accurately—that the noise level didn't interfere at all with his comprehension."

Ethan knew that Steve Jankowski had reported accurately what he heard. How could he have failed initially to recognize Jankowski when the blogger stopped by the booth at Martin's Tavern and said hello while Owen Peterborough was heading toward the rest room? It was only when Jankowski reappeared at the edge of the booth—where the chief of staff couldn't see him—that Ethan finally connected the man's face to his occupation. It was a minute—maybe two—after Owen Peterborough had confessed to his and his brother's interest in the same woman. Ethan couldn't prevent Peterborough from what he said next--that which Jankowski heard plainly and then placed on his site later that night. A mere fourteen hours later, Ethan stood before the press and stared helplessly at Tim Gerard.

Ethan now looked for the squirrels. They were gone, and he hadn't even seen them leave, although he hadn't diverted his eyes from them at all.

. . .

The cracking from inside the wood stove relaxed him. The weather had dropped to 6 Celsius—43 degrees Fahrenheit—making Ethan ponder a winter in Kingston, which, while likely not colder than his winters in Vermont and New York State, would still be a new experience. For example, Blair had told him how long the locals left up Christmas lights after the New Year. That the city enjoyed extending the holiday illumination charmed him. The previous Christmas season he was deep in study and in meetings in preparation for his job as White House Press Secretary. He hardly had time to enjoy the season as he usually did. Because of work, he had to forgo Christmas dinner with his sister Holly and her family. This Christmas he'd be looking forward to getting even more distance between him and the disastrous events of early July.

Nursing a beer and waiting for the pasta water to boil, Ethan tried once more to understand Blair's cut-out from the *New York Times*. Was it just a coincidence that she had taken the photo and/or story from the front page, which surely included fallout from the press conference and his resignation? Yet he hadn't seen the *Times* or the *Washington Post* that day, leaving him at least some doubt that the photo and/or story Blair excised was of or about him. His mind ran rapidly through the possibilities. Mere coincidence? Was there any such thing? If she took out the story/photo of him, did she necessarily recognize that Ethan Brooks was the same man he purported to be now—Ethan Matthews? If she knew he was the former press secretary all along, then why did she allow him to lie to her about his identity? Someone who had seen him—or perhaps one of the photos she took of him on her cell phone—might have more recently given her a copy of the *Times* from early July and connected her new love interest to the notorious expatriate Ethan Brooks? But he was dead sure his appearance was altered enough—the beard, the contacts, the longer hair—to fool anyone in Kingston. How could Blair know and say nothing? She had only just confided in him more fully about her past mistakes and present fears.

The last three months had either revealed a latent or a newly formed side of his personality Brooks found disturbing. He tended to look now for that which fueled negative suspicions about the motives of others. Since the events of early July, he reevaluated his impressions of those in his life and substituted new takes on what they had said and done. Regarding Aashna's shocking rejection of him, Ethan pondered hitherto unperceived evidence of her capriciousness—or so he deemed it—and her failure to hold him in the same affections he had held her. Everyone from the president to members of the White House press corps was subjected to reassessment. Brooks realized he was wasting his time by sifting everything through his feelings of being betrayed and wrongly portrayed as the villain of the most stunning White House drama since Clinton and the infamous blue dress. But he couldn't help feeling the way he did. His grandfather used to tell him that emotions have to play themselves out. "Don't fight these thoughts Ethan, whether they're love or hate. Give them their space and expression. Just make sure they never dictate what you actually say and do."

Coming to Canada had allowed him immediate relief from his pessimism. The sense of crossing a border was palpable. He took solace in the fact that all he experienced in early July happened *there* and not *here*. But now he was bedeviled by concerns about Blair Babineaux. If she knew who he was and wouldn't admit to knowing his true identity, why not? The worst-case scenarios bullied their way into his imagination. Was she working with a journalist from the States and learning what she could about him—all for the purpose of contributing to a blockbuster story? Or was she planning to identify him publicly, complete with a story she penned alone?

"Oh, Jesus Christ." Having given allowed such dire and tawdry possibilities their expression, Ethan felt ashamed for having done so. He found amusing though comforting the simplicity of his next thought. "Blair is a Canadian; she would never do such a thing."

Ethan had just dropped the pasta into the boiling water when his cell phone rang. He knew it could only be one of three callers—Blair, his sister Holly, or the same person who called twice from

Washington D.C. but wouldn't leave a message. That person he wanted to believe was journalist Tim Gerard, who had twice been in touch with Holly about her brother's whereabouts. Holly informed Ethan of Gerard's calls, twice relaying the reporter's message that he wasn't trying to get information for a story; he was merely worried about his friend. Gerard promised Holly he wouldn't reveal Ethan's whereabouts or write a single word about him. Holly almost pleaded with her brother to touch base with the journalist. "He's your friend, Ethan. It would do you good to talk with him. It might help put all this behind you." Brooks didn't want to deal with the possibility that Holly gave Tim the cell number after promising she wouldn't tell *anyone* where he was or how to reach him. As for his parents, his mother died at age fifty-eight, a little less than a year before her son went to Washington—and his father stopped making contact by mutual agreement after his and Ethan's final and bitter meeting when his son graduated from college. The last time Brooks looked at Tim Gerard, the reporter's eyes were fully expanded after Ethan's response to his question at the early July press briefing. Ethan wouldn't meet with Tim or take his calls later that day or the next morning. After that, Ethan was out of his Washington apartment and heading for Chicago.

Brooks checked the number on his cell phone. It was Blair. He was briefly inclined to let it ring, out of concern he would question her about the newspaper clippings he discovered at her place. He could have gone through her scrapbooks to see if she had kept a story or photograph of him from the *New York* Times, but he didn't-- not simply because he felt he shouldn't pry but also because he feared what he might find.

"It's me, Ethan." Her voice sounded cheery, suggesting that she was having a good time with her friend Lisa.

"How's it going?" She filled him in on what she and her friend had been doing, everything from listening to Nora Jones to critiquing the late summer's major film releases. "We just returned from a delicious dinner at Richmond Station. I'll have to take you there. Have you eaten yet?"

He moved to the stove to stir the pasta. "I'm making it now."

"What?"

"Pasta."

She laughed. "So you're still being stubborn, eh?"

Brooks grinned as he recalled Blair's teasing him about his faulty pronunciation of "pasta" in the Italian form, when it should "properly" be pronounced "pass-tah." As she moreover reminded him, "Darling Ethan, you must always use the long 'o' for 'progress.'" Punctuated by occasional pinches and soft punches, Blair pressed into his vocabulary such British- and Canadian-isms as "kerfuffle" and "dodgy" as well as asking him to erase all definite articles before "hospital" and "university." "You Americans overuse 'the' way too much, regardless of whether you pronounce it 'thuh' or 'thee.'"

Her voice warmed him. He wouldn't mention now the man walking behind her townhouse or ask her, no matter how cleverly, about Jordan Essex's physical appearance. That could wait until she returned to Kingston.

"Ethan, have you seen Tim today?" Once more her voice sounded playful.

He froze.

"Ethan?"

"Blair, how the hell could you know about…" His voice trailed off as his mind jerked him back to the cut-out from the *New York Times*. He couldn't get a handle on how she knew about Tim Gerard and what she was trying to do with her jocular demeanor on the phone.

"Oh, so you did see him. I understand everything clearly now, Ethan. As soon as I leave town, all your promises start to be broken. I should have known you'd have to see him." Her mock disappointment only made her designs even more incomprehensible to him.

"Blair, what are you saying? How the hell did you know about Tim?"

Her hesitation suggested that she didn't comprehend either his question or the tone of his voice. "Ethan, I'm confused. Are you mad at me? I was just having fun with you."

"But you mentioned Tim, and I don't understand how you…could know. Oh. Blair, I'm sorry."

Tim. The familiar name for Tim Horton's—the favorite chain of coffee shops in Ontario. Saying "Tim" or "Timmy" was simply a colloquial way of identifying the coffee or the establishment. He had promised that he'd never go there without her.

"Ethan? You're not making sense. Can I ask again if you're upset with me?"

"Of course not. It was just a bad attempt at play acting."

"Is everything all right at my place?"

"Yes. Don't worry about anything. Just have a good time with Lisa."

"I'd have a better time if you'd come over tomorrow. But I understand."

"Thank you. You know I have this thing going with old Tim, so…"

"Tell him I said hello. Love you. Bye." Once more she hung up without giving him time to reply.

Checking the pasta, Ethan poured the jarred marinara sauce into a sauce pan and searched the refrigerator for some greens. His cell phone rang again. Perhaps Blair was still worried that he was mad about something. No. It was an 802 area code.

# CHAPTER 10

"Hi, Ethan." The quiver in her voice let Ethan know she was upset.

"Is everything all right, Holly?"

"Yes, we're all fine. The girls send their love."

"Send mine back. Tell them I miss them."

"I will." She seemed at a loss for what to say.

"Jeff okay?"

Oh, yes. He wants to know if you've caught any Canadian fish."

"Holly, I'm guessing Tim called again and you told him where I was." Ethan's tone was light enough so she wouldn't think he was accusing her of breaking her promise.

Her response was forceful, without any trace of a quiver. "No, I did not. I said I wouldn't and I haven't. And without your permission I never will."

Ethan thought to ask if she gave Gerard his cell number, but he didn't wish to hurt or anger her. "I'm sorry, Holly. I didn't mean anything by that. So, what's on your mind? If you're wondering how I am, I'm good. Tell Jeff I haven't dropped a line in water since I've been here. Anyway, Richard's house is just the best place to stay. You'll love it when you come up. As far as my state of mind, I'm sorting things out a little at a time." He hadn't intended to tell her yet, but he reasoned it would make her worry less about him if he said something about his social life. "And Holly, I'm seeing someone."

"You are? That's wonderful, Ethan." The reemergence of the shakiness in her voice belied her stated pleasure.

"Holly, there's something wrong, isn't there. What is it?"

"Tim did call again. He asked for a number where he could reach you, and I…"

"Oh Holly, why did you give it to him?" Now that his suspicions were confirmed about the call he received at Fort Henry.

"No, no. I didn't, Ethan. I swear I didn't. It's just that I promised him I'd give you *his* number. I know you probably don't want it, but please take it down. He said he wants to talk with you whenever you feel comfortable doing so. He's your friend, Ethan. He's worried about you and he wants to help if he can. I can't believe he'd write a story about you and betray your trust. Please call him—for me. I hate that you're so isolated like this. Every bone in my body tells me it would do you good to talk to him. Please? Can I give you his number?"

Ethan felt utterly foolish and ashamed for having doubted his sister. Her voice quivered only because she was afraid he'd be mad at her. What was wrong with him? How could he have made her fearful of his reaction?

"Yes of course, let me have his number. I can't promise when or if I'll call him, but I promise you I'll think very seriously about doing so." The pause was only momentary. "Thank you so much for your love and concern."

"You know there's nothing I wouldn't do for you. I just want to do more, that's all."

"I don't deserve you. Wait, let me get a pad and something to write with. Okay, I'm ready."

After she shared Tim's number, repeating it once, she hesitated for a long moment. "So, who's this woman you're seeing?"

"I'll tell you when I see you."

. . .

Brooks set his cell phone on the table and moved to the stove to strain the pasta. He'd let it cook too long. Refusing to eat the clotted linguini, he decided to make do with a frozen pizza and salad. Before he opened the freezer compartment, he cast a glance at his phone and knew something was wrong. He checked his recent calls—from Holly, Blair, and the number from the caller in Washington. He compared the last number and the one his sister gave him. They weren't the same. Yet the simple fact that the number Gerard gave to Holly was different really didn't mean much. Tim could have called from his office yet given Holly his home number. Tim and his wife recently had a baby boy in June; therefore, Vicki Gerard would likely be home and could take a message for her husband. Still, if he called earlier how would he have gotten Ethan's cell number? Why would he ask Holly to share his number if he already knew Ethan's? The call at Fort Henry had to be from someone else. Brooks decided to dismiss it as a wrong number, because not to do so would leave him with only one other conclusion—the call had come from someone more hostile to him or to his desire for privacy.

. . .

In July, when he returned to his apartment after his final Oval Office visit, Ethan found a dozen messages on his apartment phone's answering machine. He hadn't bothered to check his cell phone's text or voice mail. He shut off his cell the moment he made his way from the Oval Office past the Roosevelt Room and around to the West Wing Lobby, on a route he took purposely to avoid going by his now former office, even though several staffers made their disappointment and disgust most clear as he passed through the halls. But it was the sound of the president's voice as Ethan left the Oval Office that reverberated as Ethan made his way outside the West Wing entrance. "We'll have your personal belongings sent to your place sometime this afternoon." Ethan had always imagined Jack Peterborough's final words to him being something along the lines of "I can't thank you enough for the excellent job you've done for me and the American people." The men would then shake hands warmly, and perhaps the president would clap him on the arm and speak of getting together again in the future. Instead, Peterborough remained standing behind his desk with arms folded across his chest and eyes staring down at the desktop—to where they had shifted when he finished his bitter monologue with a terse and contemptuous "That will be all, Ethan."

As he headed up Connecticut Avenue NW toward Farragut Square, Brooks felt shoved forward by both anger and shame—the latter more powerful, even though he believed anger and a sense of betrayal should have been his only emotions. But betrayal had shifted sides as Ethan felt the lash of the president's words, "You've betrayed me, Ethan. You've betrayed us all." How could he have stood before the press and done what his conscience told him was the right thing and immediately felt the full force of censure? How could he have expected understanding, let alone admiration for his decision? And why did he head toward Farragut Square—the center of the city's business and commercial district after leaving the White House grounds? He and Aashna had attended one of the summer concerts there three weeks earlier, and coming back from the event she gave him hope that she'd seriously consider marriage after the end of Peterborough's first term. Was he presently seeking some connection to her while she was at the time away from the city with the First Lady? Or did he simply need to get his feet off polished floors and outdoor cement and stand on grass and dirt while he regained control of himself? He looked at the others sharing the area and wondered why they weren't pointing fingers at the man just fired by the president of the United States.

During the hour he spent among the pedestrian traffic in Farragut Square, he accepted that he'd have to heal; he'd have to leave everything behind and start again. But the public wouldn't give him the necessary time to nurse his wounds or reconstruct his life. He'd have to leave, disappear, and with time re-emerge as another person—newly forged from trauma and reshaped into a man whose painful experience would never again allow a sense of self-confidence, vanity, or belief in principle and fairness to leave him so vulnerable. That time had not yet come, however, and here in the Montroses' designer kitchen he was still reliving what happened and castigating himself for his unforgiveable naiveté.

Fortunately cutting through the grating sound of self-censure was his grandfather's calm and supportive voice when young Ethan had confessed to dwelling on all that was going wrong with his life—namely problems with teenage girls and the humiliation and sadness that accompany a missing father from a boy's life. Dan Brooks told his grandson that he too had those moments of depression—he was a widower and had the misfortune of watching his son do considerable emotional damage his daughter-in-law and grandchildren Ethan and Holly. "Ethan, whenever you feel really bad, just take up a hobby or choose a topic you want to read about." Other than their books, Ethan and Holly had both enjoyed puzzles of all kinds, and, as an adult,

Brooks had occasionally treated himself to crossword puzzles when he had the time. Coincidentally, Tina Montrose was an unapologetic puzzle fanatic, and the night before she and Richard left she showed Ethan where she kept her crossword puzzle books and jigsaw puzzle boxes--"In case you get too bored with just sitting around the house. Don't worry about doing puzzles in a book I've already started. I have many more than I need anyway."

Ethan examined Tina's collection and chose one that was rated a six on the ten-point difficulty scale. The book was clean. He guessed that Tina kept it for a houseguest who wasn't as proficient with crossword puzzles as she was. He finished four other puzzles easily enough, although his stomach hardened when he read one of the clues— "Washington Betrayer." Six letters—the second letter being an r. He saw how "Brooks" would fit perfectly, even though the obvious and correct answer was "Arnold." Ethan bravely decided to increase the degree of difficulty and found a compilation of 300 *New York Times* Sunday puzzles—the most difficult challenge available. He briefly held the paperback book in his hands but then put it back. He felt certain that in one of these puzzles, which had many contemporaneous clues, the name "Ethan Brooks" might well serve as an answer.

Under the pile of crossword puzzles, Tina had stacked several jigsaw puzzle boxes. Brooks recalled with pleasure the many nights he and Holly worked together on some fairly tough ones—or so they thought then. He now chose one of the puzzles, which he'd construct on the impressive table in the formal dining room—a room he didn't use. The one he selected would do perfectly and would likely keep him occupied for quite some time. A puzzle of 1000 pieces--Jackson Pollock's abstract painting *Convergence* (1952), described as a "visually chaotic, explosively intricate, and expressively powerful piece"—a most "difficult and challenging" jigsaw image. Looking at the painting as reproduced on the box cover, Ethan saw that the description contained not a bit of hyperbole. The reconstruction would take considerable time and thought, likely frustrating and fatiguing him and daring him to sweep all the pieces back in the box before he lost either his temper or his mind. And yet he felt the challenge worthy of an attempt. If nothing but to provide an escape from his recent memories, the puzzle would do him some good, even if he failed to piece it all together.

Ethan spent his initial session putting together the outside frame of the puzzle. But as he did so, he continued to examine the photo of the finished product on the box cover. As a teenager he had dismissed the abstract school as many had with an immature swipe: "Looks like someone just poured paint on a canvas and rubbed it around." But now the painting intrigued him. The spirals and sweeps of red, blue, yellow, white, and black drew him in, giving him a sense of a clearly defined image—or "answer"—lying just beneath the convergence of these colors. Something was there trying to speak to him, but the sound was muffled by the sirenesque voices of the clashing yet harmonious colors. Eerie, tortured, and intimidating faces came into focus, as well as the exploded and collapsed geometric patterns that suggested to him a moment of utter chaos and transformation. But the shapes and colors also hinted at a resurrection of order and stability— a goal to be reached or at least an inevitability to be welcomed.

And then there was the title *Convergence*. Did it simply mean all things meeting and interacting—or the safety and sameness of ideas and cherished beliefs completely obscured or altered to the point of mutation or unrecognizability? What was Pollock thinking when he named the work? That the viewer would step away distrusting and lamenting all he or she had formerly accepted as truth or was it accepting and becoming healthier in mind because of the irresistible challenge of reevaluation? Ethan had never before given any work of art such deep thought, and doing so invigorated and inspired more than depressed and perplexed him. If he could analyze with a critic's eye the events and decisions of his life, he might be able to put the past behind him and find a way toward serenity in whatever was to come.

So motivated, he quickly stepped back into the kitchen and picked up his cell phone. He punched in the number and waited.

"Hello?"

"Hey, Vicki. This is Ethan Brooks. How are you? Say, is Tim there by any chance?"

She was at a loss for words. "Ethan? This is quite a…well, are you all right? Tim and I have been so worried about you these past three months."

"Vicki, I'm fine—I really am. I just needed to leave Washington and hide out in the woods for a while." Ethan was gratified by this evidence of continuing friendship and concern from the Gerards.

"Ethan, I can't believe the timing of your call. Tim left town late this morning. He'll be gone for two days but he'll be home on Monday. Wait. What's wrong with me? I can give you his cell number. He's changed it since you were…well, do you have a pen?"

"Yes, go ahead." As did Holly, Vicki Gerard gave the number and repeated it once. Brooks was disappointed that the number didn't match the one he saw while he was at Fort Henry.

"Ethan, I'm so happy you called. Is there anything I can do for you?"

"No, Vicki, but thank you anyway. It means a lot that you care, believe me."

"Of course we care. Ethan…" She paused. "Did you read what Tim wrote about you three days after you left Washington?"

"No, I really haven't read anything but the sports page since early July."

"I understand. Well if you want me to send you…never mind. Please call Tim when you can. Can I tell him you called if I speak to him before you do?"

"I think I'd rather call him first. And I promise to do so before he flies home. Where did he go, if I may ask?"

"He's in Canada."

Ethan felt his head hum with surprise and confusion. "Canada?"

"Yes, he's gone up to Ottawa to give a talk for members of the Canadian Association of Journalists. He was supposed to attend their big conference last May, but you might remember he tore his MCL and could barely move around at the time."

Ethan laughed. "And you were about to deliver a baby as well. I do remember him dropping his crutches during a presidential news conference. The president was thrown off balance by the noise." There it was. He had actually reminisced about his former job without bitterness. "Anyway, does he have nice accommodations?"

"Oh, yes. He's staying at the *Chateau Laurier* right in downtown Ottawa. Tim told me that the *crème de la crème* have either stayed or visited the hotel—from Queen Elizabeth and Winston Churchill to John Lennon and George Harrison. I can't wait to hear more about it when he gets home."

After ending the call, Ethan wondered if Tim Gerard's being in Canada was coincidence--or was it rather convergence.

# CHAPTER 11

The following morning broke pleasantly—with clear skies and a slightly cooler than usual temperature for early fall in this part of Canada. But Ethan hadn't been awake to mark the rising of the sun. He had slept as soundly as he could remember—his eyes not popping open until 9:50 a.m. Finally speaking with someone from his previous life, other than Holly and the girls, released a considerable amount of tension. Although he had gone to bed undecided as to when he would call Tim, he now made up his mind not to call him at all. Instead he would drive up to Ottawa and surprise him at the *Château Laurie*. But he would do that tomorrow—on Sunday—assuming that Tim's talk was scheduled for tonight. Today, Ethan wanted to treat himself to a football game at Richardson Stadium.

This wouldn't be soccer, as most in the States assumed "football" meant to everyone living outside the U.S. Rather, Queen's had a Canadian football team—the slightly amended form of American football, with its 110-yard field, 20-yard end zones, and three downs instead of four. Brooks was sure Richard Montrose wouldn't mind if he borrowed one of his absentee-host's Queen's University sweatshirts. For a man who wished to blend in with his local surroundings, Ethan could do no better than to dress in the home team's colors. As his head disappeared under the sweat shirt, the flash of darkness triggered yet another memory. He had similarly slipped on a Washington Redskins sweatshirt a few weeks before Jack Peterborough's January inauguration and took in an NFL game. The seats at FedEx Field were choice—a "welcome" gift to the incoming press secretary, with an assurance that he'd have season tickets for the following season beginning in September. Ethan had been accompanied by Leggett Humphrey—whom Jack Peterborough had picked as the next White House Communications Director. The idea for their going together belonged to Owen Peterborough, who reminded both men that they would have to work together in perfect harmony so that the new president's message would be delivered consistently and effectively, whether it was presented at press conferences, in short statements, or on radio and television addresses—and of course in all major speeches. "Plan your strategy, gentlemen, and be sure everyone is not simply on the same page, but also on the same goddamned line."

During the pre-game activities, Brooks and Leggett Humphrey talked about the uses and dangers of social media and the importance of Ethan's relationship with members of the media, who were in late December still intrigued--and many of them pleased--by the incoming press secretary's being one of them and someone completely inexperienced in the world of politics. Humphrey made clear that he had little trust in the media and fully expected the new administration to be treated unfairly by the press. Ignoring the fact that Brooks had recently worked as a journalist, Humphrey cast his aspersions and unloaded his trunk of profanities directed at all correspondents during his pre-game monologue. Seeing that the kickoff was only minutes away and needing a break from Humphreys' diatribe, Ethan excused himself and headed to the concession stand.

As Ethan waited in line, he felt a tap on the shoulder. "You're Ethan Brooks, aren't you?" Ethan nodded and the other man extended his hand. "I'm Tim Gerard."

Ethan was delighted finally to meet the journalist, whose reputation as one of the best White House reporters was well known. Gerard had corresponded via email after Ethan's big New York corruption story appeared a few months earlier.

"Hey, Tim. Great to meet you at last."

After the men exchanged further pleasantries, they made arrangements to meet the following night for beers and watch some basketball at Penn Quarter Sports Tavern just off 7th Street, slightly north of the Capitol. They shook hands again and Ethan collected his concessions and returned to his seat next to Leggett Humphrey, who spent the time between plays dourly predicting all the media trouble the administration would have and warning Ethan not to be "taken in" by any initial friendliness on the part of the "jackals" of the Washington press corps.

In stark contrast, the next evening Ethan thoroughly enjoyed several beers, wings, and basketball viewing with one of the "jackals"—Tim Gerard, who never asked a single question about the new administration's media strategy. They talked about the Albany story and half a dozen other topics of mutual interest, including the *Godfather* films. Brooks was at first annoyed by the nagging thought that Gerard was trying to establish a relationship that might serve him well after Jack Peterborough's inauguration, but Ethan realized Gerard might think the incoming press secretary had the same motive. There was no need to analyze the cordiality between them—the men just hit it off. After he began his job and faced his new friend in formal press sessions, Ethan saw the quality that gave Gerard his reputation as a dogged journalist. And yet, even after Tim pushed Ethan with follow-up questions, he always came up after the briefing and winked, as if to say, "This is the life we've chosen. It's just business—it's nothing personal." Throughout the five and a half months Ethan served as press secretary, the two men continued to see each other socially when they could—and Ethan enjoyed several meals at the Gerard home. Brooks knew Tim respected him and truly appreciated Ethan's own respect for the press and his accommodating manner. Ethan heard that Gerard defended him from attacks by some in the journalistic community, who saw Brooks as less forthcoming than they had initially hoped, by reminding them how different the environment might be with someone else—namely Leggett Humphrey—as press secretary.

Gerard was thirty-seven—a few years older than Ethan—and Ethan came to think of him as the big brother he never had. Ethan adored Vicki Gerard, although he had often to ward off her insistence that he bring Aashna Malini to the house for dinner. He lamely offered the "she's so busy" excuse—which of course was often true, but Aashna was in fact uncomfortable with the idea of sitting around with a married couple in a suburban setting talking of neighbors, lawns, and children. In short, his affection for the Gerards only made his concluding day as press secretary more painful. The expression on Tim's face on July 7 when Ethan uttered his final answer was painful enough that Ethan judged it as complete shock and great disappointment. Because he couldn't help believing the worst, Ethan didn't answer any of Tim's messages or return his calls. He didn't want to hear his best friend express anything that even hinted at disapproval.

But as he pulled at the sleeves of the Queen's University sweatshirt, Ethan understood that Vicki Gerard was still in his corner and her implications were that Tim was as well. Yes, he would drive up to Ottawa the next morning, but first he would try to put all else out of his mind and enjoy a football game.

. . .

The home team's defense stopped the visitors on the last series and walked off the field with a close and hard-earned win. The afternoon had flown by. Brooks kept his mental wandering pretty much in check by adding the yardage totals for Queen's offense in his head and keeping his eyes moving around the stadium between plays. The modest size of the stadium and crowd reminded him of those at New England schools, although the spirit level on both the student and alumni sides was consistent and for the size of the crowd fairly boisterous. He wanted to take Blair to the next home game so that she might explain to him what it was the Queen's fans chanted and sung. He was sure it was in Gaelic, and the woman who sat next to him on the alumni side had punched him playfully on the arm after Queens' first score and told him to get up, as if he knew he should have. She wrapped her arm around his shoulder and began the chant, accompanied by some kind of shuffle step reminiscent of a Broadway kick line—without the precision. Ethan also enjoyed the bagpipes included in the home team's band. The weather held for the entire game, and he was able to chat a bit with others in his section. He merely introduced himself as Ethan and was relieved when no one asked if his last name was Brooks.

He left the stadium with the happy crowd, able to walk a rapidly as he wished. Leaving FedEx Field late in December hadn't afforded him such pleasure, especially with Leggett Humphrey whining in his ear about the media. Always somewhat claustrophobic in public settings, Ethan didn't care to be trapped in the stadium exits with so many others pressing him from behind. A horde of reporters making their way toward him in the White House or on Air Force One also affected him, but as soon as they began their give-and-take he relaxed and enjoyed the company. Feeling grateful for his anonymity, Brooks headed toward his parking spot without anyone walking alongside him. But as he came closer to where he had parked, he saw someone standing near the driver's side door of his car, looking into the window. Ethan stopped. The man looked at Brooks and then turned and walked away.

By the time Ethan reached his car, the man had gotten into his own vehicle and pulled out of the parking space. It was the same silver Lexus Ethan saw yesterday at Blair's. Since the car drove away from and not toward him, Ethan was again too far away to read the license tag. As for the man, he wore khaki trousers and a deep blue or black sweatshirt and a gold and red ski cap—or toque as Blair called it. The man's body seemed the same height and weight of the person Brooks saw the day before. The clothing was far more casual, although its cost was impossible to judge at such a distance. Assuming the man was Jordan Essex, what was he looking for inside Ethan's car? Brooks concluded that the man was searching for any evidence of Blair's having been in the vehicle—perhaps something lying on the passenger seat, such as a woman's sweater, scarf, or hair band. There was nothing visible of that kind as far as Ethan could recall. Besides, had Essex spotted lipstick on a tissue or an emery board lying on the console, he might well have waited by the car to confront Blair or Ethan. Brooks curled his hands into fists. He'd have no hesitation stepping in if Essex attempted to harm or harass Blair in any way. As he was accustomed to doing since he left Washington, Ethan's mind raced ahead to possible and often dire scenarios. He'd step to the side if Essex simply wished to make a final plea to his former lover and then, when Blair expressed the desire not to see him again, Ethan would politely ask—at first—that he leave her alone. If a physical confrontation was inevitable, then he'd be ready.

Yet he wondered why Essex didn't wait for him to return to the car. How could Essex know for sure Blair didn't go to the game? Ethan stood by the car door and pondered other questions. How did

Essex identify Ethan's vehicle? Yes, he must have seen it when he walked behind Blair's condo, but how did he connect it to Ethan? Had he seen them together in the car or seen them together and then watched Ethan get into his vehicle after he and Blair parted? When would that have been? How long had Essex been in Kingston and when did he first learn that Blair was living in the city? She recently saw him down the street as she was going to the brew pub, but had he seen her before or after that time?

Ethan entered his vehicle and inserted the ignition key, but before he could turn it, another question stumbled into his consciousness. What if Essex was really after him and not Blair—or after the both of them—fully intent on some act of violence? Since Essex obviously knew which one was Ethan's car, he could have waited until Ethan returned from Richardson Stadium and confronted him. Then why didn't he? The first answer that came to mind was that there were too many witnesses in the area and that Essex wished to confront his "rival" alone. If so, Essex's visual search through the car's window remained problematic, unless Essex was planning to tinker with the automobile in some fashion. Ethan had no time to reflect on these questions when another possibility struck him. What if Essex wished to find Ethan and Blair together before making his move?

Ethan slammed his hands on the steering wheel. He cursed himself for entering such a web of fanciful assumptions. He decided to look for that silver Lexus and have a talk with its driver. He'd try to reason with Essex and, if that failed, he would warn him that he'd notify the Kingston Police. Then if Essex became aggressive, Ethan would defend himself. No, he wouldn't allow himself to live in dread of something that sprang from his imagination. Now that he had a plan of action, he calmed down and started his car. But before heading back the Montrose house, he would head to Blair's apartment for a quick check.

The late afternoon sun gave additional luster to the turning leaves, making his drive more enjoyable. He watched the orange and red leaves ready to fall, needing only the gentle persuasion of the breeze to separate them from the trees, where they had blithely hung for the previous six months. That they would fall was of no surprise—instead their dropping was anticipated with pleasure. But as Ethan reminded himself, there were other recent events that were completely unexpected, with results he couldn't possibly have anticipated. Such as his final drink with Owen Peterborough at Martin's Tavern in early July.

. . .

"That's right, Ethan. My brother and I were both, at the very same time, in love with the future First Lady." Ethan attempted to signal Owen Peterborough to lower his voice, but the chief of staff had become animated and in his present state of inebriation was in no condition to heed such warnings. "My God, I thought I'd have to kill him at one point." Peterborough laughed, downed the rest of his third martini, and looked for the server. "Where the hell is that girl?" Peterborough's voice caught the attention of several at a nearby table.

"I'll find her, Owen."

"Order me another. You get another beer too."

Ethan located the server and reluctantly asked for another martini and draft. She wouldn't budge until Brooks assured her that Peterborough wasn't going to operate a vehicle. Believing that he couldn't afford to upset Peterborough by refusing to order the cocktail, Ethan had to think of some way to get him out of Martin's Tavern before the chief of staff said something more damaging.

"Drink's on its way, Owen. Again, this should be the last one. I know I'll be done after the next beer.

"Okay. You're right."

Ethan hadn't expected the response. Peterborough was in agreement, as the softer tone of his voice also suggested. Now Ethan needed to come up with a safe topic they could discuss while they had their last drink.

"Have you been to any Nationals games this season, Owen?"

"Too damn busy, but I'll try to get to the old ball park later this month. My brother tells me I need to take a few days off."

"You should. No one's worked harder than you since the inauguration—or even before that." Ethan didn't have to exaggerate the compliment.

"Why don't you come with me to a game?"

Brooks doubted that a sober Owen Peterborough would extend such an invitation, but he would humor him now. "Of course. That will be fun. I haven't been either."

"Yeah, my brother, the current president of the United States, says I need to get out of the way for a while."

"I don't think he meant it like that, Owen."

"My fucking brother…" The server arrived with their drinks. "Thank you, honey." She nodded, looked at Brooks for assurance, and went back to the bar. "Pretty girl, but I don't get the tattoos. Do you?" Ethan shrugged. "How old do you think she is, Ethan?"

"I don't know. Twenty five — twenty six maybe."

"Right. At the very same age." Peterborough offered no context for the remark, and Ethan thought better of asking for elaboration. "The same goddamn age." Peterborough sighed heavily and took a full swallow of his martini, after which he tossed the speared olives toward Ethan. "I've had enough of these damn things." With a full meal, topped off by dessert, and all the alcohol he had consumed, it was miracle the chief of staff hadn't passed out.

"Owen, are you all right?" Like a passenger in a doomed aircraft, Ethan sat rigidly in the booth, awaiting the inevitable, knowing he couldn't do anything to prevent its coming.

Peterborough dropped his head and repeated a series of facts as if they were part of a White House report. "She was almost twenty six when I fell in love with her. I was thirty-five. We were both working on a campaign. We went out seven or eight times, but had no sex. I didn't want to blow it by rushing things. Then Jack met her. He was always so much better looking than I was. I had my father's granite rock build, while my brother inherited the softer and sleeker features of our mother. I was the smarter one, but that goddamn Jack and his irresistible fucking charm. Anyway, she saw him while she was still seeing me. God damn it, I *loved* her. I fucking loved her. But I eventually forgave the both of them, even though I still…ah, shit — fuck it." The chief of staff finished the martini in one gulp, some of it spilling out on his broad chin and dripping like tears onto the table top.

Ethan began to get out of the booth. "Okay, now that you've finished your drink, let's go. Meet me outside. I'll pay the check. Come on, Owen."

"You're not getting the fucking check!"

"Damn it, Owen, lower your voice."

Peterborough pointed his finger at Ethan. "I can talk to you, Ethan. I can trust you. Hey. You want to know something?"

"Tell me outside, Owen."

"No, no. I'm going to tell you…right…here." In spite of his intelligence and normally intimidating manner, his cadence at this moment was the same as the silliest drunk.

"Owen, quiet. Please."

"Okay, laddybuck, I'll lower my voice. How's this?" It wasn't quite a whisper but it was soft enough to get the others nearby to return to their own conversations. Peterborough leaned over the table, knocking over his martini glass as he did so. "Let me tell you, my young wide eyed and still sober friend--my feelings haven't abated in the twenty plus years since I fell in love with her, even though I married and had three kids."

"Owen…" Ethan's attempt to silence the chief of staff was halted by the appearance of someone who had stepped from the bar and stood just behind Peterborough. It was the man who had stopped by the table and greeted Ethan when Peterborough went to the restroom. Ethan finally put a name to a face the moment the chief of staff offered his next remark.

"Let me tell you, my boy. I think our First Lady's as desirable as she's ever been, even now, right now. Sometimes when I look at her I can't help thinking how badly I still want to fuck her."

The man standing behind Peterborough, whom Ethan now knew was the D.C. blogger Steve Jankowski, turned and took his place back at the bar.

# CHAPTER 12

Back at Blair's place, Brooks realized he had a problem with the timing of his trip to Ottawa, around a two-hour drive. Would he be able to drive to Ottawa, locate and talk with Tim, and drive back before Blair returned and found him gone from Kingston? It might work if he'd just call Tim and arrange a specific time for them to meet. Still, what if Tim had breakfast plans and wouldn't be available until the afternoon? Exasperated, Ethan decided to drop his cloak and dagger efforts and call both Blair and Tim so that the timing of the visit would work out. But he still couldn't tell Blair the reason for his going to Ottawa.

Following a quick inspection of all the rooms in the town house, Ethan stepped out the back door and walked to side parking area looking for the silver Lexus. Not finding it there or in the street, he returned to the kitchen and thought Blair wouldn't mind if he consumed the other half of the Turkey Club she brought home from a place called The Toucan on Princess Street. But his assumption of several quiet minutes alone was broken by the sound of footsteps in Blair's bedroom, which was right above the kitchen.

Brooks was sure he had locked the front door behind him, but could someone have snuck in the back way? Since he had turned his back to the door when he surveyed the side parking area and street, he concluded that it was possible. Ethan searched for something to use as a weapon. He ignored the impulse to find the largest kitchen knife and instead opened the storage closet and pulled out a wooden baseball bat that Blair kept for the purpose of defending herself from "mad dogs and promiscuous aliens." So armed, Ethan made his way to the foot of the stairs. He heard a loud thud coming from the bedroom. Was Essex going through Blair's drawers and closet, perhaps moving the bed to see what she might have under it? Brooks stared at the baseball bat in his hand. What good would it do him if Essex had a firearm? Believing his odds of surviving enhanced if he remained at the bottom of the stairs until the intruder came back down, Ethan took his place alongside the staircase, squatting so he wouldn't be seen until he could get a jump on the trespasser.

He waited a full minute before he heard the bedroom toilet flush. Something intruders never do in movies, he perversely thought. And then the sound of footsteps moving rapidly down the stairs. Still crouched and unable to see Essex descending, Ethan waited until the footsteps hit the wooden floor at the bottom of the carpeted staircase before he emerged from his hiding place with the baseball bat raised over his right shoulder.

The figure jumped back. "Ethan! What are you doing? You're scaring me!" Blair was back a full day before expected.

"I heard someone upstairs, and I thought..."

She released an exaggerated romantic sigh. "And my hero was going to protect me."

"Not quite, I was all about protecting myself. I thought you were still with Lisa in Toronto."

"Oh. Well, I love you anyway." She embraced and kissed him, while he hugged her with the bat still in his hand.

She informed him that her boss called to say her cover for the weekend received word of a family illness and left immediately for Winnipeg. "So I have to work tonight and then have to be there for the lunch crowd tomorrow. I'll be working until early evening." She shook her head at the sight of the bat still in his hand. "I saw your car out front and called your name as soon as I opened the door. I thought you were out walking, so I took my things upstairs and came down only to have my brains nearly dashed out by a handsome Neanderthal with a club. Even so, I missed you." She kissed him again.

"I was out back...checking the scenery. Why didn't you call and let me know you were coming? I would have had something waiting for you."

"Something?" She was being her usual naughty self.

"Champagne, caviar, roses--that sort of thing."

"I *did* call you—five times. And I left three messages on your cell phone."

"Jesus." He explained that he left his cell in the glove compartment of his car when he went to the game. It was there still.

"Well, Ethan, are you going to hold on to that bat until I leave for work? If I may risk offending your sensibilities, I wouldn't need that kind of convincing if you wanted to have your way with me. Although I'm beginning to feel that *you* might."

"Sorry. When I was a kid I used to carry my bat around all the time and even slept with it from time to time."

"Oh, so *that* explains it." She meant her remark as good-natured kidding, but he sensed there was something in her voice that revealed concern and frustration over his refusal to act on her hints and bolder invitations to have more intimate relations.

Could he satisfy himself—and her—by classifying his hesitance as merely "postponing" and not "refusing?" Was Owen Peterborough's remark about dating the First Lady—"I didn't want to blow it by rushing things"— serving now as avuncular advice? There was no question the softness of her body, the texture of her hair, the fullness of her lips, and the lower sound of her "bedroom" voice never failed to stimulate him. Her playfulness, when her voice modulated to fit the situation or "character" she portrayed, never took away from her sexual charm. But still he resisted. He wondered if he was cautious because he couldn't be sure how long she would feel attraction for him. How would she judge him after he announced his true identity, which he now planned to do when he returned from Ottawa? To make love to Blair and then be dismissed because he had misled her. He already knew how painful that experience was.

Aashna. An intrusion now unwanted yet impossible to suppress. Over six months of memories from the time they shared drinks at the Round Robin Bar at the Willard Hotel. Memories of his initial infatuation and then deeply committed love. Memories of his frustrations over her hesitancy and joy over her concessions. Memories of all he admired about her—her intelligence, grace, bearing, and self-assuredness. She was always calm under pressure and even-tempered when under considerable stress. Never harried; always feminine. Respected by her peers and adored by the First

Lady. Aashna's sense of humor was subdued and quiet, and he always felt a sense of accomplishment whenever he made her laugh. She refused to suffer fools, and Ethan did his best not to be one of the insufferable. Until early July, she never complained or whined about anything he did—therefore belying the assumption by some that she was very "high maintenance"—but Ethan took meticulous care nonetheless to please her in every way he could imagine, with surprise gifts, pampering sessions, and reservations always at her favorite restaurants. He remembered contradicting her only once, when she said she was "lucky" to have him. He was the lucky one, he insisted without contradiction.

Converging in his mind were also memories of what she wore and how she smelled. Her style was impeccable and, he thought, often regal, even if she was wearing "work clothes." He recalled every piece of jewelry and other accessory she placed around her neck, on her fingers and wrist—and occasionally on her left ankle. He was also stimulated by her chosen scent, which strangely she never identified or wanted him to purchase for her. This was only one of several "forbidden areas" of her life to which he wasn't permitted access. Yet such reserve in these matters only made her more desirable to him. He finally determined that it was her erotic aloofness that captivated him more than any of her other qualities. When they made love, she accepted him only when he lay on top of her or against her from the side. She wasn't completely passive but neither was she ardent. She preferred that he not kiss her on the mouth while they engaged in sex, but rather invited him, by the way she adjusted her head, to limit his kisses to her neck, where her scent was most pronounced. She cared nothing for sexual aggression or light-hearted teasing. She merely expressed her desire or approval with her eyes and lowering of her bottom lip, almost always accompanied by a soft brush of the side of his neck with the back of her hand.

Each time he lay with her afterwards, he experienced a nagging doubt—less doubt that he pleased her than fear that he would never have the opportunity again. As for his hesitancy with Blair's sincere offering of physical affection, he knew that his misguided loyalty to Aashna—or to the memory of what they had and how he had loved her—wasn't the only cause. He also feared impotence—the failure even to approach the passionate intensity of this incredible woman from Canada, who for some reason desired him and wanted a serious relationship with him. When would it be all right to love Blair and enjoy the pleasures she could bring? What penance had he left to do?

"I hate to ask this, Ethan, but have you seen anyone who might fit the description of you-know-who?" Blair tried to put a comic emphasis on the question, but her eyes betrayed her deep concern.

"Well, Blair, you never told me what he looked like."

"I didn't? Just shows how much I want to erase him from my memory. He's just a bit taller than you. Fit. Trim but not thin. Clean shaven. Shorter hair than yours."

"What color?"

"Ethan, have you seen him?" She was shaken by the possibility.

He couldn't bring himself to frighten her any further. "I just want to know what he looks like. Hair color is…?'

"Dark brown."

Ethan's stomach tensed. "Anything else?"

"A blackened soul." Her attempt at levity was half-hearted. "Sorry. No scars or tattoos, so the only other thing would be his blue eyes, I guess."

Ethan hadn't gotten close enough to the man to determine eye color—but he had seen enough to validate his conclusion that the man who was behind Blair's place and near his car earlier today was indeed Jordan Essex.

"Okay. Enough of that. How was your stay with Lisa in Toronto?"

"Much fun. We ate like farm animals. And gave each other foot massages. It was great being with her again. She can't wait to meet you."

"I'm sure."

"Stop that. She said that you sound 'dreamy.'"

"Blair…"

"Or did she say 'steamy'? I can't remember."

"Blair, remind me to call Lisa so I can apologize for whatever false description you gave of me."

"You're blushing." Once more she kissed him. "You'll stay with me until I go to work?"

"I'll take you to work."

"You'll spend the night when I get back?" She sounded as though she were a teenager asking her father for the keys to the car.

"Of course."

"In my bed, right?"

"If I must." He surprised himself with his playful retort.

"Remind me to poison your breakfast the next morning. Anyway, I'll be more awake than I was last time we slept together." She offered him a conspirator's smile that prevented any satisfactory reply on his part. "Oh, I forgot to tell you. Lisa and I went to hear one of our own local authors read from his latest book. He was hilarious. He's reading in Kingston Monday night and I don't have to work—so do you want to go?"

"Why not? I could use a little laughter in my life."

"And I don't give you that?" Blair feigned the sad-puppy-dog look.

"I meant a 'little *literary* laughter.' You entertain me like no one I've ever known."

"Now I'm blushing."

Given his painful past and a menacing present in the form of Jordan Essex, Ethan needed all the laughter he could get.

. . .

"Ethan, I can't believe you called. Hell, I can't believe you're actually in Canada."

After dropping Blair off at the pub, Brooks returned to the Montrose's house and placed the call to Tim Gerard's cell. Ethan caught him near the end of dinner with friends in Ottawa; therefore, he quickly explained where he was and invited Tim to call the Montrose's phone number when his friend returned to his hotel room. Ten minutes later, the Montrose phone rang.

"Jesus Christ, Ethan, have you been in Kingston the whole time since you left Washington?"

Ethan filled Gerard in on his comings and goings and apologized for waiting almost three months to touch base.

"Tim, I'd like to drive up to Ottawa and see you tomorrow afternoon, if that's possible."

"You bet. Just let me know when and I'll be waiting for you downstairs in the lounge."

The men agreed on a time, and Ethan was gratified by Gerard's excited tone. "Just one thing, Tim. You've got to promise me that you'll not write anything unless I give you the go-ahead. Not even the basic fact of where I am or that you saw or heard from me. Don't tell a soul. You have to promise me that."

"I won't even tell Vicki."

"You don't have to, Tim. I already did."

.   .   .

Ethan began the evening sitting outside on the Montrose's rear deck, contemplating both the present situation with Blair and Essex and tomorrow's meeting with Tim Gerard. Blair was at work and therefore safe enough, he reasoned. Perhaps Essex had satisfied himself with the knowledge that his former lover had another male interest and would accordingly dismiss her from his mind and return to Montreal. But Ethan feared the odds of that happening were slight. He expected a confrontation; he just didn't want it to be between Blair and Essex.

The two black squirrels made their appearance and in tandem feasted on black walnuts or whatever it was they held between their paws, glaring at Ethan and seeming to mock him for not having any food or drink of his own. Brooks stood up to get himself a beer from the kitchen, but the squirrels remained in their position, nibbling away. On one of their walks, Blair had told him that black squirrels had the reputation of being fearless and that was why they were such a conspicuous presence in downtown Toronto. Ethan felt envious of these creatures, whether their reputation was justified or not. They were disinclined to run away, while the former press secretary wasted no time fleeing Washington. The pair of black squirrels came out of hiding, whereas he was presently concealing himself from everyone he formerly knew, with the exception of his sister and her family, the Montroses, and now Tim and Vicki Gerard. Ethan felt a wave of anxious relief as he anticipated tomorrow's reunion with Tim — the next step in his coming out of hiding. How far he'd come out he didn't yet know, but that question would be answered in due time. He playfully waved to his two friends in the yard, and they made their slow way into the bushes, refusing to show any anxiety of their own. Fearless indeed. Good role models but probably impossible to follow, he reasoned.

. . .

Around nine that evening, Brooks stepped into the formal dining room to do a little more work on the jigsaw puzzle of Jackson Pollock's *Convergence.* He would leave for Blair's pub in half an hour, have a beer or two and perhaps some bar food. He'd wait until she finished up and then drive her home. Living by a schedule had been important to him long before he took the job as presidential press secretary, which of course demanded a Spartan adherence to a daily agenda. Still, too often since he arrived in Kingston, he was unsure what his daily plans were, never mind what he was going to do with the rest of his life. Blair was the spontaneous one, although she never went as far as suggesting anything that made him uncomfortable. He believed preparation was his guidepost, and when he made errors or felt off his game it was always owing to something he wasn't able to prepare for or couldn't possibly have prepared for—most significantly, Owen Peterborough's brutal and tasteless remark about the First Lady and Aashna Malini's rejection of him. Perhaps that was another reason why he hesitated to enjoy the affections Blair Babineaux wished to bestow. Would she ever be as steady and predictable as Aashna? Then again, would he really want her to be?

Glancing at the photo of the Pollock reproduced on the box cover, Ethan once more allowed his imagination to sink into the enticing turbulence of color represented in the painting. But now the red, white, blue, yellow, and black in *Convergence* turned his mind to the memory of these colors on the last day he served as press secretary. The flashes of recall flitted before him like the travel slide-shows his paternal grandfather took such delight in presenting. The red, white, and blue American flag on the podium behind him when he gave his press briefings. The blue chairs in which the media members sat. The blue, red, and yellow ties on the male and the black, blue, and off-white dresses and pant suits donned by the female members of the media. All of these colors merged as he felt shaping in his mind the enormity of his response to Tim Gerard's question at his last press briefing. The moment had weakened his body and spirits, but he strongly articulated his succinct reply to Tim's pointed question "Is that true, Ethan?"

. . .

On his way to the pub, Brooks drove to Blair's and checked for any evidence of a break-in or a message from Jordan Essex. There was nothing pinned to the door, and inside all again appeared undisturbed. Ethan glanced at the Waterhouse portrait *The Lady Clare* and stared into the lonely and frightened eyes of the subject. He was even more convinced now that if Blair darkened her hair she would look eerily like the painting's subject. Ethan feared that, if the situation with Essex wasn't resolved, Blair's eyes might become similarly frozen in fear and despair. He made up his mind that he wouldn't be the cause of her loneliness and would do all he could to banish the fear she'd been experiencing since she left Montreal. If it came to blows, he'd rely on the boxing lessons Dan Brooks gave him, along with the admonition, "Once you've decided to fight, don't ever hesitate. Just keep punching."

Making a quick check of the upstairs, Ethan peered into Blair's bedroom and saw that she had placed a small pile of clothing at the edge of the bed—apparently what she had worn while in Toronto but hadn't had time to wash--an attractive green blouse, a pair of jeans, a black t-shirt, a pair of socks, a bra, and two pairs of her panties. There was more in the pile, but he wasn't about to take a full inventory. The panties were of course the most intimate of her garments—and he realized that he had only once caught sight of them on her body—when she fell asleep wearing her hockey jersey. He had agreed to spend the night in Blair's bed, but would he act on her willingness to make love? Would it be right or fair to do so?

. . .

The pub was full of patrons when Brooks arrived at 9:50 p.m., and there were still almost four hours left before it closed. Fortunately for Blair, her boss said she could leave at 11:00, given the last-minute rearrangement of her schedule and her being out of town when it was made. When she first saw Ethan in the doorway, she could only shrug because every seat was taken. A large wedding party had claimed most of the seating—in the main area, in the banquet room, and on the front patio. Ethan asked one of the more sober merry-makers about the gathering.

"We had a rehearsal late this afternoon and the couple wanted to come here rather than have a sit-down at some stuffy hall. As you can tell, we'll need to drag everyone out—oh--in about half an hour. Big day tomorrow. A Sunday wedding at 2:00. Unfortunately for many here, that means the reception comes the night before everyone has to go back to work. At least half the guests have a two-hour drive or more." The man paused. "I'm sorry. I'm Kelvin Logan."

"Nice to meet you, Kelvin. I'm Ethan..." For a second he had forgotten his alias. ". . . Matthews."

"Do you live in K-Town, Ethan?"

"Yes. I love it here. How about you?"

"Me too. On Victoria Street just past Queen's. I'm the bride-to-be's uncle. See that woman in the blue sparkly dress?"

Ethan wondered how anyone could miss her. She was flirting shamelessly with one of the bartenders, moving her hips to a tune she must have heard in her head.

"I see her."

"That's my big sister. The bride-to-be's mother. The young woman shaking her head in evident agony is the bride-to-be. My darling niece."

Now Ethan realized why Blair's boss was generous about her schedule tonight. The wedding party and guests would be leaving at a reasonable hour in preparation for the big event early tomorrow afternoon. But Ethan was delighted being a small part of what was going on, learning some facts from a very nice guy about a family in the midst of a joyous occasion.

"Here, Ethan. I'm looking for a place for you to sit." Blair handed him a draft. She looked a bit of a wreck. Half her pinned-up hair hung loosely over her left eye. The perspiration bubbled on her brow. And she had apparently banged her hand into something that didn't give, because there were four bloody splotches on the four knuckles of her left hand.

"Are you all right, Blair?" He couldn't help laughing at her harried expression.

"At least two-thirds of these people are supposed to leave at 10:30."

"Hang in there. You can go in an hour right?"

"Oh, God. I do so hope. There, there!"

Blair pointed to a couple getting up from one of the tables outside on the front patio area. She pushed Ethan toward the spot, and two-swallows-worth of beer jumped from the glass and trickled down his left hand and wrist, but at least he had found his seat for the next half hour. After the wedding party left, he'd move inside—perhaps taking a place at the bar until Blair was free to go.

"Do you want something to eat?" Blair surveyed all of her tables, three of which signaled to her.

"Chicken wings."

"When we get back home I want something from you, and I'm not going to take no for an answer."

Surely she wasn't going to get bawdy on him now. "And that would be?"

"A long discussion on why I need to get another job."

Ethan admired how quick and attentive she was to her tables. Other than healthy tips, he was certain she received plenty of flattery and the occasional invitation from her customers. But if anyone could handle these pleasures and aggravations, it was Blair Babineaux. Ethan smiled as he took his first sip of beer. It was such a delightful early autumn evening. Clear, with only a slight breeze. The temperature, as he heard on the car radio, was 13 Celsius—about 54-55 degrees Fahrenheit. Resisting the urge to eavesdrop on the various discussions going on around him, Ethan took in the pedestrian traffic on his and on the other side of Clarence Street. As his grandfather liked to say about a person's physical appearance, "It's amazing what God can do with two eyes, a nose, and a mouth." In the span of a minute, he saw the alluring and the repellant as well as the graceful and the oafish. Such dichotomies he also recalled in the faces and forms of those in Washington whose job it was to elicit information and explanation from the press secretary. Given what had happened, he hated to admit that he missed them all, because he never believed he wasn't one of them—or that he was "the enemy" of the media.

Ethan turned and glanced inside the pub. Poor Blair hustled about, checking all her tables and moving the drink and food orders as quickly as possible. He admired her ability to chat with her customers. She was free with a laugh and a playful pat on the shoulder. Ethan felt almost chivalric in the urge to give her a hand. Yes, her "shining knight," as she called him. Swirling the remaining beer around inside the pint glass, Ethan returned to his street observations. He had no sooner done so, when he saw Jordan Essex standing directly across the street.

# CHAPTER 13

"Excuse me, but will you be sure no one takes this table? I have to run across the street for just a minute."

The twenty-something woman sitting near Brooks cautiously nodded, and he bolted from his seat, leaving his nearly-empty pint glass on the table. Trusting that Blair didn't see him leave, Ethan struggled past several patrons clogging his way, repeating "Sorry, sorry" as he banged into those standing on the deck and on the sidewalk. An approaching line of cars delayed his crossing Clarence, and when he finally got out in the street he looked to where he had seen Essex. The man was gone.

Brooks stopped when he reached the opposite sidewalk and peered to his left and right hoping to spot Essex walking away. Brooks made his choice. He turned to his right and walked quickly toward the corner of Clarence and Ontario Street. There he spotted a man wearing the same combination of black pants and black short jacket Essex had on moving briskly into Confederation Park. Ethan crossed Ontario and when he reached the park he ran toward the spot where he saw the man disappear from sight. Making his way to the distinctive low-arched fountain, Brooks looked back toward the street and down toward the waterfront. The lighting wasn't bright enough to provide a wide enough vista, and after walking another fifty yards without spotting Essex, he headed back to the pub.

Although he didn't confront him, Ethan felt invigorated by his active pursuit of the man who posed a threat to Blair. The dominating metaphor of his present life had been reversed. Instead of running away from, he was running toward active engagement. Realization that Essex might have been armed and that finding him might have led to serious injury still didn't dampen Ethan's spirits. Perhaps within the hour he would judge his feelings as nothing more than a temporary release, but for now he would enjoy the fact that the pursuit had stimulated him. He thought his friends the black squirrels might look at him differently now.

"Where did you go?" Blair had just placed the wings and another draft on the table.

"Thought I saw someone I knew across the street."

"Who?"

He couldn't come up with even a half-truth. "One of Richard's neighbors."

"Was it a him—or a her?"

"A him—of course."

"Good answer." She flicked him with her bar towel.

"Well, it's seems I just wasted a good sprint."

"That's my Ethan." She returned to the crowded pub and her still-thirsty customers.

.  .  .

Blair agreed to work an additional half-hour, seeing that the wedding party was taking its sweet time finishing their "one for the road" beverages. She and Ethan left the pub at 11:35 p.m. and walked to where he had parked his car.

"Ethan, what are you looking at—or for?" His head must have appeared on a swivel as he glanced behind them so frequently. "Kingston's ladies of the night aren't that discreet, Ethan. They're not going to sneak up behind you with an estimate."

He laughed as much at the delivery of the line—complete with Blair's amusing facial expressions—as at the content. Yet the humorous moment only made him feel more protective of her, as was evident in his behavior once he started the car.

"Ethan, you're spending more time staring in the rear-view mirror than at the road in front of you. Did you do something illegal tonight when you went across Clarence Street? Make a drug deal? Snatch a purse? If the police stop us, I'll swear you kidnapped me at gunpoint."

"I'm on the look-out for extra-terrestrials."

"Oh. Why didn't you say so?" Blair rubbed his knee and lower thigh and sat back fatigued from work but seemingly satisfied that all was well.

Then it hit him. Given that she had earlier seen Jordan Essex and must have assumed he was still in town, why wasn't she the one looking behind them?

. . .

"I'm going up to bed, Ethan. I can barely keep my eyes open. I know I promised to be more awake, but..." It was 1:15 a.m. They had shared a bottle of sparkling wine while they watched the local news and sports recap and talked about Blair's abbreviated stay in Toronto.

"What time to you have to be up tomorrow?" He waited for her to complete her yawn.

"Oh, I guess 8:45 to 9:00. I have to be in by 10:15. Are you going to drive me to work again?"

He smiled as he nodded. "I love the way you Canadians pronounce 'again.'"

She smiled more broadly. "Because we pronounce it the proper way — a-gayne,' not 'a-gen' as you Yanks do."

"And do properly."

She turned her body on the sofa so that she could rear up on her knees and stare down into his eyes. "Pronounce the word 'g-a-i-n.'" He did as she instructed. "So put an "a" in front of it and what do you have?"

"Okay, you have me there."

She dropped her head and pressed her mouth against his. "As I said, I need to go to bed."

"Can I escort you upstairs?"

She paused. "You're weakening, Ethan. At this rate, you'll be mine in seven or eight years — I can just feel it."

As they made it to the door of her bedroom, she turned and kissed him on the cheek. "Thank you for a wonderful evening, Ethan. I had a great time. Maybe we can do it again in the future. Call me. I'm usually home in the evenings."

"Will do. Well, I guess I'll just sleep here in the hall, but..."

"But…?" Her eyes lit up in mock anticipation of something wonderful.

"But I want to make sure you're able to get into the bed all right—I mean, seeing that you can barely keep your eyes open."

"Oh, I think that would be a good idea. I can't tell you how many nights I've fallen on the floor beside my bed because I couldn't keep my eyes open."

They went inside the darkened bedroom, and Ethan turned on one of the bedside lights. He saw the pile of worn clothing still on the foot of her bed. "Shall I remove your laundry?"

"By all means. But you don't have to wash it."

He scooped up the pile and placed it on the chest of drawers.

"Ethan, do you realize that you've just handled some of my unmentionables?"

"But I handled them respectfully, you'll have to admit."

"Then this shouldn't shock you." She removed her work shirt and began unbuttoning her jeans.

"Well, Blair, I guess that's my hint to head out into the hall. Is the blanket and pillow in the same place?" He was clearly quite comfortable right where he was.

"Ethan, you are the all-time worst hint-taker I have ever met, do you know that?" Her jeans were down to her ankles.

"I grew up in a household of orthodox literalists."

"Poor baby. Before you leave, will you do me the favor of pulling these jeans off my ankles?" She dropped on the bed and dangled her legs over the edge.

"I would be honored." He dutifully knelt down and removed her jeans, allowing the inside of his wrists to slide across the inside of her bare feet. He had never rubbed or massaged that part of her body, and the feeling was particularly stimulating.

Blair got off the bed, wearing only her bra and panties. "Will you pull the covers back for me before you go and leave me all alone to mourn my loneliness?" She began removing her bra.

Ethan again did as she requested. "There you go, my lady. The bed is open for your loveliness."

She walked around the bed and stood before him, her modest yet beautiful breasts pressed lightly against his chest. "Then I guess I should say goodnight before my eyes close for the next seven hours or so." She kissed him gently. "Thanks so much for taking care of me." She slipped under the covers and pulled them up to her neck. "I hope you sleep tight, Ethan." She turned her body in a semi-fetal position. He took one more look at her in the bed and felt the full effects of his desires. With also a palpable feeling of disappointment, he turned off the bed stand light and headed toward the door wondering if the game he was playing went too far. Had she forgotten that he had agreed to sleep in her bed tonight?

"Oh, Ethan. Would you put this somewhere for me?" He made his way to the other side of the bed, where he could see her extended arm in the darkness. When he reached out, he felt the top of her clenched fist. As soon as he touched it, she turned her hand and opened it. She placed her panties in his hand. "Ethan, my love, you know I think I could keep my eyes open for another half hour or so—that is, if you'd like to stay and keep me company."

. . .

Ethan lifted his head above Blair's sleeping body to note the time. A little past 4:30 a.m. He was surprised he had awakened, given the release of his passion and the rapidity in which he had fallen asleep after they had finished enjoying each other fully. But he was more astonished by how Blair had responded when he finally acted on her playful hints and slid under the covers bringing their bodies together. He had fully expected her to take the lead in the commencement and duration of their lovemaking. In his recent fanciful imaginings, he had flashes of her astride him and articulating in graphic detail all she would do to him. Yet when they came together and kissed passionately, she remained on her back as she took him inside her and did nothing more than gently kiss and caress his face. Only his name escaping her lips disturbed the relative silence of their blissful moments. When it was over, she offered no witty postscript or suggestion of a next time. She merely rested her head on his chest until she fell asleep.

Ethan softly stroked her hip and upper leg and drifted back to sleep.

. . .

Ethan, let's go out for breakfast before you drop me off at work."

He thought Blair looked fabulous in her light blue thigh-length terry cloth robe, with her hair still damp from her shower and her make-up not yet applied. Since they had awakened, Blair had made no mention of their intimacy. Rather, she acted as though waking up with Ethan was the most natural thing in the world.

"Sounds like a good idea. Where we shall we go?"

Blair dropped her robe in front of him and slipped into her panties, again without a hint of discomfort or nod toward decorum. It was all he could do not to remark favorably on her actions—but he wouldn't risk saying anything to alter the special atmosphere she had either deliberately or inadvertently created.

"I haven't taken you to Pan Chancho yet, so we'll go there." She hooked her bra and grabbed her jeans. "I've been craving their three-egg Spanish Torta all week—even when I was in Toronto."

Yes, this was the moment where she would usually add with her elfish twinkle, "What have you been craving all week, Ethan?" But she didn't, and for a brief moment Ethan feared that she would never again show him her playful side now that they had consummated their relationship.

She took one of her work shirts and excused herself. "I'll be right out—with hair and face far more presentable than what you're seeing now." There it was—the exaggerated facial grimace and flailing hands. He hadn't lost that Blair at all. But it was the other Blair—from the night before—that continued to enchant him.


. . .


Blair kissed him when he pulled in front of the pub. "Remember, I'm getting off at 7:00."

"No earlier than that?"

She was evidently pleased by his query. "I'm afraid not. If anything, I might be asked to work until 8:00—but definitely no earlier than 7:00. I'll call you if it's going to be later."

"I'll miss you."

"You can always come over and have lunch—drink a dozen pints—and stay for dinner."

"I wish I could. I'm going to use the time to get some work done."

"Research?"

"You could say that."

Once more he was unhappy offering these half- and quarter-truths. He just couldn't come up with a sellable reason for driving to Ottawa.

Blair put up her hair as she reached the front door of the pub. She took one more look at Ethan at the same time an impatient driver hit his horn.

. . .

Having checked the route on the Montrose's computer, Brooks headed east on the 401. He would go just past Prescott and then turn north on the 416, which he assumed would lead him directly to Ottawa. Knowing it would take two hours or so to get to the capital city, Ethan made a mental note that he'd have to leave around 4:30 to make it back in time to pick up Blair—that is, if she got off at 7:00. He guessed that he'd arrive at the *Chateau Laurier* between 12:30 and 1:00, giving him a good three hours with Tim before he needed to return to Kingston. Accompanying him on the trip were a large cup of Tim Horton's coffee and a cheddar scone from Pan Chancho, the latter highly recommended by Blair.

After making the turn north on the 416, Ethan replayed the pleasures of the previous night and realized that, although he experienced some doubt as to the wisdom of his intimacy with Blair at this time, he felt no guilt for having betrayed the memory of his love for Aashna. This freedom surprised him, because he had assumed it would take him a year at least to drive her enough out of his mind to permit his heart to accept a new object of affection. By the time he crossed the Rideau River, Brooks knew he wouldn't entertain, as he had so often since he left Washington, a fantasy of Aashna lying beneath him. He was confident that his sexual imaginings would be restricted to the woman for whom he now had both chivalric and passionate longings. With no other way to reach out to Blair at this moment, he took a bite out of the cheddar scone. She was right. It was delicious.

# CHAPTER 14

"Love your new look, man." Gerard slammed his right hand into Ethan's and grabbed his forearm with his left as he studied his old friend's appearance. "The longer hair and beard suit you. You're wearing contacts now?"

"I am. Well, Tim. You haven't changed a bit in three months."

"Not true. I've lost eight pounds and gained a new crown on one of my teeth. And you look fitter than you did last summer."

After further reunion chat about Vicki Gerard, the new baby, and Ethan's sister Holly and her family, the men ordered cocktails, crispy prawns, and some chips and herbed truffle dip to munch on. Brooks was particularly impressed by the elegance of the *Chateau Laurier's* Zoé's Lounge and its glass adorned atrium. Tim permitted him a long look around before continuing their discussion.

"Ethan, how the hell are you and where the hell have you been all this time?"

"I'm good—well, better now than I was when I first came to Canada." Ethan explained his short stays in Chicago and Atlanta and his relationship with Richard Montrose and the use of his home in Kingston.

"So how long are you planning to stay in Kingston—or in Canada?"

Ethan shook his head and lifted his shoulders. He truly had no idea how long he'd be out of his own country. He just knew he had no present plans to leave his place of refuge.

"Don't tell me. You met a nice Canadian girl. *Zum whol.*" Tim toasted Ethan with his recently-delivered cocktail.

Ethan was delighted. It had been too long since he had last heard Gerard's familiar German toast "to health." "Yes, I have met someone. Not sure where it's going yet, but…"

"But you like where it's been so far—right?"

Ethan flashed a broad smile. "You could say that, Tim."

The men looked at each other. Both understood what the expected follow-up question would be. They just weren't sure who should ask it. Finally, Tim made the move.

"Ethan, are you interested to know about Aashna?"

Brooks answered quickly to disguise his fear of knowing. "Sure."

Gerard repeated the facts as he knew them—in a manner befitting an experienced journalist calling in a story. He began by sharing what he had learned regarding the immediate days after Ethan left the city.

"The president wasn't happy that the press and the tabloids sought her out for information about you and your relationship with her. As you know, it was no secret that you two were an item. Anyway, he wanted her out of the White House, but the First Lady wouldn't hear of it. So she sent Aashna on a 'fact-finding' excursion to Europe before the first lady's big trip in late August. But Aashna was actually holed up in San Diego for two weeks—as we later found out. She then returned to Washington and resumed her duties, under strict orders not to discuss you in any manner. After another two to three weeks of hounding, the media left her pretty much alone. She's still press secretary to the First Lady."

"I assume she's well."

"She trimmed her hair so that she doesn't wear it up anymore. But otherwise, she looks the same."

Ethan smiled wearily. He loved her hair up for no other reason than the dramatic contrast whenever she let it down. When he told her as much, she wanted to know why it was so important to him how she wore her hair, intimating that she desired to cut it shorter and dispense with the trouble of putting it up for work. From a compliment to a perceived criticism of her appearance—a pattern Ethan knew only too well.

"And in case you were wondering, Ethan, she's not in a serious relationship."

Brooks laughed. "And you would know this how, Tim? Don't tell me you're moonlighting for one of the D.C gossip blogs."

"I know because she told me."

"What do you mean?"

"Since the beginning of August, she's called me every couple of weeks to see if I've heard from you."

"I don't understand." Ethan truly didn't.

"It's obvious she's interested to know where you are and, I assume, how you are."

"I really doubt that." The memory of her cold dismissal blocked his giving any credence to Tim's assessment.

"I guess I can tell you this. This past Tuesday, she and I met for lunch."

Ethan tried his best to present a carefree expression with a teasing "Does Vicki know?"

"Yes, she knows. In fact, she encouraged my accepting Aashna's invitation. My wife's curiosity was as piqued as mine was."

"Okay."

"Aashna almost grilled me on your whereabouts. It took all my efforts to convince her that I had no idea." Gerard chuckled. "That woman has no patience for small talk, in case you didn't know."

Ethan knew. "So she was merely keen to know where I was?"

"And how you were—although she asked that question only after she accepted that I couldn't tell her the where. When I expressed regret that all had ended the way it had, she didn't want to talk about it. She excused herself for a moment, and when she returned she informed me that she had to get back to the White House—so our lunch never got beyond the delivery of water to our table. But after she offered an apology for leaving early, she leaned toward me—I was still sitting—and placed her hand on the top of mine. I thought she was going to press her nails through my flesh. She said, 'You've got to promise me that you'll let me know where Ethan is just as soon as you find out. Or at the very least tell him I want very much to hear from him. Say I want him to call me, wherever he is. I had to change my number. Here.' She wrote it down and insisted I put it in my wallet. I just nodded and she left without even a goodbye. I don't know what to tell you, buddy. You didn't run off with one of her prized possessions did you?"

"Didn't take a damn thing, Tim." Ethan's reply was mechanical. He was surprised he could articulate anything coherent, given the contradictory thoughts that had suddenly flooded his mind.

"Well, she might be regretting how it ended between you. Or she might want you back, I don't know. But I'm not saying anything to her — or to anyone — about seeing you the next time she contacts me — that is, unless you want me to deliver a message."

"Let me think about it, Tim."

"Do you want her phone number?"

Ethan didn't move. After a moment, Gerard pulled out his wallet and placed the folded paper on the table. Ethan stared at but didn't take it.

"Well, here's the food. Ethan, let's switch topics if you'd like. Have you kept up with the Skins or Ravens? Do you get any NFL games in Kingston?" Gerard's face suggested a man full of regret for having acted against his better judgment.

Brooks stood. "I'll be right back. Where's the nearest restroom?"

Gerard gave him directions. "You're returning, right?" Ethan smiled at Tim's response, but his friend seemed serious.

"I am. And I won't be leaving early — I promise."

He had to get away from the table and collect his thoughts and pose his questions. Was Aashna truly sorry for how she treated him in early July? Did she still love him? Had the past three months altered her perspective in his favor? Why else was she so insistent with Gerard? Should he take the number and call her? Flushes of hope and caution coursed through him before clashing. Then another thought intruded. Why would she have cut her hair if she hoped to renew their relationship? He splashed on his face cold water from the restroom sink to help purge such juvenile reasoning. When he lifted his head and looked in the mirror, he felt ashamed of the image looking back at him. All these thoughts about Aashna, and it was Blair Babineaux who had made loved to him the night before.

. . .

"Glad to see you came back, Ethan."

"Did you think I'd run off?"

"Seriously, I feel badly about scraping at an old wound. I just thought you'd prefer knowing about Aashna's contacts with me."

"No, no. It's fine. I'm glad you told me." In truth, although Ethan did indeed prefer knowing, he wasn't at all glad about it.

"If there's anything more I can tell you about the aftermath of your leaving, just let me know. I don't want to--"

"No, no. Tell me. I'm interested to know." So much for talking about the NFL. "Am I still a national *persona non grata*?"

"Hardly that, Ethan. Jack Peterborough's opponents still hold you in high regard. They think you're the best thing that's happened since the election."

"Wonderful."

"But in all honesty, it's easier on the conscience and far more convenient for the members of your party to hang you in effigy."

"I was a registered independent before January, in case you didn't know. I only signed on after I took the job. Not very principled of me, was it."

"I don't want to hear that you're not principled, my friend. Jesus, how come we didn't know you were an independent?"

"Poor journalism on your part, Tim."

Gerard signaled for another drink. "Another, Ethan?"

"I think I'll need it. But after that, I better stop. I have to drive back later this afternoon."

"Why don't you stay in Ottawa tonight? We can have dinner and continue reminiscing. My room has two beds. We can have breakfast and you can go back in the morning."

"Can't. I have to be somewhere at 7:00 tonight." Brooks was troubled. Why didn't he say that he needed to pick up his new love interest from work?

"Okay. Well, did you read my column in support of what you did?"

"I haven't read a single thing, Tim."

"Okay, I'll send it to you when I get back. Before we part, let me have your friend's address in Kingston."

Ethan didn't respond. He couldn't even trust his best friend to keep the Montrose address confidential. "Tim, what's going on with the administration?"

"Hasn't been the same since you left town."

"Come on, I'm being serious." The revelation about Aashna had opened the door to his curiosity about all he had left behind.

"I *am* being serious, Ethan. The administration's relationship with the media deteriorated over the summer and shows no signs of repairing."

"Paula's the new press secretary, right?"

"Boy, you *are* in the dark. No, she's not. The president chose neither of your chief deputies, but gave the job to Larry Donato."

"Unbelievable." Ethan had no use for Donato, Jack Peterborough's deputy campaign manager and later adviser to the president. "I never judged Larry as a people person."

"You judged correctly, Ethan. Donato lost all of us when he announced that he'd only be taking questions based on the subject of his briefing. Anything else we wanted to inquire about had to be asked informally in his office sessions before we could ask it at the briefing. But if he didn't like the question, he'd simply dodge—and there'd be no camera to catch his doing so. As you can guess, we complained, but Donato and the president dug in their heels, blaming us for damaging the administration and hurting the country by our supposed fascination with things tawdry in nature. Namely, what his brother said about the First Lady that night he was with you—as if he expected all of us to ignore the story. In one sense, the change in our relationship with the White House was what we all had predicted. That is, we expected the end of the honeymoon period by March and that the president would become less accessible to the serious media as his term went on—the familiar pattern. But we were all surprised by the relationship we had with you and the administration all the way through June. Most of that had to do with you—we all agreed on that. I know that if you had stayed, it would have continued to be different, even if the honeymoon had to end. We miss you, Ethan. I think the country does as well."

Brooks shook his head. He couldn't accept Gerard's estimation. After all, his political party, which often indulged in knee-jerk championing of open government, remained bitter—as Tim noted--seeing how the incident was likely to affect the president's poll numbers and the outcome of next year's mid-term elections. Members of the other party might indeed have sung his praises for what the press secretary did, but only because the event spoke poorly of Jack Peterborough on both political and moral grounds. They would ask why the president didn't understand the coarser nature of his brother's temperament and the fact that he had a drinking problem—even if there was no evidence of such problems that anyone had seen up to that night. And how unseemly was the fact, they would argue, that both brothers had sexual desires for the same woman—the loser in the courtship still harboring lewd thoughts, so ineloquently expressed in a public place within earshot of a gossip-mongering Washington blogger?

Tim pointed his index finger at Brooks, in the same manner he had done so often when he asked a question at formal press briefings. "No, I mean that, Ethan. When you were press secretary, we knew the information was managed, but the filter was much wider than it is now. Everything we get from the White House these days has to squeeze through pin pricks. The number of document dumps on Fridays has increased and the president hasn't granted a one-on-one with a serious journalist since you left. And whereas we never sensed from him or from you even the subtlest clue that access would be denied to any of us, Mr. Lawrence Donato has no hesitation in hinting and in a few cases overtly stating that it wouldn't be wise to get on his bad side. Like all other press secretaries before you, you used to say, "I'll get back to you on that" and, unlike many of them, you actually did—but Donato hasn't once said it as far as I know. He's much more comfortable with the "I'll leave it at that" cut-off line. If I didn't mind insulting all Italians—including my wife and her family—I'd write that Donato is trying too hard to be a knock-off Mafioso in the job. We're all surprised he doesn't stand before us in a black shirt, white tie, and fedora."

Brooks released a good bit of his accumulating tension by laughing along with Gerard. "You're very kind to say what you have about my short stay in the job, Tim."

"Ethan, you always seemed completely comfortable standing before us in the formal briefings--just as comfortable, it seemed to me, as you did when we all jammed into your office for the morning press gaggle. You should have gone into the theatre."

"Well, I did. I spent over five months in the theatre of the absurd." Gerard rolled his eyes. "Sorry, Tim—bad joke."

"It's good to hear you joking—whether the product is good or bad—and it wasn't that bad, I have to admit. You know I especially admired the fact that you were never defensive."

"I was one of you guys, remember?"

Now a melancholy memory, Brooks recalled the pride and pleasure he took walking to the podium with the White House seal mounted behind him and looking out at the nearly fifty assigned seats in the room, with standees and cameras along the back and sides. Even the difficult questions and follow-ups, usually twenty to thirty minutes worth of questions, were exhilarating—with the media's accompanying and often cacophonous requests to be recognized and the senior reporter's final words "Thank you," which ended these briefings on a note of respect. Even those occasional distracting moments, from the impolite chatting by reporters while he was trying to answer a difficult question to the appreciation of the more fashionably conscious members of the media, provided challenges of differing types, which he always met successfully. He especially loved the post-combat banter with the media, often poking fun at his own performance in the face of their questions. And when his day was over at the White House, he relished sharing with Aashna all that happened. She usually said very little about her own work, even though Ethan always asked. Most often, she seemed more like a proud parent than a delighted lover as he spoke about his day, always praising him with "You are doing such a great job for the president, Ethan," followed by a firm and business-like kiss on his lips. Flattery and small gifts had far less effect on her passions than evidence of Ethan's success on the job.

"Tim, since I'm conceding to my curiosity, how well has Owen Peterborough come through the crisis?"

Gerard's head reared back as if he had suddenly come upon a dead body. "You don't know?"

"No, I have no idea?"

"Then you really didn't keep up with the story, did you?"

"Really, I read nothing and watched no television news since I left the White House. So, what happened with Owen?"

"Jesus. I thought for sure that you knew. All right. Soon after they announced your leaving, the president sent his brother up to Camp David and joined him two days later. The next day, Larry Donato told us that the chief of staff had resigned."

"You're kidding."

"No, I'm quite serious. Donato merely remarked that given recent events, Owen Peterborough and the president decided that it would be best for someone else to take the job of chief of staff."

"Did Owen take another job in the administration?"

"No—or not yet. He went to Great Britain right after his resignation and has been seen in several cities in north England and Scotland. He's like you; he wants to disappear. He fell on his sword for his brother."

"Even though they both felt it should have been shoved deeply into me."

"You might say that."

"Did the First Lady respond to what Owen said at Martin's Tavern?"

"Not a word. She's remained above it all, refusing to speak about her brother-in-law or answer any questions about their previous relationship, the fact of which came out soon after you left. Jankowski's gang did their job and quoted a witness to it from back then, and they even posted an old photo of Owen and the First Lady lying on the beach all snuggled up. In any event, Owen had to go— especially given your response at the press conference. He had revealed his continued longing for the First Lady using a lewd Anglo-Saxon profanity. There was no choice but for him to resign."

"Yes, Tim. There was a choice. The choice I made."

# CHAPTER 15

"I've told no one but my sister about any of this, Tim."

"I understand. Again, I won't say or write a thing—unless you give me permission to do so."

Brooks knew his friend dearly wanted that permission—and not just for journalistic and selfish reasons. Since Tim had written in his defense in July, he would love to revisit the matter with further evidence that justified that defense.

"Tim, early in the morning after the events at Martin's Tavern, I was called into the Oval Office. The president was there, with one of his senior advisors."

"Which one?"

"Susan O'Bannon." She had worked for Jack Peterborough for seventeen years.

"Anyone else?"

"Yes, Mark Lattimore of his legal team and the First Lady's chief of staff."

"Heidi Korman was actually called in?"

"Right."

"Interesting. Was Owen there or did he come in later?"

"Neither. The president told me his brother wanted desperately to speak with me about the previous night, but that the president thought it was a bad idea."

"I see."

Ethan took another sip of his drink and toyed with his cocktail napkin as he recounted the events of that early July morning in the Oval Office.

. . .

"Have a seat Ethan. You know everyone." Jack Peterborough stepped from behind the famous resolute desk and sat on one of the two striped chairs in the comfort area of the Oval Office. He gestured for Ethan to sit in the other chair. Lattimore and O'Bannon were on one of the two sofas—Korman on the other. As Brooks took his seat, he glanced at the framed portrait of George Washington above the fireplace. The first thing that came to mind was Parson Weems's story of the cherry tree and Washington's supposed refusal ever to tell a lie. Long ago Ethan had committed to heart what Washington's father supposedly said, "My son, that you should not be afraid to tell the truth is more to me than a thousand trees! Yes--though they were blossomed with silver and had leaves of the purest gold!'" When he was in high school his grandfather let him know the story was apocryphal, but that the lesson drawn from it shouldn't be casually dismissed.

The president continued. "First Ethan, I want to tell you how unhappy I am that matters got to the point they did last night in Georgetown."

"Mr. President, I want to assure you that I said nothing to Steve Jankowski or to any member of the press." Brooks hadn't even returned Tim Gerard's call, fearful he might say something he couldn't take back. "I promise you. I didn't speak to *anyone* after the fact." That fact was Owen Peterborough's crude admission regarding the First Lady—words Ethan knew he'd never forget: "Let me tell you, my boy. I think she's as desirable as she's ever been, even now, right now. Sometimes when I look at her I can't help thinking how badly I still want to fuck her."

The president tapped Ethan on the thigh. "I know you didn't. I never even entertained that possibility. I would be curious to know if anyone contacted you when you got home last night or this morning."

"I received four phone calls and several voice messages."

"I see. Was one of those from Jankowski?"

"Yes, but I didn't answer any of them. I regretted not having something ready to say, but the whole situation was…well."

"I know; I know." The president stood and commenced pacing behind Ethan's chair.

"Mr. President, I want you to understand that last night I did everything I could to make the chief of staff stop drinking and to take our conversation outside, but I couldn't convince him."

"You might have simply left or refused to go with him to Martin's Tavern so he wouldn't have had a drinking partner. Then all of this could have been averted." Heidi Korman had evidently made up her mind that the fault was Ethan's.

"No, Heidi, you're wrong," the president countered. "Ethan's not the villain here. I thought my brother had long ago gotten past his...never mind. Now we have to address the incident publicly."

Ethan couldn't imagine what the administration could say to tamp down the political wildfire that had begun earlier in the morning with the publication of Jankowski's account. Every media outlet had run with it, and the newspapers would devote the front page to the story the following morning. Coming over to the White House, Ethan decided to recommend that the chief of staff offer a simple but sincere apology to the First Lady, to his brother, and to the American people. He would continue with an assurance that such behavior would never happen again, followed by a firm but tactful refusal to take any questions now or afterward. It was important that the chief of staff project genuine sorrow and embarrassment—which Ethan was certain Owen Peterborough felt—or the resistance to questions would be viewed as nothing more than a dodge or cover-up.

"Mr. President, I've thought about the matter a great deal this morning and if I might suggest--"

"I'm sure you have Ethan, but we've already decided on a course of action. All you have to do is implement it."

Ethan was troubled by the president's choice of language. It seemed to him too much in the military vein. And yet now he could offer no suggestions unless he was asked for them.

"Mark, tell Ethan what we're going to do."

Lattimore walked around and sat on the arm of the sofa nearest to Ethan's chair. The president grimaced. It was apparent he didn't like anyone sitting so casually on the Oval Office furniture.

Lattimore smacked his knee with the palm of his hand. "Here's the deal, Ethan." How different Lattimore seemed from when he was part of the nervous quartet who dined with Owen Peterborough at the Willard in the late fall. Now Lattimore knew he had the president's confidence, which only magnified his own. "After you've read the formal statement, the chief of staff is going to address the media with a short comment. Susan, will you read the exact wording for Ethan?"

O'Bannon remained seated and lifted the folded paper Ethan noticed in her lap when he entered the room. "The chief of staff is going to say, 'I truly regret the embarrassment caused to my brother the president and especially to the First Lady...'"

Ethan's torso began to relax. What he would have suggested was evidently what the president had decided on.

"... by a gross misunderstanding of the context of my remark by a fringe member of the journalistic community."

Ethan pressed his palm down on the arm of the blue and gold striped chair.

O'Bannon went on. "He'll also say that earlier you, Ethan, had explained the situation fully and there was nothing else to add. He won't identify the person he was only quoting, given the unforgiveable and lewd nature of the remark."

Heidi Korman jumped up. "I think we all agreed--right Mr. President?--that the chief of staff will reiterate his regret that the First Lady had to be embarrassed and end by praising her and the work she's been doing for the country."

The four others stared at Brooks, all apparently pleased by the plan they had agreed upon. There was just one aspect they hadn't shared with the press secretary, who was trying to absorb what he had just heard—the part about the person Owen Peterborough was "quoting."

"Well, what exactly am I to say to the media?" Ethan's voice disguised none of his incredulity. Korman and Lattimore returned to their seats on the sofas and the president again sat next to Ethan, after coming up behind him and pressing his hands into his press secretary's upper shoulders and briefly giving him an abbreviated fraternal massage.

"Ethan, I think this will be the best for all concerned. I thank everyone here for putting their heads together with me on this." It was evident the president wasn't quite sure how his press secretary would react to the plan. Ethan could only imagine the look on his own face at this moment.

Mr. President, I'm not sure--"

"You know what, Ethan." Jack Peterborough was always very quick to interrupt if he didn't like the direction of the conversation. "Maybe it would be best if you didn't give the explanation."

"Sir?" Lattimore, O'Bannon, and Korman uttered the word almost simultaneously."

"No, no, wait. We'll release the explanation rather than have Ethan announce it. Mark, make the necessary changes in the wording. Then when Ethan goes before the cameras, he'll endorse what we've released and simply say 'Everything you need is in the statement.'"

O'Bannon was the only one of the three advisors who nodded with approval. "Then Ethan can tell them that the chief of staff will speak to them shortly."

"But not right away," Lattimore offered.

O'Bannon shook her head. "I don't know, Mark. We need to get this out and over with as quickly as possible."

The president waved off her concern. "No, Susan. I think Mark may be right. It will appear too artificial and orchestrated if Ethan introduces my brother. Let's all behave as if we're not so worried about public reaction—since we have the explanation on our side."

Heidi Korman again quickly stood. "Just as long as the First Lady isn't embarrassed any longer than is necessary."

"Jesus Christ, Heidi. She's my wife—remember? I think I'm sensitive about that point."

"I'm sorry, Mr. President. I was just--"

"Heidi, just keep looking out after the First Lady. That's what I love about you—your loyalty to her. Keep it up."

Ethan watched the conversation among the other four and felt as if he were no longer in the room. He couldn't believe it, but he had just raised his hand to be recognized.

"Yes, Ethan? The president wore a pleasant smile—quite content with how well this meeting was going.

"Sir, you haven't yet told me what I'm endorsing."

"Excuse me?" The president was genuinely confused.

"What the statement is going to say—that I'm then to endorse."

"Holy Mary mother of…I'm sorry, Ethan. We haven't told you, have we?"

"No, sir." The president's face had lost its benign expression. There was worry on it now.

"Mark—read the statement you drafted—revise as you read to get Ethan out of it."

Lattimore walked down to Ethan's left, forcing the press secretary to turn his neck ninety degrees, which aggravated him. He wanted to look at the president when he heard the statement.

"Okay. Here it is. 'This administration deeply regrets the events of last night, but protests vigorously the implication that the chief of staff was speaking his own words and thoughts.'"

Ethan curled his fingers into fists as Lattimore continued.

"'All of us understand that the daily give and take of politics can occasionally result in anger, when certain things are expressed that one regrets almost immediately. In such cases all of us should be more careful to watch what we say in the heat of the moment. There are, however, times when matters become too personal and reactions are even more difficult to restrain. Such was the case last night with the chief of staff.'"

Ethan was perplexed. What the hell were they trying to say? He and Owen Peterborough weren't talking politics or anything that was said about anyone else.

"'It is with both embarrassment and sadness to admit that the chief of staff was quoting the exact words of someone he had spoken with earlier that day. The chief of staff was angry and disgusted by the remark and his anger and disgust led to his sharing the remark with me.' No, no, I'll cut that and change to 'led to his sharing the remark with the press secretary.'"

"Good, Mark." The president looked at Ethan. "See, we'll keep you out it. Go ahead Mark, read the rest."

"Yes, sir. 'Unfortunately, the remark was overheard by a Washington blogger and immediately disseminated. It is also regrettable that this blogger did not discuss the remark with the chief of staff or with…the press secretary in order to determine accurately the source of the crude remark about the First Lady. You will of course wish to know who made the remark, but it is not our intention to identify the person. Why he made this statement to the chief of staff—the brother-in-law of the First Lady, is not our desire to know. Again, neither the source of the remark nor the position the man holds will be revealed. We ask that you refrain from asking the chief of staff or...the press secretary--or anyone else in the administration— the identity of the person who made the remark. Please respect the First Lady's feelings on this matter. She has been embarrassed enough.'"

Lattimore returned to his seat. The president placed his hand on Ethan's shoulder.

"Again Ethan, we think this will be the best response—for all concerned."

Ethan felt a paralyzing sensation affect his entire body. He wondered if he could even speak.

The president stood and clapped his hands together. "Well, that's that. Thank you everyone for doing this service. Mark, make sure this goes out right away." He escorted them to the door of the Oval Office. None of them said a word to the press secretary, who struggled to his feet.

"Ethan, stay for a minute, will you?" The president gently pushed him back into the chair and then took the other one and pulled it around so that it was directly in front of Brooks. The president sat and leaned forward. "Ethan, tell me what you think."

"Mr. President, I don't know what to say. Honestly, I don't."

"Would you like some coffee? Are you hungry? I heard your stomach growl a minute ago."

Ethan hadn't been aware of it. "No thank you, sir."

"Coffee though, right?" The president stepped to the northeast door of the Oval Office. "Bonnie, two coffees for the press secretary and me—and put them in mugs. We're going to take a little stroll."

"Sir..." Ethan didn't want coffee; he just wanted to head around the hall to his office. He needed to be alone with his thoughts, but he was unable to protest.

The president walked to the door heading out to the Rose Garden. "It's a beautiful morning, Ethan. They don't expect rain for the next five to six days. Be a shame for the clouds to usher in and spoil what we can look forward to."

Ethan understood the president's metaphor. In truth, the clouds would have mitigated the mid-90s expected for the next five to six days. "Mr. President, if I may. I feel that I--"

"Ah, here we go. Thank you so much, Bonnie." He took the two mugs from his secretary. "Come on, Ethan."

He opened the door to the colonnade. "The grounds were quite beautiful this spring, weren't they, Ethan."

"They were, sir."

"Members of the crew told me this was the most colorful spring out here in at least six years. My wife almost cried when the spring blooms began to fade. I assured her that next spring would be just as beautiful."

Ethan was certain the president was still speaking metaphorically. They continued down the west colonnade. Ethan finally stopped, unwilling to listen to more of the president's indirect attempt to elicit an acceptance of and cooperation with the plan they were at present implementing.

"Mr. President, I deeply regret telling you that I don't feel comfortable with what we've decided to do."

"Come on, Ethan. Let's go into the Rose Garden." What was the president trying to do by leading him there? As the men stepped from the colonnade, Ethan forgot he was holding a mug of hot coffee. Some spilled out and mildly scalded the top of his hand. "Be careful, Ethan." The president withdrew a handkerchief and blotted Ethan's hand. "There. That should do it." He tossed the now stained handkerchief back on the colonnade. "Your hand okay, Ethan?" His demeanor and voice suggested how well he understood his press secretary's discomfort with the decision. When they reached the center of the small lawn between the colonnade and the garden, the president stopped and both men faced each other, the president lifting the coffee mug to his lips. "Tell me what you're thinking, Ethan."

"Sir, with all respect, I can't stand in front of the media and lie."

"Ethan, I think you failed to understand that I've made it so you don't have to lie. I know we talked about your endorsing the statement and what the chief of staff would subsequently say, but you don't have to do that. You simply come out and announce that everything the media needs to know is in the statement and that the chief of staff would shortly speak for himself." For the first time, a twinge of impatience and frustration was evident in the president's words.

"Can someone else make that announcement, sir? One of my deputies?"

"No, it has to be you. The media would seek you out and insist that you tell them."

"I appreciate that, Mr. President, but I'd still have to go out there and field questions—not only today but for weeks or perhaps even months to come."

"Surely not months, Ethan. In any event, that's why we've included the comment that we won't be speaking any more about it. Sure, that will hang uncomfortably for a while, but it will pass. Whenever they ask, just politely remind them of what we said in the statement. They respect the hell out of you, Ethan. They'll soon concede that we won't be talking about the matter any further."

"Sir, I'm afraid this will damage my relationship with them, which will only hurt the administration. Perhaps I should resign? I mean I don't know what else--"

"God damn it, Ethan, I don't want you to resign. That would really harm every single one of us." The president fought to corral his anger. "I don't get it. I've made it so that you won't have to say anything more than that we stand by the statement." He paused, took a few steps closer to the Rose Garden and reached his hand out to Brooks, who came forward. The president gently grabbed the press secretary's upper arm and brought him close. "Ethan, I'm sorry for the outburst. This whole damn thing has gotten me pretty upset."

"I understand, Mr. President. I'm upset too."

"I know you are. Look, don't even say 'we'—say 'the administration'—no, say 'the president says' that we'll not answer further questions. You can even look sad about it, which you apparently are, so they blame me and not you. How's that?"

Ethan couldn't accept that such a response or look would be enough—for him. He wanted to offer another option. "Mr. President, is there any way we could simply admit that the chief of staff was under the influence, which then led him to say something he would otherwise never have articulated? I could say that."

"Do you know how damned naïve you sound? That my brother said what he said—even under the influence—wouldn't take away from the fact that he felt a desire for Amanda." It was the first time the president had ever used his wife's first name in front of Ethan.

Brooks felt properly chastised. "Of course, I know you're right. I was just trying to…"

"You were just trying to make everything come out so that there won't be any mud on any of us, but we're in an untidy business, Ethan. Nothing—and I'm afraid no one, remains pristine. Look. Can you see that?" He stepped further toward the garden and pointed to several wilted summer flowers that marred the overall look of the area. Ethan easily saw the point the president was trying to make about imperfection, but the conventional metaphor suggested the importance of removing what had lost its power to please, what marred the overall impression of the rest of the summer blooms. Would the president ask for his resignation if he continued to be unsupportive?

"It's getting hot out here," the president announced. "Let's go back inside and finish our coffee." Brooks had yet to take a sip of his.

They walked through the Oval Office and made their way to the Roosevelt Room across the hall. Standing at the end of the long conference table, the president surveyed the surroundings. "This is my favorite room in the White House. We've already gotten a lot of work done for the country in this room."

"I know, sir." Ethan finally took a sip of coffee. It was lukewarm.

"The reason I always sit in the middle chair on this side of the table is that I can look at that portrait of FDR. I find this portrait one of the most inspiring in the White House." The portrait did not have the pride of place in the room. The larger portrait of Teddy Roosevelt took the prime position above the fireplace.

"It is a striking portrait of FDR, Mr. President."

"He looks in perfect health—mature in years, yet virile and determined. No evidence as he sits in that chair of the polio that inhibited his movements. I think it was important to keep his debility a secret from the public—as much as p0ssible—don't you, Ethan?"

The president finished his coffee and put down the mug as he waited for a reply. Brooks knew what the president was driving at.

"I wonder, sir."

"What do you mean?"

"I don't think he lost any respect or significance when he was seen with his braces or in his wheelchair."

"Can you really argue that he would have been as effective—at least in first term—if the American people saw evidence of his paralysis? Would he even have been elected?"

"I guess I couldn't say, sir."

"Ethan, in politics sometimes being completely open and honest causes far more harm than any good it can possibly serve. I'm not arguing Watergate here. In our situation, no crime was committed or even ethics breached. My brother simply shot off his mouth when he shouldn't have. He revealed to you a feeling he harbored in the past. He committed a highly embarrassing *faux pas;* he didn't pass on a secret or order an illegal action. I thought he was done with the occasional excessive drinking years ago—as I thought his feelings for my wife had abated from what they were when I first started seeing her socially. I might well have been wrong to assume that, but I can have no doubt, nor can you, that he won't ever allow himself to drink to excess again—for as long as I'm in the White House—and never again allow himself to say anything of that kind about his sister-in-law the First Lady. He's deeply ashamed, and he has yet to face my wife and ask for her forgiveness. No one is really getting away with anything here, Ethan."

Brooks had to get off his feet. He pulled out a chair and waited for the president to gesture that it was all right to sit. Jack Peterborough walked to the fireplace and looked up at the portrait of Teddy Roosevelt astride his mount in his Rough Rider uniform.

"Ethan, my brother loves this country and has worked extremely hard for me and for the American people. I can't afford to lose him over this. So I'm asking you to get on board with what we are doing. Jesus, can't you see how I'm trying to make it as easy on you as possible?"

"I can and I deeply appreciate it, Mr. President. If only I wasn't the chief witness to what happened."

"I wish it wasn't so, Ethan, but unfortunately it is. And still I'm doing everything I can to give you satisfaction on this. Like my brother you've been a vital part of this administration. Your relationship with the media has given us the benefit of the doubt a number of times. To repeat, they respect and like you—everyone in the administration respects and likes you. I sincerely believe that without you as well as without my brother, I wouldn't be half effective as president."

Ethan's forehead now rested in his hand. "But their respect for me would diminish if they felt I was lying to them."

"God damn it, you've not been asked to lie!" The president turned from the fireplace and rushed to the table. Brooks immediately stood, unsure if Jack Peterborough would take a swing at him. "How many god-damn times do I have to tell you that you won't be lying or misleading anyone?"

"Sir, I simply meant that if they sense that I'm not being forthcoming..."

"Okay, okay!" The president walked the full length of the conference table and after a moment regained control. "Ethan, when anyone asks why you're not saying more, I want you to display as much disappointment as I'm sure you really feel and then say, 'The president has instructed me to say no more to you than what I have about the released statement.' Tell them also that when I address the media I will be happy to verify what I instructed you to say and not say. That way, I'll take the heat if they persist. How's that, Ethan? Good enough?"

"Sir, I didn't mean to anger you." Brooks was as disappointed with himself as he had ever been.

The president closed his eyes for several seconds. When he reopened them, he went on. "My brother did more for me than anyone in the public knows. Being older, he protected me not only from neighborhood punks but also from an abusive father. I'm telling you what I've told no one other than my wife. One night, my old man came back smashed from several hours drinking at one of his watering holes and accused my mother of cheating on him. He slapped her twice, cutting her lip and sending her to the floor. When I took her side, he shoved me against the bathroom door and told me he was going to kick my ass. I was thirteen—without a toned muscle in my body. I tried to run out the front door, but he caught me near the garage, slammed me up against the garage door, and clutched his fat hand around my throat. Just then Owen drove up after finishing football practice and pulled him off me by the hair. My father cursed him and swung wildly, but Owen was pretty good with his fists and broke the old man's nose. I can still see my father moaning on all fours in the grass. I had never seen him look so helpless. Owen got my mother and me out of there—and a day later our father took off and later agreed to a divorce if no charges were pressed against him. Owen was just seventeen. I really believe he saved my life and even my mother's that night. Given what I owe him, I can't turn my back on him now. I have no problem fudging the truth enough to save him. I hope you can see why."

Ethan felt further shame at causing the president to explode in anger and to make concessions to his press secretary. And what made Ethan feel even worse than the personal history the president confided in him was the fact that Jack Peterborough truly liked him.

"Yes, sir. That's good enough. Please forgive me for being such a pain in the ass over this. It's just that--"

"Ethan, just shut the hell up—okay?" The president flashed a smile. "I'll see you after the briefing." Peterborough walked out, leaving Brooks to contemplate the historic nature of the Roosevelt Room. His inspiration had returned. He truly felt he was doing his country some good as press secretary. He loved his job; he didn't want to leave it.

# CHAPTER 16

Ethan headed west on the Queensway, intending to return the same way he had come. But as he approached the turn south on 416, Blair called to say that she'd have to work until eight. The additional time encouraged him to take another route back to Kingston—one promising a more scenic drive, going through a number of the charming small towns and villages Blair had spoken of. Often, as the pace of his life became more hectic, he had lamented his inability to take the time to focus on and appreciate the everyday, the simple, and the more scenic aspects of his surroundings. Feeling relaxed, he passed through Kanata and turned down the more rural byways that would take him through small towns such as Smiths Falls, Portland, Morton, Seeley's Bay and finally into Kingston—or so his GPS informed him.

Heading in the direction of Carleton Place, he slowed down as a vehicle turned into the long unpaved driveway of a charming old house, with a white rail porch fence in the front and a visible barn structure in the back--likely a "hobby farm," as Blair had described such dwellings. The driver stopped his vehicle in front of a metal or aluminum swinging gate. Ethan could see a woman—likely the man's wife—coming down to open the gate accompanied by a beautiful white Great Pyrenees dog and a haughty duck or fowl of some kind. As he passed the farm, Ethan thought of the life he imagined the couple to lead as something approaching ideal. Close enough to take advantage of all Ottawa had to offer, yet far enough away from the city and with generous space between the house and others nearby to provide a sense of privacy and anonymity. Brooks took a last look over his shoulder as he drove on and saw the vehicle pulling through the gate. He also noticed smoke rising from either a chimney or wood burning stove. It was as benign a scene as he could imagine on this early autumn afternoon. He smiled as he imagined walking up to the couple, making an offer on their land and home, and then listening to all the reasons why the couple felt their life at the hobby farm had plenty of the quite difficult to water down the purely idyllic.

But the delightful image of driving home to be greeted by a loving spouse and family dog disappeared when he felt in his pocket Aashna Malini's new phone number, which Gerard had left on the table when the men parted at the *Chateau Laurier*. Tim didn't remind him that the number was still lying there; nor did he look at it when they said goodbye. Brooks knew he could have memorized the number and left the paper where it was, but his conscience wouldn't let him commit the number to memory or leave it for someone else to possess--yet it still gave grudging permission for him to put the number in his front pocket. Even though he hadn't made the determination to call Aashna and even though he and Blair had never made a vow or even a loose promise of a future together, Ethan still sensed he was betraying the woman waiting for him in Kingston. He debated whether it would be fair to move the relationship with Blair further along if he still felt strongly enough about Aashna to take her new phone number. Would he actually call his former lover — and if so what would he say? Would she do all the talking? After all, she was the one who stated a desire to see and hear from him again. He held none of her possessions; they had signed nothing together; and she was quite definite in ending the relationship. If he could accept that she had a change of heart about keeping him out of her life, was he obligated to hear her out? Could he permit himself to reconcile with her after what had happened in July? Was he willing to destroy his relationship with Blair for a chance to renew the one with Aashna? He couldn't believe he would do anything to risk losing Blair, but there was something about his feelings for Aashna that hadn't completely died — something he couldn't identify. Would talking to her reveal what that something was?

· · ·

Stopping for coffee after he passed through Smiths Falls, Brooks reached into his pocket for two one-dollar coins — called loonies--and felt the other folded paper he had taken from Zoé's Lounge. Tim had written down his P.O. Box number in case Ethan wished to send anything through the mail. "Just use an alias and your P.O. Box number for the return address. Wait. Don't use 'Ethan Matthews.' The 'Ethan' might give you away. Try 'Robert Zimmerman' or something like that." Brooks reminded Gerard that the alias was Bob Dylan's real name, and the men mirthfully applied the name of Dylan compositions to Ethan's present situation— "All Along the Watchtower," "A Hard Rain's a-Gonna Fall," "I Threw It All Away," and "It's All Over Now, Baby Blue."

Ethan found the sparse traffic on the way back to Kingston conducive to further thoughts about what Tim had told him regarding the immediate aftermath of Ethan's leaving the White House. Within an hour, the president issued a statement, a copy of which Gerard called up on his iPhone and read to Ethan. "We deeply regret the resignation of Ethan Brooks and will dearly miss him, as I'm sure all of you will. Unfortunately, the events of last night, complete with a salacious blogger's failure to understand the context of the chief of staff's remark combined with Mr. Brooks' confusion and unfortunate comment to the press have now made impossible the press secretary's continuing in the job—the decision to resign being that of both the president and Mr. Brooks."

Ethan assured Gerard that on that July morning he had misunderstood nothing and that he signed off on a resignation letter already prepared for him. He did concede that the president was correct in saying that the events of that night—including the "explanation" released by the White House did in fact make remaining as press secretary impossible, although he burned with anger at being handed a *fait accompli* when he returned to the Oval Office after addressing the press.

As Gerard explained, "We of course didn't buy the 'I was only quoting someone' defense after you came before us. They tried for two days to sell the story, but the opposition and sixty-eight percent of the public, according to a snap poll, didn't buy it either. For two days the media shook its collective head over both the explanation and the nature of the relationship between the First Lady and Owen Peterborough, although on the third day the White House explanation was more or less dismissed as the by-product of panic. The press instead focused most on the past relationship of the president's wife and his brother and speculated about the present feelings between the two. After the chief of staff went up to Camp David and told his brother he would resign, the administration started laying more of the blame on your doorstep. Their relationship with the press and media, as I've already said, deteriorated and revisionist takes on that night at Martin's Tavern have been forwarded—one storyline being that you fed Owen martinis and brought up the subject of Amanda Peterborough's pulchritude and almost badgered the chief of staff into a vulgar admission of his feelings. There's also the tale that you promised Owen and the president that you wouldn't bring disgrace to the First Family—including brother Owen, but that you broke your word when you addressed us."

Brooks was sickened by Tim's account, even though he assumed something like that had happened after he left Washington. Gerard reiterated his willingness to "set the record straight" and repair Ethan's reputation, but the former press secretary wouldn't give him permission. Speaking to Tim was a needed release, but it didn't alter Ethan's desire to remain apart from the turbulent and lingering effects of that day.

Owen Peterborough. Even after all that happened, Brooks couldn't harbor any resentment for the former chief of staff. He only wished that he could. That way, he could divest himself of the guilt he felt for ruining the man's career and reputation. As unwelcome as Peterborough's war stories and advice were at times, Brooks sensed that the chief of staff looked on him as a kind of protégé. Ethan knew of no one else Peterborough asked to accompany him for dinner and drinks. Yes, he was highly inebriated that night, but even so, such confiding of private feelings for the First Lady had to say something about the chief of staff's fondness for and trust of the press secretary. And yet with a single word, Ethan had ruined everything for Owen Peterborough and perhaps altered the direction the administration would go, at least in its relationship with the media. A single word he could have refrained from articulating, but at the critical moment couldn't keep to himself.

Of the several discussions Owen Peterborough had with the incoming press secretary, Ethan recalled the one they had on January 5th, fifteen days before the inauguration. He and Peterborough had been at the White House for a transition team meeting with members of the outgoing administration. After lunch, Peterborough asked Ethan to accompany him on a walk down 15th, across Constitution Avenue, then over 17th to the reflecting pool. As they started toward the Lincoln Memorial, Peterborough was as happy as Ethan would ever see him. "We've got the next four years—hopefully eight—to come over here and elsewhere and absorb every inch of history this city affords. I don't know about you, Ethan, but I can even smell its history in the air. I hope you're grateful for the opportunity you have to help make a difference in this country."

"It's beginning to dawn on me what a great opportunity we do have, Owen."

"You're going to be in a position to facilitate so much of what we hope to do. You're not one of the junior advisors or assistant secretary to whoever or whatever. You're going to be one of the faces of the administration. The president, the secretaries of state and defense, the attorney general, the First Lady, and you. You have to be careful, laddybuck—very careful to do your job always with the president in mind. I know we've gone over this already, but I want you to drill these responsibilities into your head, so there are never any mistakes."

"I understand, Owen."

As they reached the bottom of the Lincoln Memorial steps, the men stopped and faced each other. Peterborough's demeanor was intense, yet there was a strong hint of vulnerability in his eyes that startled Ethan. "You have to put the president first, because when you do that you put the country first. Ethan, it's your job to protect him— take the blows for him if necessary. Prep him well for what will be asked at formal press conferences and do what you can to direct the media's questions to that for which he's most fully prepared. At times you'll have to build a wall around him—at times to protect him from what he might otherwise know if you told him. There will be so much that he won't need to know—because if he doesn't know, he can't be put in an embarrassing position. Never—and I mean never—tie his hands, Ethan. He may need them to shrug off his ignorance or point in another direction. I know we've talked about honesty, and I again assure you that neither I nor the president ever wants you to lie. But being evasive isn't tantamount to lying—you have to understand that. Sometimes it becomes little more than an adult form of "keep-away." Remember that no one should make news except the president—not you, not anyone else."

Instead of walking up the steps to the statue of the sitting Lincoln, Peterborough turned and looked in the direction of the Vietnam Memorial. Without turning back to Brooks, he concluded his remarks. "Ethan, you must devote all of your time to making sure that the president maintains his credibility with the American people."

Further contemplation of that cold and clear January afternoon was suspended by what Ethan now saw ahead of him. On the two-lane road, an SUV was directly in front of his car going slightly below the speed limit. Ethan considered passing the vehicle, but just then he caught sight of a deer coming from the tree line and bounding across the meadow toward the road. Judging the speed of the vehicle in front of him and the speed of the bounding deer, Ethan was certain that if the deer jumped the fence separating the road from the meadow, the animal would slam into the SUV. The deer maintained its speed and Ethan watched it leap over the fence. A second later, it rammed into the front side of the SUV. Somehow the deer wobbled for several steps but regained speed as it ran parallel to the fence passing Ethan's car. Ethan jerked his head around in time to see the shaken but still graceful animal re-leap the fence and head back across the meadow to the tree line from which it had come. Ethan pulled up behind the stopped SUV and checked to see if the driver and her child were all right. The child was animated while the mother was shaken, but she assured Ethan she was fine and grateful that the deer survived the collision.

Ethan was affected most by his momentary sense of omniscience—knowing exactly what was going to happen to the deer only moments before it actually did. Yet, this wasn't the first time he felt such omniscience. Three months earlier on that muggy morning in Washington, he knew something dire was going to happen as soon as he mounted the platform and faced the media.

. . .

"So how was your day?"

"Very busy, very long, and very frustrating." Blair had her arm inside Ethan's as they walked out of the pub.

"Why frustrating?" He assumed she'd now say something about missing him.

"I've never waited on such a long string of such parsimonious tippers."

"Oh."

"Ethan, how much do you normally tip in the States?"

"I think it's still true that fifteen percent is the expected amount for okay service and twenty for exceptional service — although recently I've found myself doing the twenty for okay service and up to twenty-five for exceptional."

"Then today I must have rated somewhere between 'boring' and 'appalling.' I actually received a paltry five percent from a pair of old women who asked, as they paid the bill, if they could request a male server next time."

"That's because they were trolling for men."

"And I ended up in the net, eh?"

. . .

When they returned to Blair's place, Ethan came close to asking if while at work she had seen any evidence of Jordan Essex, but she seemed so content that he assumed she couldn't have. As he waited downstairs enjoying a short bourbon and water, he debated whether to stay the night. Blair would make dinner and invite him to stay. Yet tonight he would prefer not to, given his discomfort over having taken and kept Aashna's phone number. He wanted to come to a final decision about whether to call her — whether to keep alive any residue of past feelings for her — before making love to Blair a second time. He just wasn't the kind of man who took his pleasure whenever he could get it. This particular principle wasn't shaped by any religious training as a boy; rather, it was more from the lessons taught by his grandfather about integrity, fairness, and consequences. Dan Brooks advised that his grandson play life like chess—always to consider effects and results of actions several steps ahead of the one he was about to take. "Don't jump around as if life's a checker board," he liked to say.

But the situation with Essex also hadn't been resolved. Ethan fully expected Blair's former lover either to knock on the front door confronting her or to take out his anger and perhaps misguided sense of humiliation out on Blair's current male interest. Grandpa Dan also taught him to ignore any challenges or provocations from those he'd not likely see again but if they were habitual, then he must confront the person—verbally or, if threatened, physically. Ethan just needed to find Essex and get it all over with. Still, if Essex was particularly disturbed and vengeful, he might well attempt to find Blair alone—and that scenario concerned Brooks the most.

"Here I am all comfy and cozy." Blair stepped into the living room wearing just her Montreal Canadiens jersey—or sweater as she called it. "See--number 9. Maurice 'Rocket' Richard."

"Blair, I have another idea. I want you to come back with me to the Montrose's. I want you to see where I'm staying. You'll really love the house—especially the kitchen and back area. There are two black squirrels I want you to meet."

"I'm flattered that you want to introduce me to your family."

"Amusing."

"I'm serious now, Ethan. I'd love to come." She volunteered to bring the food and cook supper. "Okay. Let me change." She started up the stairs. "Should I...um, never mind."

Ethan smiled at her transparent attempt to gauge his intentions. "Yes, Blair, you should." In a few minutes she bounded down the stairs in her jeans and a soft blue blouse covered by a light sweater. Her overnight bag was slung over her shoulder.

. . .

"It's even more impressive than you described, Ethan." He had finished giving her the tour of the inside. "I adore everything about it, especially that bay window and the living and dining rooms—and of course the kitchen. I should also say something complimentary about the bathroom at the top of the stairs. This is a house worth cleaning if there ever was one."

"Now come outside."

"It's dark."

"I'll flip on the lights."

Brooks poured some sparkling wine they had bought on the way over--and they sat on the rear deck enjoying the darkness and cooling temperature in complete silence. Ethan could never be silent with Aashna. He feared that silence equated to boredom on her part and failure on his to entertain her adequately.

After several serene minutes of listening to the intoxicating sounds of the night, Ethan felt Blair's hand on his. "Let's make dinner, Ethan."

By the time they began putting together Blair's chosen dish—a Kefta, Tomato, and Egg Tangine—Blair was her normal chatty self.

"I didn't know you were a gourmet chef, Blair."

"I didn't either. Actually, I'm merely an ambitious cook interested in Middle-Eastern, Asian, and Indian dishes."

Ethan let out an involuntary puff of breath. Aashna had introduced him to the joys of quality Indian food, missing no opportunity to denigrate those lesser establishments who purported to serve the cuisine. His increasing tension and guilt informed Brooks that he couldn't wait much longer to make up his mind about calling her. Fortunately, Blair's dish was Moroccan.

About forty-five minutes after she finished prepping the ingredients and began cooking the Kefta, Blair said it was time for the final touch. "Can you get the egg carton from the frig now, my love?"

He did as she instructed and heard her say that one egg was enough. He pulled one from the carton and handed it to her.

"I'll need three more, sweetie pie."

"I thought you said that one would be enough."

"That's right. So could you hand me three more?"

Ethan didn't notice the smile on her face. "Okay, what's the deal? You originally said that one egg is enough."

"That's right—and it's true. So can I have three more eggs now?" It was then that she burst out laughing. "Didn't you take French at university, Ethan?"

"No, I took Italian. Wait. I learned enough French on my own. Jesus. That was mean, Blair."

"As I always say to all my non-French Canadian friends, 'Remember, one egg is an *oeuf.*'"

Playfully indignant, Ethan whispered menacingly, "I won't say when it will happen, but I swear I'll embarrass you in public with an Italian word—or an Americanism—so that you'll know how humiliated you've just made me feel."

They both looked at each other with wonder. If for no other reason than their shared sense of humor, they had each found someone both had never imagined would come into their lives.

. . .

"That was very good. No, far better than that. I've had nothing like it."

"You're sweet, but it's really only pasta and meatballs without the pasta and with lamb instead of beef." But she was pleased with what she had served. "The next time I'll do something Asian—spicy Asian—hot and spicy Asian."

"Okay, so would you like another glass of wine? Then we can go downstairs to my lair and watch something on the TV."

"The wine would be nice, but I'd rather go into the formal dining room and look at that puzzle you started. I barely got a look when you gave me the tour."

"All right. I'll open some wine, and then you can see what little I've gotten accomplished on Pollock's *Convergence.*"

"Jackson Pollock?"

"Yes." Ethan bent down to retrieve under the counter a fresh bottle of wine.

"I'll have you know, Ethan, that he's the author of one of my favorite quotations. One of the few I remember from my art history class."

Ethan grabbed the bottle of Pinot Grigio and started lifting his torso. He felt the folded paper with Aashna's phone number crinkle inside his pocket. "What was the quotation, Blair?"

"He said, 'Art is coming face to face with yourself.'"

# CHAPTER 17

"Are you dressed?"

"Would it matter? Come on in. I'm just about to put on my face—if I can find it."

Blair looked as lovely as always—even though she was merely adorned in her "work togs"–jeans and her brew pub t-shirt. She had showered, made the bed in one of the upstairs guest rooms, and packed her overnight bag. She and Ethan were headed out for breakfast and then a walk on the Queen's campus before she had to report for work at 10:00. Ethan would drop by for a small bite to eat around 1:30 and in the evening they would go and listen to the Kingston author Blair had seen in Toronto. The morning was sunny though rather crisp for early autumn. Had Jordan Essex and Aashna Malini not existed, the day would have been as perfect as Ethan could have hoped.

Blair finished tying her second shoe and grabbed her bag. "Ethan, I hope you weren't insulted when I suggested we sleep apart last night."

"Of course not. After a good cry, I finally dozed off."

"I wish that was true. But I did miss and think of you being down there all alone. I was tempted to pay a surprise visit, but I reminded myself that I was a guest in a home belonging to a couple I've never met—a couple who had no idea I was sleeping over."

"I won't say anything if you won't."

"My lips are sealed." She paused as they reached the top of the stairs. "I said my lips are sealed."

"Blair, you know I trust you to be discreet."

"Ethan, your mental reflexes are so aggravatingly turtle-like that you can't catch my little hints. I meant--my lips are sealed and ready for a kiss, you unromantic cur."

"Sorry. I think my mother dropped me on my head when I was a baby."

"Well I that case, I forgive you." She gave him a stabbing peck on the lips, one far more aggressive than tender--by a mile.

. . .

After a breakfast of BLTs and homefries at Windmills on Princess Street, Ethan and Blair strolled over to the northern quadrant of Queen's campus, and Blair lamented her inability to commit to a regular exercise regimen.

"I walk a great deal, but I hate running. I wish I were as dedicated as you are, Ethan."

"I'm only newly dedicated, Blair. And only since I came to Canada. I'll be anxious to see how much I'll want to run this winter—and next summer. I'll probably be in shape only in the fall and spring—and a muddled mass of flab the other two seasons."

When they started back toward the pub, Brooks realized he had playfully implied that he'd be exercising in Kingston next summer. Had Blair caught that suggestion? Yet did he really imagine he'd remain in Canada for a full year? Perhaps not, but he absolutely knew he didn't want to leave Kingston—at least right now.

"I wonder what joys are in store for me today?" Blair made the remark blithely, as if she hadn't a care in the world. Again, where was her concern for the possibility that Jordan Essex wanted to do her harm? Did she believe he had returned to Montreal? Ethan knew he could chill her sunny temperament by noting that he had seen Essex on three occasions—at her place, standing near his car after the Queen's football game, and across the street from the brew pub. But he couldn't do it. He would bear all the worry and vigilance for her. Better she remain unaware. As for her enjoying her job as much as she did, Ethan understood why she wouldn't wish to return to banking, but surely she had plans to move beyond a career in food services. But for the first time he felt uncomfortable with the idea that she would aspire to something more, because if she did it might take her away from Kingston.

"Well, Blair. I hate to be the bearer of bad news but we better pick up the pace. It's almost ten."

. . .

In the wake of their talk about exercise, Brooks decided to change into a sweatshirt and shorts at the Montroses' and drive out to his favorite spot off the Thousand Island Parkway, where he could work off some of his concerns with a good run. As he drove out to the Parkway, he found himself looking into the rear view mirror every few miles for any sign of Jordan Essex's following him. Twice he believed Essex was driving the car behind him, but in each case, as the distance closed between them, he saw that the vehicle wasn't a Lexus and that the driver didn't at all resemble the man who had now become his nemesis as well as Blair's.

Once again Brooks contemplated the proximity of his location to the United States directly across Lake Ontario and then, as he headed further east, across the St. Lawrence. So close geographically and yet so distant from everything he knew — everything that made him the man he was. Admittedly, he had fled Washington and shortly afterward his country and hadn't waited until the initial tide of negative publicity had run its course. Yet from what Tim Gerard informed him at the *Chateau Laurier*, only a few — namely Tim — publicly defended the press secretary's actions as evidence of considerable courage and integrity. Dismissing the political opposition's desire to make him a martyr in order to use him as evidence of the administration's moral deficiencies, Brooks found unsurprising yet still painful Tim's account of how supporters of the president voiced puzzlement and outrage over the press secretary's "betrayal" of the president and his administration. In subsequent polls, Tim added, a majority of independents had also disapproved of Ethan's handling of the situation. "What the hell is wrong with people?" he asked Gerard.

Pulling his car to his usual spot, Ethan noticed a forbidding rock formation jutting up some twenty yards off the road to his left. He wondered how many had tried to ascend it, especially since it had few visible ledges and exposed rock for a climber's hands and feet. A daunting prospect he thought, although no climb could ever challenge him as much as the short step he took up to the podium in the Brady Press Briefing Room on the morning of his final day in the White House.

As he left his office in the West Wing, Brooks reminded himself that the president had done all he could to protect his press secretary's sense of honor and integrity. Ethan was merely to address any questions about the incident at Martin's Tavern by stating to those in the room that the president had instructed him to say nothing further and by asking the media to consult the official statement. He also had permission to encourage the media to question the president if they wanted corroboration of his instructions to his press secretary. But Ethan began his short walk to the briefing room feeling almost debilitated by all the classic symptoms of severe stage fright — the humming sensation in the face, the dry mouth, the irregular breaths, the quivering of muscles in the hands and forearm.

As he mounted the platform and made his way to the podium, he looked back at the American Flag standing next to the White House seal, something he had never done before. Did he expect strength or comfort from his nation's emblem? He grabbed the podium with both hands--again something he had never needed to do previously.

"Good morning, everyone." It was his familiar greeting, although he could tell his voice didn't deliver the words in the usual cheerful fashion. "The president would like to announce formally the name of his choice to succeed George McMahon as Chairman of the Council of Economic Advisors. As you all know, the McMahon family has health issues that require the Chairman's resignation at this time. The president has named Frances Smithson as his replacement. You have Dr. Smithson's bio, I believe, but if you need a copy just let me know. The president hopes she will be confirmed with little delay."

As he delivered the prepared script, Ethan kept his eyes lowered until he finished. He then asked if there were any questions.

He looked up and saw Malory Nealon's hand shoot up from the fourth row. In the moment between recognition and acknowledgement, Ethan took in the living photograph before him. Only one lone empty seat in the back row. Marcus O'Donnell and Caleb Sensabaugh sat together third row center. Jovita Henry and

Mariall Fernandez in their usual spots front row center. And of course Tim Gerard to Ethan's right in the last seat of the first row. The color in everyone's clothing seemed to fade to the point that Ethan only saw the grays, blacks, and dark blues in the jackets and ties of the men and the grays, blacks, and burgundy in the jackets and blouses of the women. It seemed to Ethan as though they had gathered for a memorial service.

"Malory."

"Thank you, Ethan. About the incident involving the chief of staff that you personally witnessed in Georgetown last night, I'd like to know if we're really supposed to--"

For the first time since he had become press secretary, Ethan put up his hand to cut her off. He looked at the back of his open hand and felt queasy. "I've been instructed by the president to ask you to refer to the official statement and to answer no further questions about what happened."

Ethan closed his eyes as he heard the first rumble of discontent from those in the room. Malory stood up. "Ethan, you mean you can't even--"

He hadn't lowered his open hand. "Malory I'm sorry—believe me, I really am sorry, but the president has asked me to say nothing further." His head and neck trembled with fear and disgust.

"I can't believe I heard that from you, Ethan. You can drop the hand now, if you like."

Ethan understood that Malory's comment as she sat back down was gratuitous, but it was also right on the mark. She was frustrated and disappointed in him—as he was in himself.

It seemed everyone's hand was now raised—except for O'Donnell's and Sensabaugh's. Each man was typing furiously onto his i-Pad. The room seemed to shake from the fusillade of male and female voices. Brooks glanced to his right and saw Tim Gerard's expression of near-horror but also concern for his good friend.

"Tim. Go ahead." It was all Ethan could do at this moment. Perhaps his good friend could get him out of this impossible situation. Gerard stood and the room fell silent. Everyone was aware of the personal friendship between the men.

"Ethan, please indulge me just one question."

Brooks stared at his friend. He knew he was at that "spot" his grandfather told him about—where a man's integrity was on the line and had to be defended. "You've got to stay true to yourself, my boy—or else your whole life will never be what it could have been." Whether Dan Brooks was paraphrasing Polonius in *Hamlet* or repeating what he had learned for himself didn't matter. Ethan heard the words and felt his grandfather's presence.

Brooks lifted his torso; he hadn't been aware of how low his shoulders and head had dropped since he took his position behind the podium. "All right. Go ahead, Tim."

"It's a simple question, Ethan. Are you telling us that the chief of staff was quoting someone else when he made the remark about the First Lady?"

"That's what's in the statement, Tim." But Ethan responded in a way that seemed to invite a follow up. The room remained silent. Even O'Donnell and Sensabaugh had ceased their pecking. A distant hum of some machine was the only sound anyone heard. Gerard lowered his head but brought it up immediately.

"But are you telling us now, Ethan—as an eye and ear witness to the very moment--that the chief of staff didn't express his *own* feelings when he spoke of the First Lady? Can you tell us that the administration's formal statement is really the truth? Can you? Can you tell us that?"

Ethan wished he could feel Dan Brooks' hand on his shoulder to steady him, but he felt nothing. His head had cleared. Every muscle was now relaxed.

"No. No, I can't, Tim."

. . .

As Brooks increased his jogging speed, he recalled how he was barely able to stagger off the platform after responding to Gerard's question. He took no others; he said nothing more, in spite of the cacophony of shouted inquiries from the room. He didn't know if Tim or any of the other members of the media would follow him to his office, but to avoid them he went down the hallway to the empty Roosevelt Room, where he and the president had talked earlier that morning. Closing the door behind him, Ethan walked to the spot behind the president's chair and stepped toward one of the two quartets of flags standing on either side of the landscape portrait on the wall. He didn't know what he would do if someone approached the door. He was too old to hide under the table, but he couldn't be sure he wouldn't step between two of the flags and try to disappear that way.

He remained in the same position for a good three minutes until he heard Bonnie Pinchot, Jack Peterborough's secretary, calling his name from the hallway. Without any other options, he opened the door and stepped out. Bonnie was in the middle of the hallway near the cabinet room. Ethan looked past her to his left and saw at the end of the hall one of his deputy press secretaries speaking with Malory Nealon, who appeared quite distressed. Also crowding the hallway were other members of the media, including Marcus O'Donnell and Caleb Sensabaugh, both typing on their iPads. Pushing his way through the others was Tim Gerard, who took four steps toward Ethan but then stopped. The president had just stepped out from the Oval Office directly across from where Ethan stood helplessly. The president crooked his index finger like a disappointed headmaster and wagged it twice without saying a word. Ethan did as he was instructed and entered the Oval Office.

.  .  .

Ethan slowed his jogging pace upon realizing he had run too far too fast. He wondered if he was trying to outdistance his memories—something his grandfather said he would never be able to do. "They go with you, Ethan. No matter how far or fast you attempt to run. They'll be with you stride for stride." Now progressing at a more moderate pace, Brooks looked back to see if his car was still in sight. Blocking his view was another runner, closing the distance between them. The man wore a dark green sweatshirt with a large designer insignia and light gray shorts. The hood of the sweatshirt covered his head, which was lowered enough so that Brooks couldn't see his face. But the physique he had seen three times before. Ethan slowed down further, looking rearward as the man came upon him. When he was some fifteen yards away, the other runner reached into the open pocket on the front of the sweatshirt and began withdrawing something. Ethan jammed his feet into the hard dirt and spun around, stepping toward the roadside. At the same time the other man jerked up his head and moved to his right—also toward the road—and slammed into Brooks, knocking him backward to the ground. Unable to stop his momentum, the man ran into Ethan's elevated legs and fell forward with his elbow and forearm crashing into the side of Ethan's head. Brooks immediately felt the blood trickle from above his eye. He twisted his body so that he could get the more advantageous body position on his assailant.

"You son-of-a-bitch!" He was able to pin the man down with his own forearm, which pressed into the back of the man's neck. Ethan jerked the hood back at the very moment an automobile pulled up a few feet away.

"Stop it, stop it!" It was a woman's voice.

"Daddy, daddy," shouted a child.

"Get the hell of me!" It was the voice of a red-headed man around thirty, looking not at all like Jordan Essex.

Ethan was aghast. "Hey, I'm sorry. I thought you were..."

The man's wife and daughter rushed to his side. The wife looked at Brooks with fury; the daughter with utter surprise.

Ethan was breathing heavily. "I'm sorry. You slammed into me...and I just thought you were attacking me."

"It looks as though your attack was a success, Zack. Are you all right, sir?" The man's wife had banished her anger upon accepting that the collision had been an accident. She grimaced as she got a closer look at Ethan's wound.

"Hey, I'm sorry about that. Here." Zack reached into his sweatshirt pocket and pulled out the small bottle of water he was reaching for before they collided. Ethan nodded and took a long swallow.

"Let me get some tissues." The man's wife rushed back to the car and pulled out a wad of tissues, folded it, and pressed it against Ethan's cut. "I'm afraid you may need a couple of stitches."

"Does it hurt?" The couple's young daughter seemed more curious than sympathetic.

Ethan smiled. "Just a little. Are you okay?" He put his hand on Zack's shoulder.

"I think so. Just had a little breath knocked out of me is all. By the way, I'm Zack Atkinson, and this is my wife Nicole and my daughter Lucy."

"Hi. I'm Ethan Brooks."

The four exchanged pleasantries, but Nicole Atkinson remained concerned about the cut near Ethan's eyebrow. "You better have that looked at."

"Here." Her husband withdrew his handkerchief and gave it to Ethan. "The blood is soaking through the tissue, so use this. Nicole, can you get the duct tape from the back seat."

Brooks was soon equipped with a makeshift bandage consisting of tissue, a cotton handkerchief, and silver tape spread across his forehead and down the side of his face. "I feel like such an idiot, Zack. Forgive my suspicions about your intentions." He didn't want to explain the Jordan Essex situation.

"No problem. If I didn't like to run with my head down, I would have seen you in plenty of time to avert the collision."

"Zack, I told you that something like this would happen." At least Nicole's "I told you so" was delivered sympathetically.

After promising to meet back in Kingston for dinner in the near future, Ethan rode back to his car with the Atkinsons, still mortified over what had happened. Lucy kept him entertained in the back seat with stories of her own recent bumps and bruises and the sad fact that one of her classmates broke her arm last Friday.

It was only after he waved goodbye and headed back to Kingston did Brooks realize that he had dropped his guard and given the Atkinsons his real last name. Surely they wouldn't remember it. Surely not.

. . .

"Love your field first aid. Very sexy." Dr. Elizabeth Greene laughed at Ethan's appearance as he sat before her at a walk-in clinic in Kingston. "Let's see what we have here." She deftly disencumbered the side of his face and forehead of the blood-soaked tissues, handkerchief, and duct tape. "Yes, I'm afraid you will need a couple of stitches."

"Sew away." Ethan hoped she wouldn't ask how he received the injury.

After she performed the procedure, Ethan asked if she worked there full time.

"No, I work ER at a hospital outside the city, but I'm here today in place of a dear physician friend who just went into labor."

Ethan found the image delightful—both of a very pregnant doctor helping patients until she went into labor and of a baby born in this delightful city with a clean slate to work with—no crises, no regrets, no memories.

"Excuse me Mr. Matthews." Dr. Greene stepped out to speak with a man who had apparently ingested too much of some substance, because he was gesticulating wildly and refusing assistance from others in the care center. He didn't speak English or French. After several seconds, Brooks recognized a few words of Russian. Then Dr. Greene addressed the man. "Сэр, я должен настоять, чтобы Вы остались спокойными." Ethan didn't understand a word of what she said, but it immediately calmed the man and he shook his head in agreement. She returned to check her stitch work.

"I told him we'd send him to a Canadian gulag in the Yukon Territory if he didn't hush up." She smiled. "No, I just told him to calm down."

"Well, he did right away."

"Maybe I sound just like his domineering mother in Minsk. Anyway, I have to tend to him—so here. This is what you should take for any pain. Come back at the time written to have the stitches taken out."

"But you won't be here to take them out."

"We're not that possessive about our stitch removing. It's the initial sewing that thrills. Okay, now you're all set. It was nice meeting you."

"Me too." Brooks couldn't imagine seeing a more impressive display in such a short time. Humor, medical proficiency, and Russian.

. . .

Ethan called Blair to say that he'd be a few minutes late for lunch, but she was too busy with her tables to take his call. He looked forward to her concern and tender ministrations, but not to the questions she'd shoot in rapid fire as soon as she saw his injury. He knew he would exaggerate the event in some fashion at first—the wound being received as a result of a mugging or a heroic attempt to chase down a street thief. Blair would probably play along for a moment before insisting on the truth. He just hoped she wouldn't laugh at him when she learned how he was injured.

Although the area over his eye was still numb from the anesthetic, Brooks lowered the window and leaned his head to the left to allow the cool autumn air to rush against the side of his head. The last twenty-four hours had been filled with events, including a reunion with an old friend in Ottawa, a mild collision with a deer, and a violent introduction to a new acquaintance right off the Thousand Island Parkway. And painful memories and several stitches over his eye to add to the discomfort. All things considered, Ethan was doubly anxious to see the effervescent Blair Babineaux. He parked the car and checked the time—1:48 p.m. He should make it inside the pub in no more than five minutes. But as soon as he stepped from the passenger seat, his cell phone rang. Blair had likely found a minute and returned his call.

He spoke before she did. "Sorry I'm running late. I should be there in less than five minutes."

"Ethan?"

It was lucky he didn't drop the phone. "Aashna?"

# CHAPTER 18

Ethan stood before the pub's entrance until he was sure he could disguise his disordered emotions from Blair. The phone conversation with Aashna had been brief. He didn't begin with anything as trite as "How are you?" and "How is everything at the White House?" He had simply said her name, and she responded, "Do you have a minute to talk?" Whether it was the result of his wounded pride or the effects of his being late for his lunch at the pub, he replied, "I'm tied up at the moment. Can we talk later this afternoon—in a couple of hours?" The request to speak again came involuntarily, and he wondered if the response was the result of his characteristic kindness and politeness or a result of the growing need to speak with the women who only three months ago was his lover and the object of all his private thoughts. Or was he trying to give her the opportunity to say "No, I won't talk later" and cut short their reunion, or whatever it was, thereby aborting any chance of reconciliation.

"Okay, Ethan. I'll call you back at 3:30." The line went dead.

Aashna sounded neither disappointed nor angry about the postponement of their conversation. Nor did the tone of her voice suggest a desire for a restoration of their relationship or an apology from him for disappointing her or betraying the president. Still, Brooks realized he needed time to prepare for their talk, whatever its nature. He didn't wish to speak while he was standing outside his car or walking to the pub.

When he stepped inside, he saw a party of six getting up from their table, with two women hanging back to speak with Blair. They seemed pleased by their meal and, Ethan was sure, by Blair's service. She noticed him as she conversed with the women. Immediately, her smile dropped. She had spied the small bandage above his eye. Excusing herself to the women, Blair literally ran to him.

"What happened to you?" She tried to inject a little humor into the question, but it was evident she was truly concerned.

"Not to worry. It's nothing."

"Nothing?" She inspected the wound—running the pad of her index finger above the area. "Stitches?"

"Afraid so?"

"Sit, sit. What can I bring you, my poor baby?"

Ethan didn't at all mind the exercise of her maternal instincts. "A Dragon's Breath Pale Ale will do for now."

"I'll be right back. Don't play with the stitches." She returned as quickly as she could. "Here's your draft. And here are two aspirins in case you begin feeling pain."

He wanted to embrace her. "Thank you. You're much too good to me."

She frowned. "You say that as if you really believe that. Excuse me, Ethan. "Another?" She nodded to one of her customers. "I'll be right back—and don't touch the stitches."

Ethan took a long swallow of his draft and felt that ale was way underrated as a medicinal application. The liquid cooled the upper half of his face and suppressed his desire to poke at the wound. Surveying the interior of the pub, Ethan nodded approvingly at the beer-barrel tables in the bar area and the various Canadian, Irish, and Scottish knick-knacks on the walls—including photos, framed documents, crests, and maple leafs. Kaitlin, the tireless bartender for this afternoon kept up a steady stream of banter with the five men and one woman sitting and standing at the bar. Kaitlin's long black hair was pulled behind her ears and matted with perspiration. Once again, Brooks saw the appeal of working here, and imagined Blair taking her place behind the bar and delighting everyone who ordered a drink or sought a willing ear. Perhaps she truly felt at one with herself in this charming establishment and that was why she didn't wish to jump to another line of work. No other place he had patronized in Washington, Albany, or in Vermont had made him feel this comfortable, even though he was a mere visitor from the States--a man in hiding, a man who had in fact run away from his own country.

"Okay, now tell me how this happened." Blair plopped down at his table, wiping her forearms with a bar towel.

He remembered his decision to tease her. "I received this injury fighting for a young lady's honor."

"Oh, so apparently she wished to keep it."

Vintage Blair. She was never pitched a comic softball she couldn't knock out of the park. Ethan laughed fully, reintroducing the discomfort to the wound above his left eye. "Ouch, ouch."

"Oh, I'm sorry, Ethan. I couldn't resist. My great uncle Cyril told me that one. I think he used to do comedy in one of the music halls in London in the 40s and 50s. But seriously, I want to know exactly what happened."

There was no way Ethan could top her or Uncle Cyril's joke, so he explained the peculiar circumstances of his collision with Zack Atkinson—leaving out his assumption that the approaching runner was really Jordan Essex. Blair alternated sighs of concern with bursts of giggling.

"I'm glad I could bring some amusement into your day, Blair."

"Just wait until I tell you about the scar on the top of my head that you can't see. You'll then have your revenge. I won't tell you everything now, but the story features an extraction of a teenage boy's front tooth from my scalp."

"Sounds hilarious."

"Ethan, I remember seeing one of the King Arthur movies--from the 80s, I believe—which included a scene in which Guinevere stitched up Arthur's wound. Did this Dr. Greene see you as a shining knight, as I and Guinevere would have?" Blair dropped her chin on her extended fingers and cooed.

"Actually, she treated me like the clumsy oaf I am."

"Poor baby. Well, out of sympathy for your suffering, I'll pay for your lunch today. But you still have to tip me. Now what would you like to eat?"

· · ·

After returning to the Montrose house, Brooks grabbed a cup of coffee and made his way to the formal dining-room table to work further on

*Convergence.* He had the border of the puzzle completed and now faced the daunting prospect of filling in the abstract center with all its color, swirling lines, and meaning—whereas at present there was nothing but the solid wood of the table showing through. He smiled at the image of the "empty picture frame," the familiar metaphor of philosophers and poets. But whereas he could have seen his life in such terms when he first came to Canada, the frame had been largely filled with his experiences in Kingston, especially by his growing relationship with Blair Babineaux. Yet could it really be possible he'd remove those puzzle pieces that formed Blair's expressive and lovely face and replace them with those that constituted the intriguing and evocative features of Aashna Malini?

He knew he was far too old to feel the way he did about speaking with Aashna. Like a lovelorn teenager, he was hopeful that the time since their parting had made her realize how much she admired him and respected his decision to answer the media the way he did. At the very least, he wanted the call to end with her professing some regret for the silence of the past three months and a promise to remain friends. Still, how could he dismiss their intimate history together? Clicking one of the jigsaw pieces into place, he fought but soon succumbed to memories of the smell of her lovely neck, the sheen of her flawless copper-colored skin, the alluring texture of her hair, and the lulling sound of her resonant voice. He adored adoring her, tending to her every need, and waiting for her smile and gesture of approval for what he had done. While staring at the frame of the puzzle, he quietly articulated her name—the euphony in the sound of "Aashna" perfectly complementing all of these stimulating memories of her.

His cell phone played its ringtone. It lay on the table not two feet from him, yet he let it ring three times before answering. "Hello?"

"Ethan?"

"I'm glad you called back, Aashna." He believed his tone was friendly but business-like.

"Ethan, I need to tell you something. I'll try to be quick about it." Because she sounded impatient, he thrust forward the one question he had for her—one he was most anxious to have answered.

"Aashna, before we talk, how did you get my cell number?" Again, only three others had it—his sister Holly, Tim Gerard, and Blair.

"I can't tell you Ethan. Please don't ask me."

He restrained his urge to insist. He'd have to determine the source later. "All right."

After an uncomfortable moment in which neither of them spoke, he continued. "How are you?"

"I'm calling because I've learned something I feel you should know."

"Okay. What is it?" What could she have possibly "learned"?

"Ethan, I have no proof that this is in any way legitimate, but someone wanted me to know that you might be in danger."

It took him several seconds to comprehend her words, given that they smashed so headlong into his previous assumptions. "Danger? What do you mean?"

"I don't know. It could have been someone playing a joke on me, but I thought it best to notify you."

"Wait. How did you hear about this danger I'm supposed to be in? Who called you?" He could hear the aggravation creeping into his voice.

"No one called me. I didn't talk to anyone. I received a text message on my phone. After thinking about it for a couple of hours, I called the number back, but it wasn't in service. It came from a 302 area code."

"Delaware?"

"Yes."

"The message said nothing specific?"

She sighed. "Here is the exact wording. 'Tell Ethan Brooks he may be in serious danger.'"

"*Serious* danger."

"Yes. The person might have assumed that we were still in contact with each other or that you had called me to…Regardless, that's the message I received."

"How long ago?"

"Almost a week now, but I had no way of getting in touch with you. You left no forwarding number or address. You evidently cancelled your old cell-phone number. No one knew where you went. I then thought that I might..." Once more she cut herself off. Ethan waited another moment to see if she would say anything further. He couldn't even hear her breathing on the other end.

"Aashna, this sounds ridiculous. Like an amateur prank."

"I'm sure that's what it was, but I couldn't afford not to tell you."

"Well, I appreciate your doing so, Aashna."

She elevated the volume of her voice. "I wish you well, Ethan. Goodbye." She hung up before he had a chance to articulate another syllable.

Brooks looked at the Pollock puzzle and considered what she had said in their abbreviated conversation. Someone—through a cell phone text message--had told her to inform him he was in "serious danger." She complied with that request as efficiently as she could, spending no time on any pleasantries. Far from what he imagined she might say, Aashna suggested a concern for him—a responsibility to notify him—and a wish for his well-being, spoken louder apparently so that it wouldn't sound intimate. At best she reacted as though she was taking care of normal business; at worst as if she was completing a reluctant chore. He let out a deep breath, looked about the dining room, and then snapped another piece of the Pollock puzzle into place.

# CHAPTER 19

He worked another forty minutes on the puzzle, delaying any thoughts about his brief "reunion" with Aashna. Stepping back and surveying what he had done so far, Brooks was pleased that the frame of *Convergence* was completed and now a good portion of the upper-right-hand section was as well. Although satisfied with his progress, he could no longer postpone the inevitable. He chose an easy chair along the fireplace in the Montrose living room, turning the chair slightly so that he could face the interior stone wall, which was decorated with a colorful tapestry, giving him the sense of sitting in the private chamber of a medieval castle.

That he felt the utter fool was the least of it. He had blithely constructed a scenario in which Aashna would express her continued love for him, her contrition at having dismissed him the day of his last press briefing, and her having sorely missed him during the past three months. He had imagined she might ask him to come back to her, forcing an excruciating choice—to play the hand he knew well and reclaim a major part of his past or to cast his lot with Blair Babineaux, with whom he had at least conceded he was falling in love and had for the first time made love to. That he had even allowed himself to spin such a scenario now seemed incredible as he sat and contemplated the stone wall before him.

Aashna Malini wasn't in love with him. The only question—to which he cared not to know the answer—was if she ever truly was. Ethan considered whether the disappearance of his love for her at present was only temporary. No—he was sure. It was over, and as much as the thought relieved him he still felt surprised. But how many times had he heard in the verses of songs or in the lines of verse the suddenness of love departing as well as arriving? Regardless, he found solace in the commonplace, seeing that sitting here in the

Montrose's living room he felt no love for Aashna and wanted her to remain out of his life but more significantly to remain completely out of his thoughts. He remembered that his grandfather had offered advice about girls and their feelings when Ethan was seventeen and dealing with the effects of a recent break-up. "My boy, if she really wants to be with you, there is nothing anyone can do to stop her—so don't worry about whether you've said the right thing or if you said enough." Ethan hadn't applied that wisdom during the three months he was away from Aashna Malini because he hadn't told her where he was or how to get in touch with him. But their conversation of an hour ago made clear that he had lost her respect and affection the second he "betrayed the president," as she termed it in July.

Ethan thought of Blair, and for a few moments, his soul was comforted and his mood lightened by images of her face—in all its fascinating manifestations—and her overt expressions of love for him. Now the relatively brief time they had known each other, as well as the previously unresolved issue of Aashna, stopped blunting his instincts to give more to her. He couldn't wait to see her at 6:00, spend the evening together, and then make love to her at her place. But soon, all of these delightful images were replaced by those tinged with shame. Yes, he would run to Blair and be more demonstrative now that Aashna had made clear her feelings. But he felt the gnawing in his stomach as he shaped the thought with appropriate sarcasm: how magnanimous of him; how flattering to Blair. He was thoroughly disgusted with himself. He had always been a one-woman guy. It was part of his nature to be loyal, to look others in the eye and be completely honest with them, never harboring something he'd be ashamed of or afraid to admit. All he could do now is try to make it up to Blair without telling her what he was trying to make up for.

But there were two other matters he had to contemplate. Aashna told him that someone left a text message warning that he was in "serious danger." If a prank—and Ethan still believed it was one— who would have played such a joke? The text came from a number in Delaware, which Aashna later found wasn't in service. Was the perpetrator someone enamored of Aashna? The list of possible suspects, Brooks sardonically imagined, could have been quite large. A jealous White House co-worker perhaps—someone on the staff who resented the First Lady's affection for Aashna? There were just too many possibilities to play "I wonder who." And what friend of his could have contacted her in the hope that she could warn him? Tim would have said something if he'd heard. And warn him of what? Was this someone on the fringes of the media who was attempting to ascertain Ethan's location for the sake of an interview or a series of photos? Ethan decided he had enough to watch out for with Jordan Essex in Kingston. He would therefore ignore the text-message warning given to Aashna Malini. He'd only drive himself to the brink if he spent his time trying to guess the sender's identity or the sender's violent intentions.

And then there was the matter of who gave his cell phone number to Aashna. She didn't want to be questioned on the matter; apparently she had promised not to reveal the person's identity. But the candidates were few—Holly, Blair, and Tim. Blair couldn't have, of course. Holly wouldn't break her promise to him—especially since she had never liked Aashna, finding her to be "too much about herself" to be deserving of her brother's love. Aashna had asked for the number from Tim, who didn't learn it until yesterday afternoon, when Ethan gave it to him at the *Chateau Laurier*. Why would he have told Aashna so soon? He had sworn he wouldn't share it with anyone—and Tim was always as good as his word. Ethan stood and turned the chair back to its normal position. The stone wall was perfectly reflective as far as the warning and the shared cell number were concerned. Ethan would ask his sister to get a new cell number for the phone or purchase a new phone, set up an account, and then mail the phone to Kingston. Aashna had the number and could give it to anyone.

. . .

"Ethan, you're sure you're all right?"

"I'm fine, Blair. Really, I am."

"Well, you aren't your usual gabby self." He smiled and asked her a series of specific questions about her shift. When they returned to her place, she invited him to have a drink and "let the sunshine in" and then headed up the stairs to take her shower and get ready to out to dinner and to attend the reading by the local author she had recently heard in Toronto.

"Ethan, it's not something I've done, said, didn't say, or alluded to — is it?"

He came up to her on the stairway and kissed her ardently. The bitterness of his guilt was at least tempered by the sweetness of her mouth.

"Wow. That was a kiss like you see on the cover of a tawdry paperback romance novel...sold in the private nook of a crumbling bookstore...in the naughtiest part of town. So, can I have another...while I lie on my back on the kitchen floor?"

She had brought in the sunshine. Brooks laughed. "Just take your shower and get ready."

Blair scampered up to the second floor, and after a minute on the sofa, Ethan felt too restless to sit and wait for her. He walked around the bottom floor, took a look out the rear door, and of all things emptied Blair's dishwasher. He also put away a dishrag and placed a pair of scissors into the cup where she kept them along with a flat-blade and a phillips-head screwdriver. The scissors brought to mind the scrapbooks he had discovered in the second upstairs bedroom and the cut-out from the early July newspaper that he was certain featured the story of his final press briefing. Ethan sat at the kitchen and looked toward the ceiling above him as he heard the shower turn on. If he could just take a quick look into those scrapbooks and satisfy his desire to know.

He walked up to the second level and heard Blair humming over the noise from the shower on the other side of the bathroom door. Her bedroom was to the left. Her work clothes lay on the bed. Without pausing to deliberate, Ethan stepped into the second bedroom. He looked first between the work desk and the book case and found still lying there the strips of newspaper he had discovered earlier. Three thick scrapbooks were stacked on top of each other on the edge of the work space. Taking a quick glance over his shoulder and still hearing the shower, he opened the top scrapbook and saw a page of photographs which showing a longer-haired Blair cavorting with friends — campus pictures during her university days, he guessed. He put his fingers in the middle of the pages and pulled the book open.

More photos of Blair, this time in academic regalia with an elderly couple—her grandparents most likely.

The album included nothing but photographs, but the one beneath contained clippings from newspapers and magazines. Still hearing the shower, Ethan pulled out the second scrapbook and placed it on top of the one he had just examined. He opened the first page and then shut it immediately. The noise from the shower seemed louder. He knew he shouldn't be intruding on Blair's privacy this way. Perhaps he could ask about this hobby of hers and she could show them to him if she wished.

"Ethan?" The voice came from behind him. The shower was still running.

Completely nude, she held a small blue bottle in her hand. "This is empty. I need to get some more body wash from the hall closet." Her eyes had expanded as if she were anticipating something dreadful.

Ethan refused to forward a lame explanation for his being upstairs in the second bedroom. "I noticed the other day that you had scrapbooks and photo-books in this room. I was curious. You said you wanted to show them to me." His pause was brief. "I'm sorry. I should have asked before I snooped around. I saw some pictures of you at the university—that's all I saw."

Blair's eyes relaxed. Ethan believed he could hear his heart beating over the sound of the water still rushing from the shower head.

Blair smiled impishly. "I'm glad that's all you saw. I have some nude photos in one of those albums and I'd be horribly embarrassed if you saw them."

"No, I didn't see any other pictures—I promise." Only after he spoke did he realize that she was teasing him. She was standing completely nude before him, after all. "You got me again, Blair."

"I hope to get you again and again and again. Hopefully all in one night. We can talk about my scrapbooking and photo-collecting later if you want. But now I have to stop wasting so much water." She opened the closet and grabbed a new bottle of body wash. "Be a darling and throw this empty one out for me, okay?" She looked at him until he left the room and headed back down the stairs.

Ethan turned on the television to pass the time while Blair finished her shower and dressed. He surfed the channels until he found the Philadelphia Flyers-Toronto Maple Leafs hockey game. It was right before the opening face-off and the American National Anthem was being played. The melody of the "Star Spangled Banner" accompanied by the visual of the American flag hit Ethan hard. Although he felt both were often misused—the former by singers making it a "performance piece" and the latter by so many in politics who used it as a prop—he often felt emotional at the sound and sight of his nation's emblems. It was trite and simple—he was just proud to be an American. But as he stood before Blair's big screen television he contemplated the power and complexity of the American anthem with its wide vocal range of almost two octaves. He couldn't help comparing it to the beauty and relative simplicity of "O Canada," which was now playing on the NHL broadcast. The latter anthem seemed much safer; the former more precarious. Ethan also saw the complexity in the American flag—its fifty white stars corralled in a field of blue, the stripes of red and white both supporting and clashing with the field of stars, which remained separated from and not at all united with the thirteen stripes. This design he found in stark contrast to the Canadian flag, with its balanced and uncomplicated red and white Maple Leaf design. Ethan shook his head, realizing how heretical his present assessment of the anthem and flag might play in the town from which he had escaped—or had been cast out from.

. . .

"What's wrong, Ethan? Overcooked?"

"Yes. It's medium well to well done."

"And you said 'medium rare.' Just send it back."

Ethan had never hesitated to send back the occasional over- or undercooked beef entrée. Dan Brooks taught him well. "You're paying a good price for it, boy. Don't be shy about getting what you asked for." But Ethan was reluctant now.

"I'm a guest of your country."

He recalled the first time he ordered a sandwich in the White House during a hectic early afternoon in his first few weeks as press secretary and it came back slathered in mayonnaise, a condiment he didn't care for. One of his deputies suggested he send it back, but Brooks thought it was insulting to the kitchen staff and for some odd reason to the White House itself. That day he let the sandwich remain on his desk until one of his staff took it upon herself to get him a new one devoid of mayo. Ethan was always polite to a fault—always conscious of others' feelings—always eager to sooth the rough edges of any situation. Yes, the very personality traits that led him to the event that cost him his job and to the decision to leave his country. Personality traits that did him absolutely no good in his discussion with the president in the Oval Office three months earlier.

Blair waited only a few seconds before she signaled for the server. "If it makes you feel better, the owner of this place is Scandinavian. He's not a Canadian citizen—so you really won't be showing yourself an ingrate to your host nation."

After the apologetic server left with the first steak, Blair set down her fork and regaled Ethan with the story of her two visits to Iceland. He learned that one of her schoolmates— "way, way smarter than I was"—married an Icelander and presently lived in Reykjavik with her husband and four children. "And she has her own online business. She exhausts me whenever I think about all she does and the very fact that she can speak Icelandic. I can't wait to go back."

Iceland. An island in the North Atlantic. Ethan smiled at the thought of ending up there. Other than its distance from Washington, there were almost twenty hours of darkness there in the winter. A better environment to hide himself in, he figured. He'd just have to go elsewhere in the summer, when the daylight situation was reversed. He could tell from Blair's joyous expression that she was thinking about the attractions of Iceland—not merely offering her the chance to see her friend again but to go to a place where her own recent past wouldn't follow her. He wanted Canada to be that place for him, but Aashna's phone call and warning, in addition to his responsibility to correctly identify himself to Blair, let him know that now he wasn't completely free from his recent history. Would there ever be such a time or such a place?

"And I'd love to go there with you, Ethan."

"During the dark or the light months?"

"Oh, in winter--during the dark months. That way I could wear bulky clothes and get fat and go without my make-up and you'd still find me desirable. The two times I visited my friend Chloe were in the late spring and late autumn. That last time I imagined making love to the man of my dreams on the edge of a fjord illuminated by the Northern Lights."

"Sounds heavenly—and pretty damned cold." Ethan was pleased that he was feeling less tense as the evening went on.

"Do you have your cell phone with you, Ethan?"

The question took him aback. There was no preparation for it, and the issue of who gave Aashna his number returned unwelcomed to his mind.

"Yes, it's in my pocket. Why?" The tone of the last word was forceful.

Blair stared into his eyes and held up her own phone. "I just wanted to text you a little note, that's all."

He was quick to recover. "Not a 'Dear John' text, I hope.

"No chance of that, Ethan. That will never happen. The Maple Leafs will win another Stanley Cup before I would ever do something as detrimental to my happiness as text you a 'Dear John.' As for *calling* you with the bad news, well, I can make no promises."

How she amused and fascinated him. "You really know how to raise a guy up—so that the fall will hurt even more."

"Look at me now." Her face was completely free of any facetiousness. "You will have to be the one to cast me away. I love you, Ethan, and I will never hurt you." Blair's face told him she knew he had been hurt by another woman. She grabbed his hand and rubbed it tenderly.

. . .

They had finished their fish and the belated medium-rare steak and were waiting for the check, when Brooks noticed two men talking to the hostess. Blair's back was to the station; therefore, she wasn't privy to what Ethan observed. Both men looked to be in their early to mid-twenties and the shorter of the two was quite animated as he pulled out something, which he showed the hostess. The taller man scanned the restaurant, apparently looking for someone. Ethan couldn't help thinking of Jordan Essex doing the same as he searched for Blair in Kingston—whether in the local banks or in the restaurants and pubs. The shorter man handed the hostess a small card. After the men left, the hostess spoke briefly with one of the servers and tore up the card.

"What are you laughing at, Ethan?"

"Nothing, just a little clumsy ballet between the hostess and one of the servers." I hate it when you have fun without me." Her pouty face made clear that she was once more only teasing.

Ethan's cell vibrated in his pocket. "Did you just dial me, Blair?"

"You have a call?"

"Yes." He looked at the number and his face lost every trace of amusement.

"Who is it?" Blair was concerned.

"It's my sister. I need to take this. Excuse me."

"Of course. Go outside. It's far too noisy in here."

"I'll be right back. Hello? Just hang on a minute." Ethan rushed through the dining room right past the hostess, who had this week likely seen dozens of patrons escaping to the street in the middle of their meals—cell phones pressed against their ears—in order to take or make a call.

He stepped away from the entrance. "Holly, is everything all right?"

"I want you to answer that."

"What do you mean?" He rarely heard his sister so upset.

"Aashna called me."

"Jesus Christ." Even outside the restaurant he had difficulty hearing her. "Look, I'm outside a restaurant. There's a lot of street noise. Can I call you later tonight?"

"Are you all right, Ethan?"

"I'm fine, Holly—really I am."

"But Aashna said that you might be in danger."

"I know. I talked to her. It's nothing, I promise you. I'll call you in a couple of hours, when I get back to the Montroses'—okay?"

"You better. But you're not lying to me—are you? You *are* all right?"

"I am and there's nothing to worry about. Somebody was just playing a prank."

"Who?"

"Holly, I can barely hear you. Let me call you later."

"All right. I'll expect your call. Bye, Ethan."

Brooks was furious. What was Aashna trying to prove by calling his sister? Didn't she realize that Holly would only worry herself sick? He remained on the sidewalk until he purged his anger and shaped a more rational thought. Aashna might have only called Holly because she doubted he would take her call and that she could at least send the warning through his sister. Which call came first—the one to him or the one to Holly?

"Ethan?" Blair had stepped from the restaurant's entrance. "I paid the bill. Is everything all right?"

"Yes, Holly came up against something she wanted my advice on. She's fine."

"Nothing like big brother's soothing assurances. It means a lot to me that you have such a close relationship with your sister. I really can't wait to..." Blair checked herself.

"And I can't wait to introduce you to her." He felt good about making this small but significant gesture suggesting a future with Blair.

Much pleased, Blair put her arms around him and turned him for a kiss.

He offered an ineffectual protest. "Blair, people will see."

"That's the idea, my love."

As he kissed her, he faced the street and heard a car beep its horn at the two of them as well as an "awwww" from three young women passing on the sidewalk. When he broke the kiss, his eye caught the figure of a man walking on the other side behind several parked cars. Although he could only see the man from his chest up, it was clear who it was.

# CHAPTER 20

"We're parked up this way, Ethan."

"I know, but I want to show you something down here before we go to the car. Come on."

"Okay."

He wanted to take her in the opposite direction from where Essex was walking and therefore prevent her from seeing him and becoming alarmed. But by the time they reached a small café and Ethan clumsily muttered something about going there the next time they were in the area, Blair asked him what was going on.

He had to start being more forthright. "I'm sorry to tell you this, Blair, but Jordan Essex is still around."

Her face took on a stoic expression. "You just saw him just then?"

"Yes. On the other side of the street, while we were kissing."

"Okay."

"I should have run across the street..."

"No, Ethan..."

". . . and had it out with him. This whole situation is getting ridiculous."

"It's okay, really it is."

"It's not okay, Blair. I've seen him three other times I haven't told you about."

Her eyes danced back and forth. "Oh, hell."

"I'm not sure what he's thinking or what he has planned, but we can't play these games anymore. I see him; he sees me, and then he goes the other way."

"Wait. Are you sure it's Jordan?"

"Blair, he was walking behind your place the first time I saw him."

"My place?"

"Yes. He matched your description of him—same height, same coloring. And he dresses well, right?"

"Yes. Very well."

"The thing is I just can't be sure he isn't really after me because he thinks I'm replacing him."

"You did that weeks ago. I know; I know. He would do something like that."

"I'm sorry to upset you like this, Blair; I really am."

"It's okay. I have to know. I'm just afraid."

"I won't let anything happen to you."

"No. I'm afraid for you, Ethan."

. . .

On the way to hear the local author read from his work, they spoke further of Ethan's physically confronting Essex. "Blair, if we're together and we see him, I want you to find a safe place—inside a restaurant or a business—and I'll head to where he is. I'll chase him down if need be." Blair questioned whether he should do so, but her protests lacked intensity. Brooks could sense her relief that something would be done to confront her former lover and with any luck get him completely out of her life. Ethan just wasn't prepared for Blair's release of tension with a hearty guffaw, however.

"What's so amusing?"

"Sorry. You see, when we were together, Jordan loved to work out, even signing up for martial arts classes."

Ethan wondered why that particular memory struck her so funny. "Well, that's encouraging."

"No, no. He always tried to present himself as some kind of modern-day gladiator, but the one time I saw him challenged, he backed out of the fight as quickly as he could, telling me afterward that he only did so because he didn't want to be responsible for the destruction of any property at *La Mouche*, his favorite nightclub in Montreal, even though the other guy invited him *outside* to settle their little disagreement. Jordan was a good dancer, but not doing the male-on-male tango, I'm afraid. That's probably why he..." Her delight over the memory evaporated instantly.

"Why he what?"

"Started carrying a folding knife in his car and sometimes on his person."

. . .

Blair's delight and raucous laughter returned less than a half hour later when she and Ethan heard the Kingston author read from his latest book, which depicted the many trials and tribulations of co-existing, as the youngest child, with his large family during the last several years of his life, as he approached and then reached thirty. "I have a confession to make about my family. My parents and older siblings—even my dear grandmother--lost the ability to add another year to each of my birthdays starting when I was twelve. To them, I'm still twelve—meaning that every assumption they had about me when I was that age they have maintained and nourished for the past eighteen years. And what's worse, they even talk to me the way they did then. For my twenty-eighth birthday, my elder brother gave me a special gift--the same facts-of-life lecture he gave me when I was fourteen and sprouting hair in embarrassing places. My brother's a scientific genius—worked on the Mars Rover and all that outer space stuff—so since I hated science and gravitated toward the creative arts, he thought I couldn't possibly retain Newton's third law of motion, as it applied to boy-girl relations, without a refresher course. Any of you incarcerated in a family like that?" With that opening, the author received boisterous cheers, a few knowing groans, and even applause. Brooks noticed a good number of the audience pointing to themselves and three or four couples lowering their heads in their hands out of embarrassment—those being parents or older siblings, no doubt. The author rode the crest of the initial wave of acceptance throughout his forty-five minutes of reading and commenting, and all in the crowd made the experience rosier by imbibing liberal amounts of Merlot and Chardonnay. Ethan was doubly entertained because he couldn't help staring at Blair's face as it revealed seemingly every nuance of its ability to look amused. She bellowed, gasped, blew, snorted, grimaced, and groaned—all in approval of what she heard.

The author received a standing ovation from all but a handful in the audience—those who had too much wine and were therefore unable to awaken the necessary muscles to lift their limbs and carcasses without outside assistance. Out of politeness, almost everyone remained to hear the poor poet chosen to end the literary festivities, but the lines depicting the march toward and then retreat from suicide, even in the style of Poe, had no chance to win the evening. Blair and Ethan felt badly enough for the young woman to offer a "We enjoyed it" after spending five minutes with the local author whom Blair kissed twice on each cheek—in some apparent French Canadian ritual Ethan didn't recognize. Ethan discovered that Blair and the author both loved popcorn punched up with a healthy sprinkle of cayenne pepper.

. . .

"Holly, see? I told you I'd call."

Ethan had excused himself to the kitchen as Blair made drinks at her portable bar.

"Are you all right, Ethan?"

It exasperated him that his sister was still frightened by Aashna's call. "Yes, Holly, I'm fine. I've had a very pleasant evening. Still having it, to be honest."

"You're with your lady friend?"

"Yes. Her name is Blair. That's okay with you, isn't it?" He asked the question with a laugh.

"Of course, but I've been worried sick about you. What kind of danger was Aashna talking about?"

Ethan explained what Aashna told him and reiterated his view that the text message his former love received was just a prank. "I only wish she didn't call you. Anyway, she learned my number from Tim, I'm afraid—although how he…never mind. I asked him not to share it with anyone, but obviously Aashna convinced him that she had to talk to me. Perhaps she told Tim, as she told you, about that text she received. I don't know what to say to Tim because I'm very disappointed in him for giving her my cell number."

"Oh, Ethan." His sister began crying.

"Holly, the text was a bad joke that's all it was. I'm not in any danger, I can assure you. Please don't cry."

"It's not that."

"Then what is it?"

"I'm the one who gave Aashna your number."

. . .

"Ethan, is everything all right with Holly?" Brooks stepped into the living room, and Blair handed him his drink.

"Yes, she's just a little upset."

"What about, if I may ask?"

"About a crank call she received." At least this time he was more comfortably close to the truth.

Brooks did all he could to suppress the anger he felt at Aashna for feeling the need to get his cell phone number. But now he was more troubled by Holly's feelings. She told him, "If you were 'very disappointed' in Tim for breaking his promise to you, how must you feel about me?" Like her brother, Holly thought one of her stellar character traits was her loyalty to family and friends. Ethan tried to ease her mind, but he accepted that he'd have to call back soon and assure her that he understood and wasn't disappointed in her. In truth, he wasn't at all, and he also regretted the comment about Tim, whom he would have forgiven without hesitation if he had in fact shared the cell number with Aashna.

Ethan noticed that Blair had become withdrawn after hearing that Holly had received a crank call. Blair was obviously thinking about Essex. She stared at the Waterhouse print of "The Lady Clare" in her living room. Ethan took in the moment as Blair's expression conveyed a desire for comfort and encouragement. With her hair down, her lips slightly opened, and her eyes slightly expanded, she looked as beautiful as he had ever seen her. Remaining silent, he refused to intrude on this living portrait of the woman he knew he truly loved. He understood that the memory of every recent thought he had of Aashna Malini would now fill him with shame.

"Ethan?" In such a blissful moment, he hadn't expected her to speak. "Do you really love me?"

Before, he had feared such a direct question and avoided any conversation that might prompt such an inquiry. But now he was grateful for the chance to answer. "I do, Blair. I really do."

She removed her gaze from Lady Clare and turned to him. "Do you love me enough to forgive me anything?"

. . .

Blair fell asleep almost immediately after they made love. She kissed him and playfully whispered, "Vigorous exercise always knocks me right out." He was pleased she hadn't said, "I always drift off right after I have sex." Aashna had said that to him after their first sexual experience — although he excused her lack of tact because she was, after all, sleepy.

Earlier, when Ethan asked Blair what she meant by loving her enough to forgive her "anything," she offered a weak smile and promised she would tell him tomorrow evening as soon as he had thought long enough about the matter to answer her question truthfully. "Don't try to answer now," she implored him.

"That's not fair," he replied.

"I know, but please think about my question and then answer me truthfully. Regardless of what you say, I promise to tell you what it is tomorrow night." He could have told her that nothing she said could change his mind about loving her, but he honored her wishes to drop the subject until the next evening.

Now she was asleep and he was wide awake. He would have preferred to replay in his mind their lovemaking, but the wound above his eyebrow was aching too much for such pleasant reminiscences. His and Blair's heads had bumped together in bed, and in his aroused state he hadn't felt anything, but now the discomfort returned with a vengeance. He rose from the bed carefully to avoid awakening her and went downstairs to take something for the pain. After finally locating and swallowing one of the pills Dr. Green left with him, he wrapped ice in a dishtowel and sat in one of the darkened living room chairs, pressing the make-shift icepack against his stitches. After a few moments, the pain began to dull.

The silence was broken by a dog's barking across the street and the sound of automobiles driving by. He wondered if Essex was behind the wheel of one of the cars. Determined to confront the man the next time he saw him, even if Blair was by his side, Brooks found little humor in pondering the number of fresh wounds he'd need stitches for. It didn't matter. The Essex business had to end.

It had been a good day for resolution in other respects as well, particularly his feelings for Aashna. Yet there was more to be resolved. When best to tell Blair who he really was and what ultimately to do about returning home to the States? The second of those decisions could wait. He wasn't going to leave Blair now—or in the future. A determination on where they could both live together would be worked out. As for his true identity, the thought struck him that he would share that information tomorrow evening when she revealed whatever it was she had been keeping from him. Perhaps her "secret" would make her understand and forgive his. Ethan rose from the chair and in the darkness walked to the fireplace, keeping his eyes on the print of The Lady Clare.

What would Blair tell him? It was obviously something she believed might affect his feelings about her. The most traumatic possibilities weren't hard to imagine. She had been married—either to Essex or to someone else. Was she was still married? Did she have a child being cared for by her parents—or the father's parents? Had she conceived and lost a child to miscarriage? Had she terminated a pregnancy? Other possibilities seemed more remote. She had been sexually active and had contracted a venereal disease. She had some kind of criminal record. Or it might be that she had a drug history. He could easily imagine her having tried marijuana, but might she also have dabbled in cocaine or something else? Had she been arrested for possession at one time? Other than these candidates, everything else seemed way too bizarre or absurd to consider. Although he would prefer that none of these possibilities was relevant to her past, Brooks assumed one of them was. Yet, not a single of them would prevent him from loving and wanting a permanent relationship with her.

Lady Clare gave him no clues; therefore, he walked back to the kitchen to deposit the ice in the sink. His head felt better. Now he could return to bed, rub Blair's hip gently, kiss her shoulder, and fall asleep. As he turned from the sink, he noticed a magnet holding a photograph on the refrigerator door, which depicted Blair and another woman standing in front of a herd of horses moving across a grassland area near a large pond with a mountain range in the background. Ethan immediately thought of Montana, but Blair said she had never been across the Canadian/U.S. border. Was it Western Canada, then? Ethan lifted the photo and read the inscription on the back. It was Blair and her good friend Chloe. The location was Iceland.

When he had gone into the Oval Office early on his last day as press secretary, the president had on the famous Resolute Desk a 5 x 7" framed photograph of himself and some hunting buddies with a Black Bear they had downed in Montana during Jack Peterborough's four-day vacation in late April. For the past two months, Peterborough had placed it on the desk whenever he worked alone or with trusted staff. The president let his press secretary know that the White House photographer was never to take a picture in the Oval Office with that 5 x 7 visible in the shot. Ethan was to volunteer nothing about the hunting trip—although he could answer truthfully if pressed. "But I'm not saying who brought down the bear, Ethan. So you don't have to lie to anyone when you say you don't know who got him. I don't need any publicity that would anger a portion of the American public." But when the president called him into the Oval Office after Ethan came out of the Roosevelt Room that final day, he found the photo gone from the desk. He had no time to comment on its absence, because the president took charge of the meeting as soon as the Oval Office door closed behind them.

"Sit down, Ethan."

Because Brooks wasn't sure where the president wanted him to sit, he hesitated.

"I said sit down, goddamn it."

Jack Peterborough had never before spoken to him in that manner.

"Yes, sir." Ethan took the same single chair he had sat in earlier when he heard the plan for responding to media questions about the events of the previous night. This time the president remained on his feet standing directly in front of Ethan. Oddly, Brooks thought, Jack

Peterborough loosened the knot of his tie—something Ethan had never seen him do during the day.

The president's normally ruddy face was flushed and his right hand quivered—a reflection of his anger—but his eyes were sunken with sorrow and shock. "Do you have any idea what you've done, Ethan?"

"Sir, I'm sorry, but I just--"

"You just what? Just decided that keeping a squeaky clean conscience was more important than the health and fate of this administration?"

"It's not that, Mr. President."

"You can come up with any rationale you want, Ethan—and for the rest of your life I'm sure you'll be consoled by whatever you come up with—but because of your damned fucking principles, you single-handedly caused grievous damage to all of us—including this country."

"I'm not sure that will be the case, sir." In truth, Ethan was only now beginning to ponder the effects of his actions. "But I understand that I no longer deserve to have this job, and if you want me to resign I will." There wasn't a trace of sarcasm in Ethan's offer.

The president folded his arms and looked to the ceiling. "Jesus Christ, Ethan, don't you see that my brother's career as a public servant is likely finished because of what you said? I'll beg him to stay on, but he won't. He'll sacrifice himself to save me as he has on several other occasions. He'll be sure that the story is all about him and we'll go on, but nothing is going to be the same. The press will bear down on us and cut us no fucking slack." Jack Peterborough was always more refined than his brother and had hardly used the f-word in front of Ethan, but in the space of a minute he had employed it twice. "From now on we'll carry the taint of having some kind of quasi-incestuous family history. Absurd conclusions will be drawn about my brother and my wife's relationship. Through no fault of her own, she'll never be viewed the same way ever again. We'll have to contend with the morality issue—never quite openly, of course, but implied and whispered. Three years from now, our opponents will be salivating over slogan choices for their candidate—'He'll bring honor and morality back to the White House' and all that fucking horse shit."

The president walked back to the Resolute Desk and picked up a framed photo of the First Lady and his grown children. He dropped his head and slammed the palm of his left hand on the desk. Ethan's body went numb.

Peterborough took a deep breath in a gesture of self-control and turned back to Ethan. His features revealed considerable emotion and strain. "And my kids are going to have to deal with all the speculation and innuendos. They're twenty-four and twenty-two now, but it will be no less painful to them. How are they going to feel about their uncle from now on?"

With that remark, Brooks felt the overwhelming force of what he had done and the damage it would cause by his refusing to lie to Tim Gerard. Ethan wished for the president to dismiss him so that he could get out of the White House. Still, he could do nothing until the president was finished. Jack Peterborough's voice now made the transition from bitterness to deep sadness.

"Ethan, this was more than your accepting the political adage that it's the way the game has always been played—and always will be. I never once wanted you to stand before the media and support something you didn't believe in or make half-ass excuses or mislead in any way. I was proud to have chosen you and thoroughly pleased by your performance in the job."

Ethan wished to interject and remind his boss that by refusing to answer Tim Gerard's question truthfully he would have greatly misled everyone. But he remained silent. Had he been strapped into the chair he couldn't have felt more helpless.

"Didn't you understand what my brother told you about how important it was that I maintain credibility with the American people?"

Ethan recalled his several discussions with Owen Peterborough, especially the ones at the Willard and near the Lincoln Memorial, when the chief of staff hammered home his two main points. "Your job is to protect the president" and "If you're not helping the president, you hand him your resignation."

"I'll be going to Camp David to confer with the inner staff and my brother. As I said, I'll try to get him to stay on—but I know he won't." The president came forward until he stood only inches away from Ethan, his voice barely above a whisper. "We will try to look forward and not backward, but I don't want you ever to forget what damage you've caused all of us for such a small, insignificant point of principle. You insisted on keeping your ass clean and you can leave here with that—no matter how much shit you left on the rest of us. You betrayed me. You've betrayed us all. I'll expect your resignation by the end of the day. We'll write it for you. That will be all, Ethan."

The president walked back to his desk. He folded his arms and stared at a report. Ethan finally marshaled enough strength to rise from the chair and make his way to the door.

Oh, Ethan." He spoke without looking up.

"Yes, sir?"

"We'll have your personal belongings sent to your place sometime this afternoon. I don't want you back here for any reason."

# CHAPTER 21

Memory of his final meeting with the president served only to stimulate his mind. After debating whether to pour himself some coffee and risk staying up half the night, Brooks decided that reading might tire his eyes and lead to welcome sleep. Yet the moment he shut off the kitchen light, a dog began barking outside the rear door. Ethan assumed it was the same dog he heard earlier, but the bark turned to a menacing growl, as if the animal had confronted something it feared or wished to attack.

Dressed in only his underwear and the Queen's University sweatshirt he had brought with him from the Montrose house, Brooks heard as he stepped out the rear door the dog's continued snarling. The animal stared at him, ceased his growling, spun around, and fled. Ethan jerked his head to the left and spotted near his car two stunned teenage girls sitting on the hood of another vehicle, drinking beers. Frantically pacing on the roof of the car was a gray cat, having likely leaped up upon beholding the dog. As soon as the girls saw Ethan, they jumped off the car and scampered off, leaving two unopened cans of beer on the car's roof—along with one confused feline.

As he returned inside, Ethan laughed, fully appreciating the humor of the moment. What must the girls have thought seeing a grown man looking at them wearing nothing but a sweatshirt and underwear? He'd be lucky if the Kingston police didn't show up and carry him away. After waiting another fifteen minutes and finally accepting that he was safe from arrest, he returned upstairs to the bedroom to find Blair still sound asleep. He took the risk of awakening her by turning on the lamp on his side of the bed and reaching for one of the books she had stacked there. On top was a thin volume with a faux brown leather cover. A collection of Shakespeare's sonnets. He thought he'd begin the paperback thriller

Blair had recently finished and recommended, but he was taken by the bookmark in the Shakespeare—all silver with a message printed in red. "Enchantment lies no further than inches away--in what you read and in what you imagine." Just a simple statement unaccompanied by artistic renderings of clouds, streams, or fairies. He thought the message so perfect for Blair, yet it also reminded him that for all her surface wit and playfulness, she had a depth of mind he could never fully plumb.

Brooks looked on the two pages between which the bookmark lay. Sonnets 28 and 29. Blair had written in light pencil above Sonnet 29 the single word "Yes!" That was enough to prompt his reading all fourteen lines.

When, in disgrace with fortune and men's eyes,
I all alone beweep my outcast state
And trouble deaf heaven with my bootless cries
And look upon myself and curse my fate,
Wishing me like to one more rich in hope,
Featured like him, like him with friends possess'd,
Desiring this man's art and that man's scope,
With what I most enjoy contented least;
Yet in these thoughts myself almost despising,
Haply I think on thee, and then my state,
Like to the lark at break of day arising
From sullen earth, sings hymns at heaven's gate;
For thy sweet love remember'd such wealth brings
That then I scorn to change my state with kings.

He too thought "Yes!" because the lines touched him personally. He was presently "in disgrace with fortune and men's eyes." He had felt alone and had cursed his fate, wishing he had the good fortune of others, who were allowed to live their lives quietly, without needing to escape attention and censure. And at a time when he could well have been lost to despair, a woman came into his life and showed him the possibility of a new day arising. Her "sweet love" was sustaining him to the point that he no longer wished to be someone else. She was lying asleep next to him. At this moment he wouldn't trade his life for anyone's.

· · ·

"Sorry to call so early."

"Not a problem, Tim. I've been up since 7:30." Blair had a short shift today ending at 4:30 and was presently breakfasting on two eggs and toast. Having seen Tim's number on his cell phone, Ethan stepped into the living room to take the call.

"Ethan, I wasn't sure about this when I saw you in Ottawa, but I've now gotten enough information to prompt my calling you."

"Information? About what?" He thought of Aashna's dire warning.

"It seems Steve Jankowski knows you're in Kingston."

"How the hell could he know that?"

"I'm not sure, but I'd imagine someone got his hands on your sister's phone records and saw that calls were made to Kingston."

Phone records—of course. For some reason, it hadn't occurred to Ethan that anyone, especially someone with government connections, could discover his whereabouts in that manner, especially if that someone saw that Holly made a call to--or received a call from—a phone listed in her name.

"Jesus."

"Ethan, I'm just guessing here—but obviously phone privacy has taken a major hit since 9/11 and it stands to reason that Jankowski or one of his minions persuaded someone to share information."

"I feel like an idiot. I should have assumed. But maybe I thought no one would go to such lengths to locate me."

"Unless someone you know there in Kingston turned you in, as it were."

"But I haven't owned up to my real identity to anyone here." He paused recalling his slip-up with the Atkinsons. And the Montroses were in Europe. "You and Holly are the only ones who know that Ethan Brooks—the former press secretary—is in Kingston. Anyone else only knows me as Ethan Matthews."

"Well, then you were discovered through phone records. Who else would your sister be calling and receiving calls from, they must have figured."

Ethan sighed. "Right. Did you hear anything else from your source, Tim?"

"Sorry to say that I did. Supposedly, Jankowski has sent a team up there to find you."

Ethan recalled the two men at the restaurant the previous evening. One of them must have shown the hostess the former press secretary's picture. The other didn't recognize him because of the beard, missing glasses, and longer hair. Ethan wondered if Jankowski had merely sent a team of two—or were there still others searching the city for him?

"Ethan, I would guess that once they locate you, Jankowski himself will fly up and attempt to pin you down for an interview. Even if you won't talk to him, he'd still have exclusive photos as well as the story of where you fled."

Ethan chose his words carefully. "Tim, are you thinking of beating Jankowski to the finish line and breaking the news?"

"I won't lie. In any other case, that's exactly what I'd do, but no one here knows I saw you and I will of course honor your wishes, whatever they may be. I would only ask, if Jankowski does find you, that you—you know, for old time's sake--refuse him the interview and let your best chum in all the world have it instead."

Ethan chuckled at his friend's comical way of making the request. "Okay—just for old time's sake—you can have the exclusive. But I already promised you that."

"You're the man, Ethan."

By the time Brooks returned to the kitchen, he had prepared an answer for Blair's inevitable question. "Was that Holly, Ethan?"

"No, it was my best friend from the States."

She inquired about Tim, and Brooks answered every question without offering Tim's name or where he worked. Ethan noted his "journalist friend's" humor, integrity, and kindness.

"Hope to meet him," Blair added.

"You will, if I have anything to say about it." Now fed up with massaging his answers and skirting by the truth, Ethan couldn't wait until later that evening when he revealed his secret to her.

.  .  .

After dropping Blair off at the pub and assuring her he'd be back for lunch, Brooks drove to the Montrose house to collect the mail and check on everything. He felt a little uncomfortable having spent a second night away from the house, since he had promised Richard Montrose he'd be there every night to keep an eye on things. Following his inspection, Ethan made coffee and moved into the formal dining room to spend time on the Jackson Pollock puzzle before returning to the pub. Now he saw the merging, twisting, and clashing colors in *Convergence* as a reflection of what the next several days were going to hold in store. Perhaps "Jankowski's Raiders" wouldn't recognize him if they saw him again. Surely, the man who scanned the dining room took measure of him and failed to make the connection. But then again, another might be smart enough to consider a possible change in the former press secretary's appearance and identify him. It was enough he had Jordan Essex to confront; Ethan certainly didn't wish to feel Steve Jankowski's hand tapping him on the shoulder as well.

It took ten more minutes of working on the puzzle before the next important thought dropped into his mind. Was Jankowski's discovery that he was in Kingston the "danger" Aashna and her anonymous text message alluded to? Surely, Jankowski wasn't out to hurt him. After all, Ethan inadvertently helped the blogger break the biggest "domestic/scandal" story in Washington since the Lewinsky/Clinton matter. Jankowski would more likely hug him to death rather than traditionally harm him in any way—especially if the former press secretary gave him an exclusive or first interview. Perhaps the anonymous correspondent with Aashna used "danger" in a looser, more figurative sense—as in Ethan's whereabouts were in danger of being revealed. Ethan' satisfaction with his reasoning lasted only a moment because he also recalled that the text message—as Aashna quoted it—said he was in *serious* danger. It was difficult to believe the full phrase could have been meant figuratively. He'd have no choice but to wait—for both his next encounter with Jordan Essex and for whoever would reveal to him the full extent of that serious danger.

"Oh, for Christ's sake." Ethan shook his head in disbelief over his own gullibility. Hadn't he already concluded that the entire warning message Aashna shared with him was nothing more than a ridiculous prank? Hadn't he already accepted that explanation? Evidently he hadn't. Ethan tried to snap the next puzzle piece into place. It wouldn't fit.

. . .

"Do you see that fellow in the olive green shirt?"

Ethan craned his neck around Blair's body and saw the man. "Yes." The pub was three-quarters full. The person in question was sitting near the railing that separated the lower bar area from the main dining area above. "What about him? Did he cheat you on a tip? Want me to go over and shake him down for another five percent?"

"How did you know? No, seriously. I've never seen him in here before."

Could it be one of Jankowski's minions, even though this wasn't one of the men at the restaurant the previous evening? "Well, is he an American?" Brooks asked.

"Not with that accent. He's a Brit. West Yorkshire accent. Probably from Leeds.""You can tell he's from West Yorkshire from his accent?"

"Sure. He said 'water' and it came out 'wah-ur.'" One again Blair blew away all traces of his gloom and worry with a refreshing spray of her wit.

"Is that so?"

"Yes, but that's not what makes him noteworthy. I'm his server and he told me he's been married three times—all to 'waste-reses,' the last of whom he would have strangled if she hadn't beaten him to the punch by breaking her neck in a fall from a horse—or so he claimed."

Brooks glanced at the man again. He seemed to be in his late sixties or early seventies—a harmless spinner of gory tales apparently. When Blair asked Ethan if he had noticed any rain clouds in the horizon on his way to the pub, he turned and looked out of the window to check the conditions. There sitting out on the deck area—in the same seat Ethan had taken the other night—was a familiar face.

Essex was decked in the same stylish sweater he wore when Ethan first saw him in the parking area behind Blair's townhouse. He sat alone, with a half drunk pint in front of him, staring into the pub, eyes looking just slightly to Ethan's right.

"He's here, Blair."

"Who, Ethan?" Her voice suggested that she knew.

"Essex."

Blair took a step back from the table. "Where? Where?"

Ethan pointed. "Right there—on the patio area, right where I sat the other night." At that moment the man's eyes caught Blair's. She tensed when Ethan touched her shoulder.

"It's time to have it out. Stay here."

Without hesitation, Brooks made his way to the entrance of the pub. Although furious, he was still conscious of the embarrassment he would cause Blair if he ran out and grabbed Essex by his expensive sweater and tossed him out of his seat. Ethan quickly determined he'd forcefully invite Blair's former lover to join him in the park across the way, where he had seen him earlier, and then do what was required to make sure the man left Kingston. But there was no time to consider the repercussions if he was arrested by the Kingston police or if Essex pulled the folding knife Blair mentioned he often carried.

By the time Ethan stepped out on the patio deck, Blair had caught up to him. She leaned toward him to whisper, although surely some of the patrons heard her panicked voice. "Ethan, don't. Don't fight--please." She tried to maneuver Brooks down to the sidewalk, but he wouldn't let her. "Don't, Ethan—please don't hurt him! You can't. Leave him alone!"

Ethan's chest collapsed as he translated her frantic words and actions. It was clear. She still cared for Jordan Essex, regardless of how the man had treated her in the past. She couldn't bear to have the man she was presently seeing battle with the one she had previously been in love with—and likely still was. Ethan experienced the comprehensive numbing sensation of those who have made similar discoveries. Thoughts of his future with Blair vanished as he began to form some course of action. But he couldn't do it standing outside the pub. He brushed past Blair and headed toward the restroom inside. As he did, he caught sight of Essex making his way off the deck and unto the sidewalk.

By the time Brooks reached the restroom door, Blair had again caught up to him. She grabbed his arm and forced Ethan to look at her. She was crying as well as breathing rapidly.

"Ethan."

"What do you want?" He had never before spoken so coldly to her.

"That man...that man isn't Jordan."

# CHAPTER 22

Chastened and embarrassed, Brooks returned to the table while a still-shaken Blair tended to one of her customers. The man he had seen several times during the last several days—a man apparently following him—wasn't Jordan Essex after all, but someone else. Blair assured Ethan that whereas the man at the pub was roughly the same height and body type as Essex, he didn't at all resemble him in the face. He was someone Blair had no memory of ever having seen previously. Ethan's profuse apology was interrupted by another patron needing Blair's attention. Her face showed Ethan that she wasn't mad or hurt by his curt remark in front of the restroom. She simply asked him to stay until she was free to speak with him again. Brooks looked over his shoulder at a pair of twenty-somethings who had apparently overheard Blair imploring him to leave the man in the fancy sweater alone. They stared at Ethan and conversed about the incident, he had no doubt. Yet no one else in the pub showed any sign that his actions had been noticed.

Taking another swallow of his draft, Brooks faced the puzzling questions of the man's identity and why he was keeping tabs on the former press secretary. The first thought coming to mind was that the "sweater man" was one of blogger Steve Jankowski's minions. But because several days had passed since Ethan first saw the sweater man in the parking area of Blair's place, Jankowski should have already flown up and made his presence felt. Was the sweater man just being sure it was Ethan? That seemed unlikely, since he was following him and was seen watching him on at least four other occasions. Who else, then, could he be?

"Here's another beer." Blair placed the pint in front of him, her shaking hand causing some of the liquid to spill on the table. "Ethan, I just don't know what to say."

"Blair, I'm truly sorry. I just thought you were protecting Essex, which meant that you still loved him. I didn't handle my sudden hurt well, I know, but--"

"No, no," she interrupted. "I'm not angry but only flattered that you thought that. It shows you care for me and...well, I love you for being afraid of what you thought I was doing but I really wasn't."

"Then you guessed what my motivation was for acting like a jealous jerk?"

"Not at first, but when I was able to unscramble my addled brain cells, I knew that's what it was. I was waiting on the heavy-set couple over there when I had my epiphany. The man got a little peeved at his girlfriend for waving at the bartender, and I overheard her assuring him that she'd never find anyone of interest but him. Then she went to his side of the booth and squeezed in next to him, which was quite a trick since the booth isn't that wide. Then she put her arms around him and kissed him passionately. They then became a 600-pound love ball."

Once more Blair had cauterized the difficult moment with her playful wit, and into Ethan's head came the unqualified and most refreshing thought that he wanted to spend the rest of his life with her. But this splendid moment of recognition was spoiled by the matter of the real Jordan Essex being in Kingston. Blair had seen him and still feared his reentry into her life.

"Ethan, stay in the pub just a little longer. I want us to make a phone call."

Brooks brought his beer out to the patio area, and Blair joined him after tending to another customer. She rubbed both her tired wrists and hands and then her temples. "Ethan, we'll have to use your cell phone for obvious reasons. I'll dial the number, and when the bank's receptionist comes on the line, ask to be connected to Jordan's office. You'll get his secretary, whose name may be Naomi. See if he's returned from Kingston and then inquire if he'll be in his office sometime next week—choose any day. If she asks you to leave your name or if you wish to schedule an appointment, just rush over her question and say you'll call back. Can you do all that?"

"I believe I'm capable."

She smiled at is mock sarcasm. "Ready?" She took his phone and punched in the number. "Here you go."

Ethan got the receptionist and then Naomi, who cheerfully gave her name. He asked if Jordan Essex had returned from Kingston yet.

"Yes, he returned two days ago. But unfortunately he's already flown to Paris for business. He'll be back at the end of next week. Would you like to leave a message?"

"No need. I'll call him back after he returns. Thank you so much, Naomi. You've been a great help." Ethan's delight was impossible to disguise.

Blair's expression broadened. "Well? What did she say? Is Jordan still in Kingston?"

When he told informed her what he learned from Naomi, Blair's puffed her cheeks and expelled a satisfied sigh. Essex wasn't at all attempting to locate Blair. He was simply in Kingston for banking business. All that worry over Blair's safety was for nothing. But the sweater man—whoever he was--was still in the city.

After his finished his pint, Ethan drove back to the Montroses' to clean up and dress for dinner. Nothing about the incident at work was mentioned after he picked up Blair from the pub and waited at her apartment while she showered and dressed. Casting a long glance at Lady Clare, Ethan finally settled on the likelihood that the sweater man was either one of Jankowski's intrepid minions or another journalist building a story about the true whereabouts of Ethan Brooks. In either case, the man would probably show himself again, and this time Ethan would more civilly confront him and determine the reason for the surveillance.

Regarding the matter of what particular danger Brooks was in, if the sweater man planned to physically harm him, why hadn't he already done so? Was he still unsure the longer-haired and bearded man without glasses was the former press secretary? Could he be biding his time by playing some kind of perverse and sadistic game? Or was the man waiting for the go-ahead from someone else? The identity of yet another player in a bizarre scheme was too much for Ethan to wrestle with tonight. He had a very important matter to tend to--one that would heal or fully tear apart his spirit if Blair reacted negatively to his confession.

After he finished dressing, he reached for his wallet and keys and saw a folded post-it note protruding from the wallet. It was a reminder to call his sister.

. . .

"Calm down, Holly. I'm fine. Nothing has happened or is likely to happen to me, I promise." Brooks explained that he wanted her to purchase a new cell phone, set up a new account and then mail the phone to him.

"Ethan, isn't this getting a bit ridiculous? I'm sorry, but I don't understand why you now need another phone account."

Ethan closed his eyes, fighting his frustration. There was no need now to explain his reasoning and risk incurring her wrath over knowing someone in the government checked on her phone records. She was an independent "don't tread on me" Yankee—on par with his fiercely independent paternal grandfather. When her brother took the job as press secretary, Holly insisted that he do all he could to convince the president to get the government's nose out of the common citizen's business. "Holly, on second thought, you can come up with the kids. Bring the phone with you, and I'll show you around this great town."

"Ethan, are you listening to yourself?"

"What do you mean?"

"If they traced your location to Kingston by checking my phone calls—and that's what you're telling me, right?—won't they just see that I've stopped calling your current number and am suddenly calling and receiving calls from a new number—*also in Kingston*?"

Ethan gazed out the rear window and saw his chums the black squirrels shaking their heads at his blatant stupidity. It surely was getting ridiculous.

Holly broke the silence with her now sympathetic and cheerful voice. "But I do want to come up and see you. How about next weekend? I'm really anxious to meet your Canadian girlfriend."

. . .

Tonight Ethan and Blair had dinner reservations at Chez Piggy, on the corner of Princess and King Streets, mere steps away from its sister establishment Pan Chancho. Blair said she had fallen in love with the restaurant the first time she came—several days after her arrival in Kingston. She told Ethan it was a "lovely place to hide out in." As she predicted, Ethan was impressed by the courtyard entrance and vintage quality of the renovated nineteenth-century building. It certainly had that private, retreat-like atmosphere, where one could escape and forget about the vicissitudes of daily life. It also featured a popular and an attractive outdoor patio area.

"Ethan, if it weren't so chilly, I'd suggest we eat on the patio. I sat out there twice this summer, and it was just heavenly. In the spring we can do it, though—that is, if you want." She waited for his response to her hint about an extended relationship, which he delayed only briefly.

"Sign me up."

Because the early October temperature had dropped to eight Celsius, Ethan was all for dining inside as well. They were led upstairs to the dining area, with its stone walls enhanced by Tunisian carpets and framed art work. The positioning of the tables gave patrons the sense that they weren't eating in a restaurant that wished to squeeze in as many tables as possible—therefore lessening the charm of the surroundings. Brooks had dined at a good number of impressive restaurants in Vermont, Albany, Manhattan, and Washington D.C. Yet here in Kingston he felt a special pleasure in all the eateries Blair had taken him to. He wasn't sure whether it was because he was a visitor to another country or whether he simply felt more at home here. And did he feel more at home because of Blair Babineaux or was it because Canada opened his arms to him when he needed sanctuary the most? It really didn't matter. He knew he'd have much to be thankful for this Thanksgiving, which Blair told him would be on a Monday in October. Still, Canada hadn't yet learned who he really was. Tonight, however, he would let a Canadian know.

But was he truly on his way to being an adopted Canadian? Could he really sever ties with the country of his birth? It was one thing to reside in Canada for a couple of months, but quite another to take up permanent residence. His instincts told him that Holly would support him if he took such a step, especially since they would be fairly close geographically, but he wondered what his grandfather would have said. Dan Brooks never gave his grandson any unvarnished patriotic advice about "My country right or wrong." It was important to Ethan to believe that his grandfather would have at least understood if his grandson decided to live out the rest of his life in Canada. It's not that he would ever refuse to return to the States for visits, vacations, and the like, but he was certain that forever he'd be seen by many or most in the U.S. as a traitor to the Peterborough administration, if not to his country. If he linked what he had done to the administration with formally transferring his allegiance to Canada, he could only imagine what the long footnote in the history books would say about him.

By the time the wine came and the main courses were ordered, Ethan had pivoted back to the main issue of the evening—his confessing to Blair his true identity. If she responded negatively, Canada would be crossed off the locations where he would spend the rest of his life.

"Ethan, let's have our entrees and then during dessert I can confess what I've needed to tell you for some time now."

Preoccupied with his own revelation, Ethan had put Blair's secret out of his mind. Although there were a number of possibilities he didn't wish to hear, perversely he wanted her admission to be serious enough to temper her possible disgust for his having lied to her for this long. He was surprised to see such an apprehensive look on her face. He expected that she would float her confession on a rapidly-flowing flood of wit and humor. "Are you okay, Blair?"

"Yes, yes. I'm fine." She put some of the usual glow back into her face. But she still hid a good deal of it. "I hope you love the food. I want to come back here often with you." She reached across the table and firmly squeezed his hand.

Following the completion of the main courses, they ordered one dessert to share. But neither of them touched it when it arrived. Blair finished her wine and cleared her throat--this time without any mock seriousness. "Ethan, I can't wait any longer to tell you something you need to know, something I should have told you weeks ago."

His natural sense of chivalry wanted to alleviate the apprehension and nervousness she manifested at the moment. "No, wait. Before you do that, I want to tell you what you need to know — something I should have told you the very first time we went out."

"Let me tell you first." She once more grabbed his hand.

"No." He put his other hand on top of hers and caressed it. "Let me speak first." Had they been in their normal states, they would have burst out laughing at their adolescent exchange. But Blair remained silent, tacitly agreeing to let him continue. Ethan hadn't rehearsed what he would say; he only promised himself he'd immediately get the point. "Blair, my real name isn't Ethan Matthews." Blair's eyes expanded and began blinking in a rhythm that reminded Ethan of a pulse beat. "My real name is Ethan Brooks and, until the first week of July, I was the press secretary to the President of the United States." Hearing these words and how he presented them left Ethan with the conclusion that no one, let alone Blair, would think he was being at all serious. "I hadn't wanted to wait this long, but I thought--"

"Ethan, can I tell you my secret now?"

He was shocked by her interruption. Didn't she appreciate the import of what he had just revealed? Was she *that* naïve about American politics that his true identity didn't register?

"Can I, Ethan--please?"

He was too flabbergasted to protest. "Of course. Go ahead. Tell me your secret."

"My secret is that I know who you really are and I've known for almost a month now."

# CHAPTER 23

"Blair, I think we better take this dessert back to your place and have a long talk." Between their leaving the restaurant and arriving at Blair's apartment, Brooks said barely a word as Blair explained how she arrived at the true identity of her new love.

"Don't misunderstand me, Ethan; I was clearly falling for you before I knew the truth. I honestly believed you were Ethan Matthews, a researcher and writer spending nine months or so in Kingston while you worked—although I was curious why you never talked more specifically about your project." She went on with her account, noting that she remained in the dark about his identity until, on September 7th, she received a stack of newspapers from one of her female co-workers. "She asked me if I wanted them for starting fires for the fall and winter. I said sure, and she handed me the bundle, which included not only issues of the *Kingston Whig-Standard*, but also the *New York Times* and the *Toronto Globe and Mail*—all copies dating from June and July." That explained the scrapbooks and newspaper clippings in Blair's spare bedroom. "I of course heard about the situation in Washington over the summer, but as I told you, I'm not really interested in American politics." She had informed Ethan early in their relationship that she didn't subscribe to any paper but went online for whatever she "needed to know."

"And you saw the story about my leaving the administration."

"Yes, but I had no interest in reading about it--until I saw your picture."

Ethan offered a weak laugh. "Even with my short hair and glasses, you recognized me?"

"It was a photo of you at your last press conference. It was snapped when you had just wiped your brow with your left hand. In your right hand were your glasses. You had taken them off."

Brooks couldn't remember having done so, but he obviously did what she described.

"I recognized your eyes. In the picture they looked troubled but still so very kind. I then went online and found the photo in color and enlarged it. I was certain it was you. Your lips and nose looked the same then, you know. I looked at the rest of the July's papers until I read that you had apparently gone into hiding. Then I knew." She grimaced.

"What is it, Blair?"

"I'm ashamed to admit that I made a copy of the photo without your glasses on and drew both a beard on your face and longer hair on your head. I put the finished product in a scrapbook upstairs, along with all the articles I found that mentioned you. You may recall that I was a little nervous when I saw you in the doorway of the second upstairs room." She further explained that she was excited when she first determined his true identity, but after she knew she was in love with him, she maintained her silence for another reason. "I was so afraid I'd somehow lose you if you realized I knew the truth."

Ethan was astounded by her account. "I don't know what to say, Blair—only that I am so sorry I didn't tell you much sooner. I shouldn't have misled you."

"No Ethan, I misled you but not telling you that I knew. I just figured you'd tell me when you thought the time was right."

"And I was petrified you'd hate me for lying or, if not that, you'd decide that you wanted nothing to do with such a notorious American fugitive."

"Your real story only made me want to care for you more. I realized that we had something in common—as we both fled to Kingston to escape ridicule and abuse. I love you Ethan Brooks. Hating you is not an option."

They spent a good two hours on Blair's living room sofa, talking more about each other's history and the evolution of their mutual love. With the help of several glasses of sparkling wine, Ethan felt immense relief, while he absorbed Blair's revelation. She knew and she loved. She had no other difficult secret to confess—of which she assured him multiple times. All potential obstacles to their devoting themselves to each other had been mirages now swatted away by the truth. But soon another image reshaped itself in his mind. A face. That of Aashna Malini.

"Blair, I want to tell you one more thing that will require your understanding and trust."

"You left someone of the female persuasion behind in Washington."

The characterization was so ludicrous, given the facts of his relationship with Aashna that Ethan almost laughed. Yet his smile was enough to puzzle Blair. He explained the nature of his former ties to the First Lady's press secretary and assured Blair that he had not only fallen out of love with Aashna but that his love for Blair made it clear that before now he didn't really know what love was.

Blair kissed him lovingly and put her head on his chest. "But she's so beautiful — so much more appealing and exotic looking than I am."

"And how would you know that?"

"One of the articles included her picture — oh, along with the notation that you and she were an 'item.'"

Brooks threw up his hands — literally. "So you already knew about her as well — Jesus."

"I like to know what I'm up against, that's all." Ethan shook his head and sensed laughter welling up. Blair cleared her throat — this time as a prelude to something Ethan had apparently not said. "Mr. Brooks, I just noted that she was far more appealing than I am, and you can say nothing by way of refutation?"

"Blair, Aashna couldn't hold your jock-strap when it comes to being desirable." He went with the first — and certainly the worst — cliché that came to mind.

"Ethan, I think you've complimented me but in a way that defies all human understanding."

They turned their conversation to the future — the area that remained blurred in the distance. Ethan enjoyed talking about Blair's meeting Holly and the girls when they came to Kingston the following week, and his enthusiasm grew when they discussed a road trip to Toronto and a flight to Vancouver. But Blair said nothing about the decisions Ethan would have to make in the near future — where their relationship would go from here; what Ethan would decide to do as far as renewing or commencing a new career; and where Ethan would decide to live for the rest of his life.

"Are you okay, Ethan?"

He hadn't realized that he had become withdrawn. "I'm just thinking."

"Ah, your favorite pastime."

Whereas, the Jordan Essex matter was resolved, Ethan still had no clue as to the identity of the sweater man and why that person was following him. And what was the "serious danger" Aashna had warned him of? He had yet to share these concerns with Blair.

．．．

Blair had fallen asleep on Ethan's lap. Had he enough strength and flexibility to lift and carry her up the stairs to bed, it would have been a lovely ending to an incredible evening. He wanted to make love to her, but it would be enough tonight to lie with her head on his chest and caress her face and body while he thanked Lady Fortune for sending him to Kingston and then to the brew pub where he first met Blair Babineaux. Blair's legs functioned well enough to get her up the stairs but the rest of her was in slumber. Ethan helped her into the bed and removed her clothing as she remained oblivious to his ministrations. He situated her under the covers and had only begun undressing when he heard his cell phone chiming downstairs. He glanced at the time. 11:25 p.m.

．．．

"Ethan, do you have some time to talk? I'm sorry for calling so late."

Brooks could tell from the tone of his voice that Tim Gerard had something important to share. "No problem Tim; I'm still up."

Gerard quickly inquired about Ethan's well-being and jumped into the latest information he had only minutes earlier discovered. "I called in a few more chips and learned from a reluctant source that the rumor of possible violence against you is valid—and that a person or persons are likely already in Kingston as we speak." Gerard was unable to ascertain from his source the name of the person who had arrived in the city, but that the flight originated from D.C. and stopped first in Toronto.

"Have you any guesses about the identity of those now in Kingston?" Brooks remained calm in the face of the information; after all, he had become used to being a possible target of the sweater man.

"Ethan, I didn't speak much about this when we met in Ottawa, but the past three months haven't lessened the hatred some have felt for you over what they believe you did to the president. The opposition continues its questions about the off-kilter "moral compass" of the administration. On the other side, some continue to blame you for diverting the nation from what they term "the best and least unimpeded path" toward genuine legislative progress. You've also been slammed for making a successful foreign policy more difficult, especially in light of Russia's and China's charge that the administration cannot be trusted, since they originally wished to lie to its citizens about a tawdry episode involving the president's brother. Hell, even New Zealand, the Netherlands, and India made the same point, although they were more forgiving. And you can imagine how the political opposition has played that up. Even a few members of my profession resent you for the latest restrictions placed upon us by the new press secretary and the communications director."

Ethan assumed the president's natural adversaries would use the event of early July to their advantage, and he was sure members of the media no longer held him in highest regard—but that he affected foreign policy as well? "So, you're saying a die-hard supporter of Jack Peterborough or a volatile cable anchor wants to do me in?"

Gerard didn't laugh at Ethan's attempt at humor. "Ethan, I'm just worried that some foot-soldier of the administration or fanatical loyalist of Peterborough's has decided to come up there and confront you."

"Tim, I'm assuming someone from the government—in whatever capacity—has informed both you and Aashna about the danger I'm in. Is it possible that at least one of these 'unfriendlies' has been here for several days now?"

"Have you seen someone you're suspicious of?"

"You might say that."

"Christ, I don't know, Ethan. Maybe so. Just watch your back, okay? Whatever else I hear I'll share with you immediately, buddy."

"I appreciate that, Tim—I really do. Look, you mentioned that I'm not warmly remembered by members of our profession." That consequence of his actions bothered him the most.

"The number isn't that large, but, as I said, there are some who hold you responsible for making our jobs more difficult."

"I understand—and I regret nothing more than that fact, believe me."

"Ethan, the younger men and women still stick up for you across the board—especially the women. They never expected you to be so respectful and open with them. The rest of us—also out of respect-- decided that when you left we weren't going to make a "Where's Waldo?" game out of your disappearance. But some of the crustier members of the press and TV have become more annoyed by the administration's obfuscation and multiple hoops they have to get their ponderous flesh and weary bones through—and they've become less sympathetic to any possible reason behind your decision. Please know that you still have strong support—and no stronger support than from me. I'll call you with any further news—and you call me if you see anything else that looks out of place. I'll notify the Kingston police myself if you won't."

Brooks was gratified by his friend's loyalty and understanding. He ended the call and checked the front door again to be sure it was securely locked. As he began his ascent up to the bedroom where Blair lay asleep, he stopped and contemplated the possibility that the sweater man was the only one he had to be wary of. It was quite possible—perhaps even probable--that the others who just flew up from Washington were Steve Jankowski and his minions, who only wanted to break a big story. With that thought, Ethan relaxed and continued his climb. He hoped that Blair was awake or only in the lightest sleep. Again, he could think of no more pleasurable ending to this day full of incident and consequence than to make love to the beautiful woman he had just placed in the bed.

"Ethan?"

Blair stood at the top of the stairs. He had never before seen such a frightened look on her face.

As soon as he reached the landing, she grabbed his arm and moved him toward the bathroom. She struggled to speak in a loud whisper.

"I woke up when my cell phone rang." She looked toward her bedroom.

"Is there someone in there?" Ethan couldn't imagine how that could be, but she was acting as though someone was.

"You weren't in bed, so I answered. I thought you had gone back to the Montroses' — or went out to get something for supper." Her fear affected her thinking.

"Blair is there anyone in your bedroom?" He grabbed her shoulders this time.

"No, no. Outside my bedroom. He told me to look out my window."

"He?"

"The man."

"What man?"

Blair had begun to regain control. "The one you thought was Jordan."

"Stay here." Ethan rushed to the bedroom window and pulled back the curtain. Still standing below was the man, wearing the same sweater he wore at the pub earlier in the day.

"Is he still there, Ethan?" Blair had come to the door of her bedroom.

"Yes."

"What does he want? What does he want?"

At that moment, the sweater man, seeing Ethan above, waved pleasantly and then crooked his finger in a gesture that said "follow me." He repeated the gesture more vigorously and began walking slowly to where his car was parked.

"Blair, please do as I ask and stay here. I'm going to find out what this guy is up to."

"I want to go with you. Let me get some clothes on."

"No time. Just stay here." He ran down the stairs; grabbed his jacket, wallet, and keys, and headed into the kitchen. He shouted, "Blair, lock the back door behind me."

She followed him down the stairs. "Ethan, should I call the police? Ethan? Ethan? Will you call me?"

He didn't answer; he was already outside looking toward the parking area. There was no time to ponder the danger in which he might be placing himself. He was going to end this nonsense once and for all.

The sweater man stood next to the driver's side of his car. The car's door was open and the motor running. After once more beckoning Brooks to follow him, the man got in the car and began driving out of the parking area—but he moved the vehicle very slowly in an obvious attempt to give Ethan enough time to get into his own car and pursue.

The sweater man had hardly progressed down the street when Ethan exited the parking area. It was clear the man was going to lead him to a pre-designated spot, where Ethan expected at least one more person to join the party.

Ethan followed the sweater man, who made doing so rather easy, until they reached the City Hall Park area. The sweater man was even kind enough to stick his arm out the window and point out a parking space for Ethan and then parked himself. The man--now some forty yards ahead of Ethan--crooked his finger once again and started into the park. Every gesture was one of accommodation; the man gave no sign that Ethan was in any danger—all the more reason, Ethan thought, to look behind and to either side of him as he walked at the moderate pace set by the sweater man. Still, with each step he believed more strongly that he would arrive at a spot where a video and still photographer would suddenly appear--on either side of Steve Jankowski.

Brooks looked past the sweater man walking ahead of him and saw that the pathway split right before a pedestal on which stood the statue of Sir John MacDonald, the transplanted Scot who became Canada's first prime minister in 1867. The air was chilly and the sky clear. The moon was in its waxing period; a fact Ethan would have thought auspicious had he not been concentrating on his immediate surroundings. He noticed a bench situated on the right a few feet from where the path split—the same bench where he and Blair had sat and enjoyed a late summer afternoon, when she told him about

MacDonald. Inhabiting the bench at present was a man sitting hunched forward with his arms folded in front of him. He wore a large blue parka and a tri-color Queen's University toque. Ethan couldn't see his face because the man was staring down at his feet, if he wasn't in fact asleep. He reminded Ethan of the many lonely souls he saw too often in Washington when he was out late at night, driving back from the White House. Then again, the man might be a dispirited student dwelling on his recent academic or personal miseries. That he felt such empathy for another at this bizarre moment surprised Ethan, who had already concluded that at the base of the statue would be where he either saw Steve Jankowski or that he'd fully understand the import of Aashna's dire warning.

The sweater man took the path to the left of the MacDonald statue, and Ethan's eyes followed his movements until he began to circle around the rear of the edifice. At that point the sweater man halted. Ethan continued moving forward until he reached the point where the path split. He stopped and stared at the sweater man, who turned his back on Ethan but remained where he was. Ethan looked to his left and right for Jankowski and any others who might accompany the blogger with cameras in tow. It was just shy of midnight, but there was enough illumination to reveal that no others had yet arrived. Ethan was about to demand from the sweater man just what the hell was going on, but the words had barely begun to form on his tongue when he heard another voice.

"Hello, Ethan."

Startled, Brooks spun around but saw no one except the man on the bench, who remained hunched over. A moment later his memory caught up with him.

"Owen?"

"Good to see you again, Ethan." Without question, the former chief of staff hid his true feelings behind the monotone delivery of the sentiment.

Ethan took a quick glance behind him and saw that the sweater man had disappeared.

Peterborough rose from the bench and removed his tri-colored toque and tossed it on the bench. "I'm sure you guessed who Greg was working for."

"Greg? You mean the guy who led me here?" Peterborough nodded. "Actually, I didn't have a clue, Owen."

"A good man, Greg Hicks. A little infatuated with the dramatic gesture, but a good and careful man. Son of Charlie Hicks, the most loyal member of my staff, who took my leaving the administration pretty hard. Died of a heart attack three weeks ago.

Anyway, Greg wanted to be sure it was you before he called me. We traced your whereabouts through your sister's phones—the one in Vermont, the other here. It was a fairly simple deduction, really. By the way, I like the new look on you, Ethan—especially the beard." Peterborough had grown one himself, an almost fully gray untrimmed appendage, which on his wide face made him look a little like Hemingway. "I started growing this the day after I resigned from the administration."

Ethan checked again for evidence of Hicks or of anyone else. Satisfied that he and Peterborough were alone, he wondered if his adversary—for that's how he viewed him at the moment—if his adversary was about to draw a weapon from one of the pockets of his parka.

"You should know that our old friend Steve Jankowski is in Kingston and is hot to find you."

"Does he know you're here, Owen?"

"Nah. If he did, he'd get his chicken-shit ass back on a plane and fly back to Washington. I'm the very last person he'd want to run into."

Brooks sensed his tension ease a bit—both he and Peterborough had a common "enemy" in Jankowski and they had both grown beards probably for the same reason—to escape detection.

Peterborough glanced around the area and began walking toward Ethan, who moved back three steps, turning his body to the right thirty degrees to better defend himself.

"Don't be alarmed, my friend. *I'm* not going to assault you. Of course, I wonder if you believe I should—or better yet, do I at least have a right to?"

Ethan was only thinking of the emphasis that Peterborough put on "*I'm* not going to assault you." Would that be Greg Hicks's job—or was Owen referring to a weapon that would do the damage?

"I understand your anger, Owen."

Peterborough ignored the feeble understatement. "I've been told that you've heard rumors that you're in some kind of danger. Have any idea why some would think that, Ethan?"

It was clear that Peterborough was attempting to wrench a *mea culpa* from the former press secretary, but Ethan couldn't see the point of apologizing. But he could honestly express his regrets. "Owen, I wish that night never happened—believe me, I do."

"That night?" Peterborough could no longer conceal his bitterness. "Not that night but the next morning, you mean. *That night* might well have meant nothing had you kept your god-damned mouth shut. You didn't even have to lie, you fucking son-of-a-bitch."

What made Peterborough's outburst more menacing was that he was stone cold sober.

"Owen, I'm not going to debate the point with you."

The words spit out. "Debate the point? Debate the fucking point? What do you think this is—an academic disagreement about some god-damned historical event?" Peterborough rubbed the expelled saliva from his beard with the inside of his fingers.

Ethan fully expected the larger man to attack him at any moment.

"Owen, I..." Nothing further came out.

"You what? You tuck your tail and run out of the country rather than face up to what you did to me—to my brother—our family—and the fucking administration." Ethan was prepared for a physical confrontation but he found Peterborough's profanity and intensity sad—almost tragic. "And so you come up here to hide out and find yourself a Canadian lady friend. A waitress, no less. Starting over, are you? Going to become a Canadian citizen and begin a new career, get married, and raise a nice family up here—that what you think?"

Ethan tensed, fully expecting some kind of threat to be leveled against Blair. He could see a young couple walking at some distance in the park, but they would be of no use to him now—even if they could hear him.

Peterborough started shaking his head. "No, no. Can't let you just turn the page and start writing a new chapter on clean white paper, laddybuck. No—just can't allow that to happen."

Peterborough reached inside the front pocket of his parka. Ethan didn't need to be told what he would draw from it.

Ethan looked at the .38 caliber revolver pointed at him. "Owen, you can't do this."

"I can't? But before I do *this*, I want you to tell me why you couldn't bring yourself to think of the larger picture before you decided to keep your conscience clean."

"Owen, it wasn't like that." Ethan immediately regretted not offering a lengthy explanation. He needed time to talk Peterborough out of shooting him where he stood.

"Oh, it wasn't?" Peterborough's voice elevated with undisguised sarcasm.

Ethan lowered his head because he knew that it *was* like that. He had refused to lie or to walk away from Tim Gerard's question on that July morning. Why couldn't he have sacrificed principle for the larger good? Didn't he know when he took the job that political utilitarianism was the operative philosophy at that level of government? Instead, he thought of "for the greater good" as the operative rationalization — a political philosophy he disdained. Was his real mistake taking the damned job in the first place? But there was no time for further reflection on that point. He was likely only seconds away from being shot.

"Owen, let me try to explain." Again the words were wrong — not at all the ones that might prevent his death or at best a serious injury.

"I know; I know. You still think you did the right thing — and you're never going to see it any differently." Peterborough's voice had calmed — resigned to whatever course of action he had apparently planned from the moment he decided to come to Kingston. "I can't let you escape what you did to all of us and live a contented and conscience-free life up here with your new lady. But I'll tell you what. I'm going to let you spend the rest of your life here if what's what you want."

Peterborough's now congenial tone belied his sadistic plan. Ethan understood: he'd be killed here so he could indeed spend "the rest" of his life in Kingston.

"Think about what you're going to do, Owen. It's not worth it. You can get past this." Now he offered advice that, from *anyone else,* might have a chance of halting Peterborough's act—but from him only enhanced the odds of his own death.

"No. I'm not going to get past this, Ethan. You've made sure of that. I'm a fucking pariah in my own family because of what I said about my sister-in-law." Peterborough was staggered by a wave of emotion. "I truly loved that woman, and even though she didn't choose me, she was in my life. She was *in my life*. Do you understand? My brother doesn't need me to protect him anymore because I put him in the worst kind of jeopardy. I fucked up what was going to be an outstanding four years. I don't really care what the fucking public thinks of me—about what they've written about me. But I care that I lost the two people I love the most. And I can't let you get away with having made that happen."

In spite of his dire circumstances, Brooks felt every word of Peterborough's conflicting admission. It was clear the former chief of staff realized his own responsibility, but he wouldn't let that realization prevent his deep hatred for the man who betrayed him and caused him such abject misery.

Peterborough's hulking frame and gray beard offered a shocking canvas for such an expression of emotional pain. After a moment of visible agony, his muscles grew rigid and his thumb pulled back the gun's trigger mechanism. The weapon was still pointed at Ethan, who dared not attempt to run. He only had his words to protect him.

"Owen, please, this won't stop the pain. It will only cause more."

Peterborough's head quivered, and a puzzled and then amused look came over his features.

"Oh, Ethan. Again a victim of your misconceptions. Didn't I tell you that you had nothing to fear from me as far as doing you bodily harm?" In fact, Ethan had forgotten that assurance. Once more he looked for Greg Hicks or someone else to come forward and do Peterborough's violent bidding.

Peterborough turned the .38 in his hand. "Ethan, I can't allow you to be free of the responsibility for what you've done. No. I'm not going to let you close the door and start over with a clean slate. You see, this way you'll never be able to wash your hands of your past, laddybuck. The memory of tonight will be with you until the day you die, which I hope will be many, many years from now." Peterborough displayed the pistol. "So the bottom line is that this will *most certainly* stop my pain--and begin yours."

"Owen, no!"

Peterborough brought the revolver up to his open mouth the moment Brooks rushed forward. Jolted, Peterborough redirected the weapon and briefly pointed it at Ethan but immediately turned it back toward his face. Before he could replace the barrel into his open mouth, Ethan was upon him. Brooks jerked Peterborough's wrist away and wrapped his index and middle finger around Peterborough's trigger finger. Peterborough groaned "No" and turned his forearm so that it was against Ethan's throat. With his superior bulk and added adrenaline, Peterborough caved himself upon Ethan, causing both men to fall upon the ground, with Ethan pinned under Peterborough, who maintained control of the pistol. Would the man shoot him first and then kill himself or simply fire a round into his mouth, which was just inches away from Ethan's face.

"Owen don't!" Ethan was stunned. The words weren't his. Peterborough's body seemed to leap off Ethan's—not the result of a voluntary action, but rather the effect of Greg Hicks having knocked him off with a flying tackle. Brooks rose quickly and saw Hicks grab the .38 and toss it toward the statue of MacDonald.

"You son of a bitch, why did you do that for?" Peterborough had risen to his knees. His shoulders slumped wearily and Ethan saw his head begin to bob up and down. His next words revealed that he had begun crying—his entire body quivered. "Huh? Greg, I wasn't going to kill Ethan. I just wanted him to see me kill myself so he'd never be able to forget." Peterborough dropped his hands to the ground and remained sobbing on all fours as two male Queen's students came running over to offer their assistance.

# CHAPTER 24

"I have to go to work. God, I hate leaving you right now."

Sitting on the edge of the bed, Blair kissed Ethan awake and ran her soft hands over his forehead. It was 10:00 a.m. He reached up and pulled her to him. He kissed her the intense way he had when he returned to her place after 1:00 a.m. and released his pent-up emotions. Blair wasn't in much better shape. She hadn't heard from him, and she couldn't call him because he left his cell phone at her place. They talked for two hours at the kitchen table after she brought from the living room a bottle of bourbon. A mix of water was superfluous as Ethan drank two stiff drinks before he began his account. By the time he was through, Blair felt completely spent from hearing all that happened in City Hall Park and what she had not previously known about Ethan's relationship with Owen Peterborough. She could offer nothing but the squeezing of her hand on his and an occasional kiss on his fingers as she raised them to her lips. She only asked if he was certain that the danger was over and that Peterborough wouldn't seek to harm him in the future.

Ethan last saw the former chief of staff being led out of the park by a shaken Greg Hicks, who, while the former chief of staff was still on all fours, assured the two Queen's students that Peterborough just had "a few too many." As soon as the young men left the scene, Hicks retrieved the .38 and swore to Ethan that he didn't know Peterborough had the gun and that he thought the former chief of staff just wanted to "punch out" the former press secretary. "He must have gotten the pistol after he flew into Canada." After that, Hicks lifted Peterborough to his feet and attempted to comfort him. "Owen, it's time to go home now." Peterborough never looked back at Brooks as he staggered from the park, but Hicks implored Ethan, "You can't say anything about this meeting. Please don't. Owen's really hurting."

Bair smoothed Ethan's brow. "I know you need time to think about everything that's happened. I'll meet you at the Montroses' as soon as I get off from work. I'll bring food, and we can talk. Then we can come back here—okay?"

Ethan smiled his approval of her plan and closed his eyes as she left. When he opened them again it was one in the afternoon.

. . .

Arriving at the Montrose house at 1:45, Brooks called Holly to assure her that all was well and would continue to be. He explained that Owen Peterborough had come to Kingston and that they talked—and that the rumor about his being in serious danger had to do with the former chief of staff's plans to confront him in Kingston. Holly was interested in every word of the exchange, but Ethan said nothing of the gun and Peterborough's plan for suicide. Nor would he tell anyone—that is, provided Greg Hicks didn't make the matter public and he wasn't asked to corroborate Hicks's account. But he thought the odds of that occurring were very long. Ethan certainly didn't need anything else to torment his conscience in the years ahead.

Satisfied that her brother was safe from harm, Holly turned the subject to her visit with the girls later in the week and the anticipation of meeting Blair. Ethan was grateful his sister made no attempt to encourage his return to Vermont. Whether she would bring up the subject while she was in Kingston was anyone's guess. He'd also have difficulty convincing her that the wound over his eye had nothing to do with his encounter with Owen Peterborough.

Not five minutes after Holly hung up, Tim Gerard called. "Ethan, I just heard from the source I told you about, and he said that Owen Peterborough was headed to Kingston to see you. The source is apparently a friend of someone close to Owen, who let him know that Peterborough has been attacking you with more intensity lately and hinting that you deserve the very worst that can happen to you. That's where all this danger business is coming from, I would imagine. Oh, and this source said he texted Aashna, hoping she'd get in touch with me."

Ethan was relieved to have the matter of the warning explained, believing that Greg Hicks might have been the one who shared Owen's state of mind to Tim's source. "Well, Tim. Your source was correct. Owen and I saw each other last night."

"Jesus Christ, what happened? What did he say?"

Ethan repeated much of what Peterborough said, again omitting any mention of the revolver, but did add, "Tim, I'm concerned that Owen's so deeply depressed that he might consider harming himself."

"Owen Peterborough—that tough son-of-a-bitch, committing suicide—is that what you're saying?"

"I don't know. Maybe. Anyway, can you keep me informed about him—that is, if you hear anything?"

"Of course. But I don't suppose you're giving me permission to report your stated concerns about him, are you?" As always, Tim never hid the hopefulness in his voice whenever he posed such a question.

"I can't give you that, Tim." Gerard sighed his disappointment in an exaggerated manner. "But I do have something else I can give you."

"And that is?"

"My story."

Gerard half-gurgled/half-shouted his delight. "Great! Wait, wait. I know Jankowski is up there hunting you down. You going to talk to him too? Look, at least give the story to me first—you promised, remember?"

"What do you take me for, Tim? I'm giving it to you and you alone, dearest chum. I'll give it to no one else—not now or in the future."

Gerard promised to keep Ethan abreast of anything he heard regarding Owen Peterborough's health and state of mind. Ethan agreed to meet Tim in two days' time again at *Zoé's Lounge* at the *Chateau Laurier* in Ottawa, where he would give him his exclusive. "Assuming that you can work that into your schedule, Tim."

"I'll book my flight as soon as I get off the phone. Ethan, please know you can always count on me for anything you need. If you'd like, I can poke around and see if there's something in the journalism field that might get you back in the game."

"Tim, right now I'm not sure where I want to go career-wise. I've got a lot of thinking to do yet. But thank you for the offer. You're the best, my friend."

"As are you. And I sincerely mean that, Ethan."

. . .

Ethan made himself some eggs and grabbed the most recent issues of the *Kingston Whig-Standard,* copies of which he had been stacking for the Montroses in case they wished to peruse back numbers when they returned in the spring. After almost three months of avoiding it, he enjoyed reading contemporary news again, even the short article about the U.S. Senate's contentious hearings on one of Jack Peterborough's nominees to the Court of Appeals. Ethan knew he'd likely resist keeping up daily with American politics, but it was liberating no longer having to hide from the topic—turning over newspapers and flipping past magazine pieces as though the print was coated with anthrax. Would he read Tim's forthcoming piece on him—that was certain to be covered extensively, even in the Canadian media? He didn't know, but he was determined to refuse all other requests—and they might well be many—for brief comments and full interviews. It was a rite of passage back to his identity and freedom he'd have to endure, but it would be worth it in the end. He hoped that eventually all interested parties would get bored and leave him alone.

Reading took up another hour, as Brooks poured through old issues of magazines and started a novel Richard Montrose had just finished the night before he left for Europe. When his eyes grew heavy and his throat dry, Ethan went to the bathroom and splashed water on his face and then to the refrigerator to grab a bottle of Moosehead. Glancing out the rear windows of the stylish kitchen area, Ethan noticed that the sun had dropped to the top level of the colorful maples at the back of the property. He opened the rear door and decided he was ready to take a seat on the deck and begin his contemplations about the future. The temperature was perfect for the long-sleeve flannel shirt and unzipped light jacket he put on. The sun shot its rays above his head after he sat on one of the deck chairs, as well as through the maple branches to his left and right. Where he sat was therefore in a reddish-hued shade—making him feel as though any decisions made while sitting there would be significant and endorsed by nature. He had over two hours before Blair would arrive--but he wouldn't be alone. His buddies the two black squirrels made their way down one of the trees and took up residence directly in front of him—some ten yards away on the grass.

With all that happened since July, including the events of the previous night, Ethan knew it had all been worth it because he now had Blair. How could he have gotten through the last month and a half without her vivaciousness, wit, gentleness, caring, and love? Although he had mistaken Greg Hicks for Jordan Essex, he was pleased with himself that he had been fully committed to protecting Blair. She had loved him in spite of learning the truth about his past, and she made it clear that she would be with him no matter where he wished to go—even going so far as promising, "And when I go to the bathroom, I'll never forget to leave the seat up—I swear it." But she and Canada were so inextricably linked in his mind that he felt he had no right to ask her to leave her country. Taking another swallow of beer and smiling at the antics of the black squirrels, Ethan's mind was replete with Blair's many charming and hilarious idiosyncrasies and demonstrations of her unique sense of humor—for example her stepping out the rear door of her apartment during a rain shower using a cast-iron skillet as an umbrella. And although they had waited until only recently to commence a sexual relationship, she aroused him in ways he had never expected—and in others he greatly anticipated. He just hoped that now—with so many issues finally resolved—they could indulge each other's desires with full freedom and contentment. He chuckled at the prospect of naming their children and how he would suggest "Clare" if a girl—in tribute to Blair's favorite Waterhouse painting—and "Jackson" if a boy—in honor of that damned jigsaw puzzle he had yet to complete.

As one of the black squirrels ran two quick circles around the other, Brooks gave Aashna Malini one last thought. He accepted that he had been madly in love with her and had enjoyed their lovemaking, although he never left her place without having doubts about her commitment to him. In short, she had never really made him feel comfortable. Although he saw no reason ever to arrange a meeting, he thought about running into her again and how he would feel looking at her beautiful features and flawless skin. But that vision was immediately replaced by Blair's quirky expressions and patches of freckles on her adorable face. In the dynamics of their physical relationship, Aashna only took; but Blair always gave—and would continue giving to the point that he would be inspired to give to her all he could. Ethan was dead certain he'd carry no torch for Aashna. If Blair Babineaux wasn't the woman of his former dreams, it was only because he previously had the wrong dreams.

Yes, so many issues were now resolved, but there was still the matter of whether he had done the right thing when he responded the way he did to Tim Gerard's question in early July. Owen Peterborough's words from the previous night still reverberated. Why didn't he simply compromise his principles just a bit and prevent not only Owen's anguish but also the difficulties the media now faced with a less forthcoming administration? Before he had clung to his grandfather's wisdom and encouragement to justify his refusing to mislead the press. He also believed a devotion to principle was the aspect of his nature he admired most. But Owen's story was far more complicated—namely his feelings for his sister-in-law the First Lady—than Ethan would admit in the aftermath of that July day. He understood that seeing this imposing and politically gifted man weeping on his hands and knees would sit heavily on his memory, because the argument that he was in large part responsible for the former chief of staff's pain would be a difficult one to refute. He also realized that should Peterborough carry out his plan and end his life, Ethan would find it impossible to separate his momentous decision in July from a far more eventful and tragic one. He could only pray that Owen Peterborough would come through his crisis, even though his return to politics—to the arena where he once impressively stood with few peers--was highly unlikely. Their names would therefore be linked—if not always in political and historical commentary—then in the minds of both men for as long as they lived.

Dan Brooks once told his grandson that "freedom" was a considerably limited concept—in that everyone's "fate" or "destiny" was often the product of "principles and limits." His grandfather added that, unfortunately, those with more principles and narrower limits pay a greater price for being who they are. "And I can tell you're one of those, Ethan," he said when the boy was about to leave for college. "But remember that you are who you are, and if you try to be someone else—even for a single moment—you'll pay an even greater price than the one you may have to pay. Don't disobey what comes from the deepest part of you and you'll always have a friend in yourself." Ethan recalled that at the time he took Dan Brooks' words less seriously than he should have, feeling some confusion as to the final part of that advice, but now he so fully understood all of what his grandfather advised. He'd have regrets about what happened, but he wouldn't regret having made the decision he did. And it might well turn out that Blair's gracious and loving remark of the previous night—"I more than love you, Ethan. I so sincerely *admire* and *respect* you"—would be all the reward he would ever need for having remained true to his principles. He heard it often from Owen Peterborough and Aashna Malini that his duty was to the president, for by serving the chief executive loyally he would also be serving his country. Yet neither of them had suggested that his duty was also to himself. The thought had always seemed too selfish and ego-driven for him to entertain, but he saw now that it was his and everyone's first loyalty—and if understood correctly, the most paramount duty. In a cynical world, an acceptance of such a realization would be laughed at for its naiveté or denigrated for its suggested vanity. So be it, Ethan concluded.

Looking at his friends the squirrels as they came closer to the steps of the deck than he had ever seen them, Ethan couldn't help addressing them. "So you guys think I'm a good guy and that I made the right decision?" The squirrels looked at each other and began gnawing on their black acorns or whatever their meal was. The bobbing of their heads up and down was enough of an endorsement for the decisions he made and the course his life had taken. He would have to seek employment after the Montroses returned, when his funds would be diminished to the point of financial discomfort. He felt fatigued by these thoughts but more as one feels after an intense but satisfying work out, and he just didn't wish to consider future job possibilities at present. He closed his eyes and immediately imagined Blair's lovely face. There was one decision he had to make right away and made it without hesitation. He would devote himself to her and marry her whenever she felt ready to do so. If she was against the institution—and so far they had not spoken of marriage--he'd live with her for rest of his life in a "state of sin," which would really be his state of bliss.

One more issue demanded consideration before he could turn off his mind and have another beer. Would he return to the States in the immediate future, accompanied by Blair, who had assured him again the previous night him she would go anywhere he wanted or had to go? "It's not as though I'm leaving a great career behind, Ethan." He was thankful--so very thankful—that she had made his decision as uncomplicated as she could. With eyes still closed, he thought of her scurrying around the Kingston brew pub with perspiration on her brow and that bright green bar towel jammed into the beltline of her jeans and of the many spots in the city she had taken him to. Kingston—Ontario—Canada had folded its arms around him and taken him in, and even though Owen Peterborough and to a lesser extent Steve Jankowski had encroached on his sanctuary, Brooks couldn't forget how important this place had been to his recovery and his hope for a serene future. Would he eventually go back to live in Vermont or in any of the other states? He just didn't know--which for a slight instant disturbed his present contentment. But he remembered his promise to Richard Montrose that he would house-sit until the spring. And surely his principles wouldn't allow him to renege on a promise. Ethan pressed his eyes tightly together and smiled. He knew right where he'd be for the next six months at least. Right where he wanted to be.

· · ·

"Ethan? Ethan?"

He awakened and felt Blair's soft kiss on his lips. She stroked his face until his eyes stopped blinking.

"I didn't want to wake you, so I put this blanket around you so you wouldn't get too cold."

He stared at the copper-colored blanket. "What time is it?"

"8:30."

"I've been asleep for over three hours."

"You needed it."

Ethan rose from the deck chair and began folding the blanket—poorly. "What time did you get here?"

Blair took the blanket from him and folded it--properly. "I've been here about an hour and a half. I knocked, but when you didn't answer I came around the side into the back yard. In the light from the kitchen I saw two squirrels standing guard over you on the second step of the deck. I was afraid they'd attack me. I whispered your name, but you didn't budge. I then navigated past the squirrels and went inside and entertained myself—but I checked on you every ten minutes or so."

He pulled her to him. "I had a dream about you, Blair." The smile returned to his face.

"Was I drowning or being lowered unto a chain saw?"

"I was making love to you while we were both drinking Tim Hortons Coffee."

Without missing a beat, she replied, "Did we spill any? No, that wasn't a dream, my love; that was a premonition. Come on inside, Ethan. I want to show you something." Blair led him to the Montrose formal dining room. "You said I could help if I wanted to."

He looked on the table and sighed with amazement. Blair had completed the jigsaw puzzle of Jackson Pollock's *Convergence.*

—The End—